THE MOTH GIRL

THE
MOTH
GIRL

HEATHER KAMINS

G. P. PUTNAM'S SONS

G. P. PUTNAM'S SONS

An imprint of Penguin Random House LLC, New York

First published in the United States of America by G. P. Putnam's Sons,
an imprint of Penguin Random House LLC, 2022

Copyright © 2022 by Heather Kamins

G. P. Putnam's Sons is a registered trademark of Penguin Random House LLC.

Visit us online at penguinrandomhouse.com

Library of Congress Cataloging-in-Publication Data is available.

Book manufactured in Canada
ISBN 9780593109366

1 3 5 7 9 10 8 6 4 2
FRI

Design by Suki Boynton
Text set in Mrs Eaves XL Serif OT

For everyone going through it,
with their own story to tell

Nobody understands what it feels like to float in the air. They think it's like floating in water. But when you lie on the surface of a pool or a lake, resting on the water's skin, your body still obeys the law of gravity, still longs for the center of the earth. Floating in the air, this illness, is different. It feels violent. Instead of letting itself be pulled down, the body pushes away. It repels the earth, rejects it. Sometimes, you hang there, feet above the ground, close enough to see what you're missing but far enough to be out of reach. Other times, you drift higher and higher, the world shrinking beneath you, and you wonder if you'll ever feel the earth's solidity again.

ONE

WHEN THE FIRST symptoms appeared on a bright afternoon in late August, I had no idea they were anything. Fall was cross-country season, and practice started a couple weeks before the first day of school. My sophomore year was about to begin, and it was a perfect day for a run, the air warm but not hot, the first few leaves beginning to turn red and gold.

It was my best friend, Smilla, who convinced me to join the team. Back in middle school, we used to watch high school girls jogging down her road and talk about how cool and strong they looked. And so, the summer before high school began, she suggested we try out for the team together. We practiced all summer, tried out just before freshman year, and both made junior varsity. It was the beginning of the nineties, the last decade of the century, and it felt like we were on the verge of something momentous. I figured that starting high school as a member of the cross-country team would turn me into the sort of cool, confident girl that Smilla and I had seen running by, but mostly I felt like my old self, quiet and always just outside the loop.

On this particular afternoon, not only was the weather perfect but I was in fine form as well. I often had trouble keeping up with Smilla, who was one of the fastest runners on JV. She seemed like one of those cool high school runners, even if I didn't. In addition to being fast, she was tall and pretty, and her pale-blond ponytail streamed out behind her like the trail from a jet engine. She'd been adopted into the cluster of the other fastest runners on the team: Jennie, Cheryl, and Min. The three of them and Smilla were usually at the front of the pack, with me struggling to break out of the middle.

But today, I matched their pace easily as we headed along the edge of the soccer field toward the entrance of the trail that ran through the woods. The varsity boys' team was doing drills along the sideline, and several of them turned, grinning, to watch us run by.

"Isn't Ben going out with Veronica Child?" said Min.

"No," Smilla replied. "They broke up over the summer."

"Oh," said Min, shooting Ben a sidelong smile.

"Hey, Smilla," said the tall senior in the middle, Jimmy Calimeris, who despite his orthodontist father had never needed braces for his perfect smile.

Smilla looked away but couldn't get the grin off her face.

As we passed them, I noticed Andy Maddox, a slim, serious junior, looking at me, and I glanced over my shoulder to catch his eye just as the sharp tweet of a whistle cut through the air. "Gentlemen," called their coach, "enough gawking. Let's focus, please?"

The girls and I laughed, partly at them for getting busted and partly from the electric joy of being noticed.

We hit the trail entrance and slipped into the woods. A warm breeze washed over us, and the sound of the rustling leaves combined with birdsong made the noise from the fields fade away and the trail feel even more like its own secret world.

"They were totally checking you guys out," said Smilla.

"And you, obviously," said Min.

Smilla scoffed. "Come on."

I poked her in the arm. "Jimmy specifically said hello to you."

"Whatever," she said, but the grin was back.

Jennie, who'd had the same boyfriend since early freshman year, asked, "Cheryl, which one of those guys would you go out with, if you had to?"

Cheryl patted her hair, her messy bun still perfect despite the exercise. "Well, Jimmy is pretty cute. But," she added with a smirk, "I would never stand in Smilla's way."

Smilla blushed as Min and Jennie egged Cheryl on. I tried to think of something to contribute to the conversation, as rare as it was to be in the middle of it like this, but it was hard to stay focused. All I could think about was the way my body felt as it soared between footfalls, bounding like a deer through the woods. Unusually light. Maybe it was because of the perfect weather, or the promise of a fresh new year of school. Maybe it was because of that look from Andy.

Whatever it was, the feeling—and I—couldn't be stopped.

Soon, I was pulling ahead. When I noticed my friends were a ways behind me, I turned and jogged back to them, but a surge of energy was bursting inside me, and I felt an almost uncontrollable urge to speed up again. So I ran on, and soon I felt like I was leaping more than running, bouncing over tree roots and rocks with incredible speed, as though I were chasing something, or being chased. But I didn't feel the panic that comes with pursuit. Instead, I felt free, exhilarated. I soared in great arcs and inhaled the sweet scent of summer beginning to turn into fall, the richness of soil and pine needles. Although I was nearing the end of the loop, part of me wanted to keep running. But my ankles were starting to ache. No surprise, considering how hard I'd hit them landing my great leaps.

I was just slowing down and about to exit the wooded trail when something appeared in the air in front of me. I stopped short to avoid running into it. It was a caterpillar, twisting and twirling just inches from my face. As fuzzy and white as a puff of cotton, it danced on an invisible strand of silk and swayed in the gentle breeze. The warm, mottled light filtered through the stirring maple branches above, and the caterpillar doubled up and straightened out, pointing and flexing and curving its body as if trying to find a place to put its tiny feet. I watched it for what felt like hours, hypnotized, until the others finally caught up to me.

"Hey!" said Smilla, and Min high-fived me.

"Wow, you're fast today!" said Jennie, and Cheryl nodded in appreciation.

None of them seemed to notice the caterpillar as they passed me and reached the soccer field again. But I couldn't stop looking at it. Sometimes, I feel like there's a part of me still standing on that trail, watching that caterpillar, unaware of all that was about to begin.

ON SATURDAY NIGHT, Smilla was at my house to get ready for a party at Cheryl's, and she was going to sleep over at my place afterward. It was the last weekend before school started, and Cheryl's parents were out of town, though I'd neglected to mention that to my own parents. Smilla had arrived with an overnight bag full of clothing options, but she seemed dissatisfied with each one after trying it on: pastel-blue top, tan skirt, pale-pink dress. "Can I try on something of yours?" she asked. "Ooh, are you going to wear that dress you got at Ophelia's last time?"

"You can try it," I said, rummaging through my closet full of thrift-store finds to get to the latest one, a lacy A-line in emerald green. "Here you go."

She pulled it on and spun, checking herself out in the full-length mirror that hung inside my closet door. "What do you think?"

"I love that color on you. Needs something else, though." I pondered for a moment, then dug into a dresser drawer and pulled out a black velvet hat. "Try this."

She put on the hat, and the whole ensemble came together. Even though she was six inches taller than me and willowy where I was muscular, the dress fit her perfectly and the entire outfit looked custom-made for her. Yet she scrunched up her face, uncertain.

"It's perfect!" I insisted. "You look amazing."

"Are you sure?"

"A million percent."

The truth was, she'd have looked good in a burlap sack, but she couldn't always see herself the way other people did. She complained about how pale she was and how her ice-blond hair had no body and never did what she wanted. But she always looked great, even the morning after a sleepover, when she was bleary-eyed and barely verbal for a full hour after waking up, her pajamas rumpled and her hair pointing in all directions.

I, on the other hand, was medium height, with tan skin and my mother's frizz of dark-brown hair that had way too much body. But I tried not to complain about my looks. I figured the discrepancy was obvious to anyone looking at the two of us, or at me next to Jennie, Cheryl, and Min, so why bother drawing attention to it?

What I did have was the ability to zero in on the best scores at all the vintage shops Smilla and I liked to go to in the city. Clothes might not fit me as well as they fit her, but I did manage to find some pretty great stuff. I tried on a couple of my favorite recent purchases, including a fuzzy purple sweater and a silver miniskirt, but I wasn't quite feeling the look.

Smilla leaned close to the mirror to put on makeup. "I can't believe school starts next week."

"I know." Smilla and I had already memorized each

other's schedules, and we'd managed to get into the same English class.

I tossed the sweater and skirt onto my bed, just one small island in the riot of color that was my room: posters and magazine collages on the walls and bright knickknacks on every surface, like the wooden Dala horses Smilla always brought home for me after her family trips to her parents' native Sweden. I changed into a pair of jeans with embroidered multicolored flowers trailing down one leg, and a black T-shirt with the logo for Into the Freeze, one of my favorite bands. I checked myself out. Not bad, actually, though I needed something to complete the outfit.

"My mom is already on me about homework," said Smilla. "And the year hasn't even started! Can you believe it?"

I pulled on a red satin blazer. Perfect. "*Your* mom? Yeah, I believe it." Last winter and spring, when cross-country was out of season, Smilla was tied up several days a week taking SAT prep courses and classes at the local community college, despite the fact that we were only freshmen. Her mom insisted it would give her an advantage on her college applications. "Well, whatever," I said. "It's going to be a great year."

Smilla applied mascara and blinked a couple times at the mirror. "I still can't believe how fast you were running the other day! Have you been training without me?"

I sat down at my desk to pick out earrings. "Of course not! You're the only reason I'm on the team in the first place."

"Anna, you would be on the team no matter what!"

There was no point in arguing about it. She wouldn't

stop trying to convince me I was great, and I wouldn't stop believing that I wouldn't be there without her.

I poked around in my jewelry box and held up a pair of dangly filigreed silver earrings. "What do you think? Or do you like these better?" I switched them for a pair of big gold stars.

"The gold ones, I think. They're bold."

I smiled and put on the stars. They *were* bold. Over freshman year, I'd built up a pretty decent wardrobe, but when it came time to get dressed for school or parties, I didn't always go as colorful, as interesting, as *bold* as I could. Maybe it was time to step out of the shadows.

Smilla finished her makeup, then I did mine while she flipped through my music collection, mostly cassette tapes with a few albums mixed in. She pulled out an old album from Standalone with a picture of the four band members silhouetted against a sunset on the cover. "We should listen to this later," she said. "I've never heard it."

"Sure." I was always pleased when I could introduce her to new music.

When we were done getting ready, we went downstairs. My father was on one of his cooking kicks, and he'd made us a homemade veggie pizza to eat before the party. We ate it in front of the little TV in the kitchen while he went to change out of his sauce-smeared HOT STUFF apron so he could drive us to Cheryl's house. Smilla was the only person in the world he could have worn that thing in front of without my being completely mortified. To his credit, the pizza was pretty good.

My mother came in and said, "You two look so cute!"

"Thanks," we said, accidentally in unison.

"Oh," said my mom, "will you tell Cheryl's mom I'd love the recipe for the stuffed mushrooms she made for the boosters' potluck?"

"Sure." As soon as my mom turned away, Smilla grinned at me, wide-eyed, and we pinched our lips together to keep from laughing.

My dad drove us to Cheryl's, where the party was already bustling. "Have fun, Anna Banana," he said, and I tried not to roll my eyes. He was getting that look like he wanted to hug me, like his baby was all grown up, and I knew I'd better hurry and get out of the car. We waved as he drove away, waiting until he was gone to skip toward the front door. And I was glad we did, because when we opened it, a bunch of senior boys came tumbling out.

The music pumped loudly as we pushed through the crowd and found Cheryl, who guided us into the kitchen, then took a step back and checked out our outfits. "Very nice," she said, and added, "Ooh, love the earrings," to me.

"Thanks," I said, and Smilla nudged me.

"You want to put your stuff in my room?" Cheryl asked, but before we could answer, she spotted one of her other friends and squealed. "Lilly!" she called, making a beeline for her. Cheryl hung out with Smilla and me and our little cross-country group, but she also traveled in circles with the football players and cheerleaders.

Smilla and I went upstairs and tossed our purses onto Cheryl's white four-poster bed. The room itself was painted a subdued pink, and everything felt neat and coordinated, from the plush white carpeting to the sleek furniture. I always felt a little silly in Cheryl's room, like my own bedroom was childish in comparison, with its wild colors and constant clutter.

I was gazing at the vintage VISIT PARIS poster that was framed on the wall when Smilla broke me out of my thoughts. "Planning a trip?"

"I wish."

"Yeah, me too. I went to England that one time, but other than that, only to Sweden."

"At least you've been somewhere." I had never even left the time zone.

"We should go backpacking across Europe," she said. "Maybe the summer after we graduate? Paris, Barcelona . . . ooh, Italy! We can eat good food, go to all the great museums . . . whatever we want!"

It sounded like a wonderful dream. But my reverie of baguettes and paintings was interrupted by a series of loud cheers from downstairs, and my mind returned to our actual surroundings.

"Ready?" asked Smilla.

"Sure."

We went back to the kitchen, where the table was piled high with bowls of chips and pretzels, packages of cookies, and bottles of soda. And beer, of course. I took a can and sipped at it, and Smilla poured herself an orange soda. The beer was lukewarm and disgusting, but having a slight buzz tended to ease my awkwardness in big social situations.

Parties always seemed like a good idea before I went to them, full of the possibility of something magical happening, but the reality almost never matched my expectations. I'd go thinking I might meet some new guy, but it was always the people I already knew from school. Or I'd be ready to dance the night away and it would end up being a dozen people in someone's living room, complaining about classes and their parents. One time, I spent over an hour in Min's basement rec room playing pool with a cute senior, thinking maybe he'd ask me out or kiss me or something, and the next time I saw him in school, he gave me a friendly wave and said, "Hey, Angela!" with his arm around another girl.

Smilla and I got some snacks and wandered into the dining room, which looked out into the chaos of the living room. One guy, a junior, was trying to do a backflip off the sofa. Several others were singing along with a silly pop song on the radio. And then, like a flock of birds all taking flight at once, they stopped what they were doing and shouted, *"Boone!"* as the front door opened and one of their buddies walked in. After they greeted one another, they started singing along with the radio again while trying to do some dance and just generally being rowdy.

On the other side of the room, I noticed Tim Frank look over at Smilla and me. Tim had been in my history class the previous year, but otherwise I probably wouldn't have known who he was. He seemed nice enough but was as average as could be: average looks, average student, average JV football player. He stood there talking to several other average-looking guys. He even dressed in an average way:

in jeans, a pale-yellow polo shirt, and a white baseball cap.

I looked away before he caught me staring, but then there he was, approaching Smilla and me. He was probably another of her admirers. "Hey, guys. I mean, girls." He shuffled awkwardly and tugged at his cap. "How's it going?"

"Fine," I said.

"How are you?" asked Smilla.

This seemed to be just the opening he was looking for. "Pretty good, pretty good." There was a moment of silence while he figured out what to say next. I could sense Smilla trying not to giggle as we watched him flounder, and I had to bite my lip too. I knew if we made eye contact with each other, we would burst out laughing, so I kept my gaze elsewhere. Neither one of us had a whole lot of experience with guys, but even still, we thought his attempt at flirtation was pretty sad. "So, uh, what classes do you have this year?" he asked.

We each rattled off our schedules, and he was starting to say that he had the same history class as Smilla when Min showed up. "Min, over here!" called Smilla, waving her over a little too enthusiastically.

"Hi, girls," she said. "Tim."

He nodded, looking even more awkward now.

"Well, okay, then," said Min. She turned to Smilla. "That dress is divine!"

"Another great Anna find," said Smilla, smiling as she shifted the compliment to me.

Min was dolled up in a formfitting black dress, and she

scanned the room for her latest crush. "Have you two seen Mark yet?"

"Not yet," Smilla and I said, accidentally in unison again. "Jinx," I added, and she laughed and poked me in the arm.

The critical mass of our girl group, with its talk of fashion and boys, must have scared off Tim, who muttered, "Okay, maybe I'll see you later," and was reabsorbed into the crowd.

"Say bye to your boyfriend," Smilla murmured after he disappeared.

I laughed. "No way. I wouldn't dream of coming between the two of you!"

We were still laughing when Jennie appeared with her boyfriend, James, who had his arm around her shoulder. Jennie glanced at my beer. "Can I have a sip?"

I handed her the can.

She took a swig and then made a face and handed it back to me. "Bleh, warm."

"I know." Not only that, but it wasn't helping me relax either. I set the half-empty can on the coffee table, and some skinny, nameless boy scooped it up, bowed at me like a knight, and then leaped, squawking, into a crowd of dancers.

I went back into the kitchen and poured myself a cup of cola to wash the beer taste out of my mouth. When I got back to my friends, Min said, "Come on, let's dance!"

Jennie looked skeptical. "To . . . this?" She waved at the crowd of boys singing along with the plodding, monotonous song that was currently blaring. They were tightly packed around the boom box and didn't seem like they'd take kindly to their song being changed.

"We have a tape," said Smilla. "But we need a diversion." She gave me a knowing look and said, "Follow me."

I pulled the cassette out of my pocket and handed it to Jennie, and she and Min tiptoed like cartoon bank robbers toward the outskirts of the crowd around the boom box.

Smilla and I wandered over to the front window, and she pointed out into the darkness, where a handful of party-goers had congregated. "Hey," she said as loud as she could without yelling. "Is that Maggie Farner?" Maggie, who had moved out of town halfway through freshman year, was the object of unrequited affection from half the boys in our class.

I looked outside. "Maggie? Is she back?"

"It looks like her." Smilla cracked the window open and called, "Hey, Maggie!" The crowd around the boom box was breaking up as boys drifted to the windows. They didn't even notice when Jennie swooped in behind them and switched tapes.

"Who are you looking at?" called Boone from near the window. "That's not Maggie."

"Weird, it looked like her!" I said. I chugged the last of my soda, finding it strangely delicious and wondering what kind it was. I wasn't the biggest soda fiend in the world, but I could have knocked back five cups of that stuff. I thought about getting more, but the good music was finally starting up, so I set down the cup, and Smilla grabbed my hands. We sang and danced along with one of my upbeat alt-rock favorites. I whirled and gyrated, feeling my lean, strong muscles stretch and flex. We twirled wildly, laughing and spinning. The song changed, and we all started bouncing around, and for just a moment, I felt like part of something bigger than myself. I jumped higher than anyone, and my ankles twinged and twanged, but I couldn't stop, didn't want to stop. I jumped and jumped. Higher and higher.

THE FIRST DAY of school dawned clear and crisp, the morning air portending autumn. I exchanged hellos and questions about our respective summers with various classmates, and sat with Jennie in first-period French and Smilla in third-period English with Ms. Meadows, our favorite teacher from the previous year. At lunch, I was going to see if Smilla wanted to sit outside and chat for a while—just the two of us—but by the time I got to the cafeteria, she was already at a table with Jennie, Cheryl, and Min. Smilla smiled and waved me over, and I tried to swallow my disappointment as I joined them.

We talked about our teachers, Ben Walden's sudden transfer to private school, Sara and Sam's tragic summer breakup, and Caroline McCall's short haircut. After we got through the details of our mornings, Min bumped her arm against Cheryl's. "Hey, great party!"

"Thanks. It was a bitch to clean up before my parents got home."

Smilla frowned, scrunching up her forehead. "I'm sorry. We should have stayed and helped."

"It's okay. It wasn't even bad when you guys left. But

a bunch of people stayed for*ever*, and then Harry broke a lamp and Boone spilled beer all over the carpet."

Min laughed. "Of course he did."

"It's all right, though," Cheryl said breezily. "Tim stayed to help me." She looked meaningfully at Smilla. "He couldn't stop talking about you."

"What?" said Smilla as the rest of them oohed. "Are you serious?"

"Very serious," Cheryl said in a singsong voice before taking a dainty bite of her sandwich.

I gave Smilla a nudge. "I told you you were meant for each other."

She laughed. "Shut up!" She shook her head and turned back to Cheryl. "What did he say?"

"Oh, just asking if you and I were still running cross-country, when he obviously knows we are, asking if we hang out a lot, that kind of thing." She took a sip of her diet soda. "He *may* have also asked if you had a boyfriend."

Jennie smiled at Smilla. "You should go out with him! Then we can double-date."

I tried to imagine Tim fumbling for words on a double date with brilliant supercouple Jennie and James. Even the fantasy version was awkward.

"Oh, I don't know," said Smilla.

Cheryl made a sad face. "You don't like him? Come on! He's . . . sweet."

Min squinted at her. "Puppies are sweet. Little baby ducklings are sweet. Tim is . . . weird."

"Okay, so he's a little . . . socially challenged, but he's nice." Cheryl's voice rose into her *clearly lying* register.

"So why don't *you* go out with him?" asked Smilla.

She laughed. "Oh god, no. He's not my type. Besides, he likes *you*. Why are you so picky anyway?"

Smilla was picky, it was true. Boys always seemed to like her, but she was seldom interested in them. And every time she turned down a date or said she wasn't into someone, I felt a wave of relief followed by a wave of shame for being relieved. It was just that I had seen it too many times: boy meets girl, boy and girl become an item, girl drops off the face of the earth and ignores her friends, at least until she breaks up with boy. It was bad enough that Smilla and I barely got to hang out alone anymore. At least with our teammates, I could tag along. With a boy in the picture, she'd be lost to me.

After lunch, I headed to geometry. Since none of my friends were in that class, I wound up sitting next to Kristi Lattzer, who briefly peeked out at me from beneath layers of black lace and fabric, her inky dyed hair hanging around her face. She used to wear pastels and giant glasses and kept her dishwater-blond hair in a ponytail, and she sort of faded into the background most of the time. But over the summer, it was like she'd transformed into an entirely different person. "Hey," I said, but she didn't respond.

Mr. Takahashi started class, and after going over his grading policy, the first thing he did was pair us with assignment partners. "You'll have some in-class work to do together, and you'll also be able to turn to each other for help with homework or to get assignments if you miss a class." He went down the rows, indicating pairs. "You and you," he said, pointing to Kristi and then me.

I turned to Kristi to give her a *Well, guess we're stuck with each other* smile, but she didn't interrupt her doodling to acknowledge me. I watched her draw for a few moments, sketchy lines emerging into a landscape and a distant castle. As Mr. Takahashi finished circulating and returned to his spot at the front of the room, I asked Kristi if she wanted to exchange numbers. She didn't reply, so I continued. "In case we have questions about—"

"Whatever," she muttered, sliding my notebook over to her desk. When she shoved it back, I saw that she had written her number in the tiniest, most precise handwriting I had ever seen, right in the middle of the page.

"Thanks," I said slowly. She didn't offer up her own notebook, so I tore off a corner of my page and wrote my number on it. I placed it on her desk, and she went back to ignoring me.

That afternoon at practice, Kristi's name came up again. "She's in my English class," said Min, rolling her eyes.

"She's in geometry with me," I said. "We're assignment partners."

"Oh, lucky you," said Cheryl. "God, that girl is intense."

"True story," said Jennie. The three of them and Kristi lived across town and had gone to the other middle school, so Smilla and I hadn't met any of them until the year before. They gave one another knowing looks and shook their heads like there was a long history there, but before they could get into it, a bug flew into Cheryl's face, and she shrieked and made us all stop to make sure it wasn't stuck in her hair or on her clothes.

As we resumed running, I thought about Kristi, about her being intense. It felt a little mean the way they'd said it, but I thought about how she'd had such an edge during geometry, and I supposed maybe she *was* kind of intense.

As practice went on, I felt myself picking up speed, and only Smilla ran fast enough to keep up with me. Soon we were well ahead of the others, and before long, I started feeling that strange lightness again. I bounded ahead. "Hey, wait up!" Smilla called, and when I turned to look back at her, she was much farther behind than I would have guessed. When she finally caught up, she was out of breath like she'd been sprinting. "Seriously," she said, "when did you get so fast?"

"I don't know," I said, and I really didn't.

THE FIRST CROSS-COUNTRY meet of the season took place on a bright Saturday morning in early September. As the bus rolled toward Ferndown High a couple towns over, Smilla asked me, "How are you feeling?"

"Good, I think." My times over the past week had been stellar beyond what I could comprehend, and the whole team had been impressed.

"If you can keep up your pace from practice, no one else has a chance. I still don't know when you got so fast."

"Hey," said Jennie from the seat behind us. "Did you see Min's manicure?"

We turned around and admired Min's nails, which she held up proudly to display the name of our town painted across them in the school's blue-and-gold colors. "Good thing 'Callington' is ten letters," said Smilla.

"Did you do that yourself?" I asked. The possibilities for doing my own nail art began to unfold in my mind.

"Yep," she said. "It only took like three tries to make it not look like blobs."

"Nice work," said Smilla.

"Go, Callington!" shouted Min, and the rest of the bus responded with whoops and hollers.

We got off the bus and stretched on the opposing team's track. It was always strange to me to see another track—the standard size and shape so familiar yet in such an unfamiliar location. Sometimes it felt like being on another planet. The scene was only made stranger by Smilla's father and mine sitting in the stands, waving when we looked over. They didn't have a lot in common—my dad was a nerdy accountant type, while Mr. Jorgensen was an intimidatingly suave history professor at one of the best colleges in the area. But they both always turned up at our meets.

As I stretched, I could feel that energy welling within me again, that same effervescent sense of vigor I had felt at practice, and I knew I had this race. Just before everyone gathered at the starting line, Coach Antee approached me with some final advice. "Remember to pace yourself and save some juice for the back half, all right?" He was a wall of a man, tall and broad, with close-cropped hair and a deep voice that had a hint of a southern drawl.

"I will," I said. "I'm ready, I promise. I've been doing the exercises we talked about and everything." The words spilled forth from me, and I nodded vigorously, although I wasn't sure how much I would be able to control my pace with all that energy bubbling up inside me. Coach gave me a strange look, and I forced my mouth into a closed smile and tried to stay still so he would move on and I could head for the beginning of the race path. I just wanted to get going, going, going already. The starting whistle was a relief.

Ferndown High had a wide spread of fields near the school, so their path went around the football, hockey, and soccer fields; through a section of woods; and along a trail cut through the high grass in the neighboring meadow. Right from the start, I pulled ahead of the pack. Coach Antee was on the sidelines, holding his hands up in an *Easy, now* gesture, and I *tried* to pace myself. But the push coming from inside me couldn't be contained. A quarter of the way into the race, I was bounding again, and although I knew Coach was going to give me a talking-to about my technique later, I didn't try to stop. As I came to the edge of the woods, I glanced over to see my father and the others in the stands cheering, and I pushed on harder.

I continued running in great soaring leaps all through the forest even though my feet and ankles were starting to ache. I knew the technique wasn't right, and I was so far ahead that I didn't need to worry about losing a little time, so I tried to rein it in. But it was like my legs were independent of me, sentient, subject only to their own will. By the time I burst out into the meadow, I was flying higher than ever, and the fans were screaming. The soreness was growing, but I was close to the finish. *Just push through it,* I told myself. I came in first by a huge margin, the crowd shouting and cheering. None of the other runners had even emerged from the woods into the meadow by the time I crossed the finish line.

My feet and ankles were really throbbing now, and all I wanted to do was sit down, but Coach Antee pulled me aside. "What did I tell you about pacing yourself?"

I nodded as if agreeing with him, but I just wanted the interaction to be over. The fizzy, bouncy energy was draining away, and my legs were getting rubbery beneath me.

"Anna, you're going to get injured if you're not careful. There's more to running than speed. And you have to be willing to take feedback if you want to improve."

He looked at me meaningfully for a long minute, as if to make sure the information was sinking in. Then he nodded and walked away, and I practically fell onto the bleachers.

One of the Ferndown runners was the next to finish, followed soon after by Smilla. I stood up when I saw her, and she rushed over and hugged me. My legs still felt jiggly, but I wasn't going to pass up the opportunity to celebrate. Jennie, Cheryl, and Min were in the top seven on our team, too, and as each of my other teammates finished the race and heard about my time, they surrounded me and gave me high fives. The trio and Smilla were often in the top seven, but it was the first time I had joined them, and for a moment, I felt like maybe I did belong there, on the team, a part of their crew.

After the meet, Smilla's father dropped us off at the old diner back in Callington. We poured through the front door and tucked ourselves into a booth. I was starving—we all were—since we hadn't had anything since early that morning other than protein bars and postrace orange slices. I ordered a banana shake and took a few sips when it arrived. They made pretty good milkshakes at the diner, but this one seemed even better than usual, cold and creamy, the flavor somewhere between real bananas and those little banana-shaped candies I got from the general store downtown.

The other girls were talking about the race, going over the play-by-play, but they were interrupted when Min looked over at me. "Wow, you must really be thirsty!" she said, eyes wide. I looked down at my glass to realize that most of my shake was already gone, while the others' drinks had barely been touched.

"The champ needs fuel!" said Smilla.

"Oh," I said, "I guess so," and I wrapped my hands around my glass, instinctively trying to conceal it.

"Well," said Cheryl, "we destroyed Ferndown, so you can drink your milkshake as quickly as you want, as far as I'm concerned." She held her glass up, and the others clinked their own to it in a toast. I clinked, too, but felt uneasy. I was proud of the win, but it didn't feel like I had actually earned it. It was that thing, that force. That energy that kept coming over me and pushing me forward.

"Thanks," I muttered. "So, Min, what's going on with you and Mark?"

She sighed dramatically, as happy to have the spotlight as I was to get rid of it. "I don't know if it's going to happen, you guys. He totally changed over the summer. But there's this junior in my gym class. Rob." Her dreamy look turned to confusion. "Or Dave? Something. Anyway, you should see him spike a volleyball."

Cheryl laughed. "Are you sure you're a one-man woman? Maybe you need a whole pack of guys on call."

"Hmm," replied Min. "I'll take it under consideration."

The others cackled and egged her on. I tried to listen but found it hard to focus. The diner had little cups of crayons on the table for kids to color the paper place mats with, and I pulled out a blue one and started doodling a moon and stars. My hands were still cold from holding the milkshake glass, and they shivered a bit as I drew. I was so focused on trying to hold them steady that I didn't notice the server come by with our food. "Are you going to eat, or can the artist not be interrupted?" asked Cheryl.

Sheepishly, I put the crayon back in the cup. The others talked with great enthusiasm as I ate my sandwich and fries, and they were back to not paying much attention to me. Which was fine. As I reached for each bite of food, I found that my hands were still shaking. I tucked them in my pockets one at a time to warm up as I ate with the opposite hand. But even by the end of the meal, when I pulled them out, they were still trembling, and they kept it up for the entire time we sat there and as my father drove us home.

When I got to my house, I turned the shower on hot enough to boil a lobster, and I let the water flow over me until my skin turned crimson. I got out and stood dripping on the mat, steam rising off my poached arms, yet my hands were still shaking. I stiffened them, tried to hold them steady, but it didn't stop. A lingering ache throbbed in my ankles too. There was a seed of worry starting to take root at my core, but I ignored it and went to bed early, hoping I was simply worn-out from the race.

I FELT THAT bounding, effervescent sensation on and off over the next few practices, but as the days went by, the lightness and energy diminished and the achiness in my ankles and feet increased. I wasn't sleeping well, either, which didn't help my performance, and I drifted from my new position at the front of the pack back to the middle.

One afternoon at practice, I wasn't sure whether I was having a good day or Smilla was having a bad one, but I miraculously managed to catch up to her. "Hey, speedster," she said.

I wasn't sure how applicable the nickname was at this point, but I kept that to myself. "Hey."

"Oh, I meant to tell you I listened to that tape you loaned me. Riley Gyre. I loved that first song! I mean, I really liked the whole thing, but that one especially."

"I'm glad." I made a mental note to put that song on a mixtape for her sometime. "I heard they're going on tour soon. Maybe we could go."

"Sure, if I'm around!" Her extracurriculars had started in earnest, and she was rarely free, but I was hoping she could plan ahead with enough notice.

"If you liked them," I said, "I should lend you P.O.P. I bet you'd be into them too."

"Cool, thanks!"

We ran together for a while. I didn't want the conversation to end, since it was growing increasingly rare to have one to ourselves. I kept pushing through the pain, but eventually I had to take a break, and I paused to stretch, hoping that doing so would unkink my sore ankles. Smilla went on for a moment before realizing I had stopped, then turned and jogged back to where I was. "Hey, are you okay?"

"I don't know," I said. "My feet have been feeling kind of weird."

"Oh." She wrinkled her face in concern. "Have you told Coach? Maybe you should ice them or something."

I put my hands on the trunk of a tree and leaned into a calf stretch. "No, he'll just freak out and tell me my form is all wrong."

"Well, maybe you should go to the trainer's office. He can probably help."

I switched legs and stretched again. I was starting to regret saying anything. The last thing I needed was for Coach or, worse, my parents to find out and make me miss practice. I gave Smilla my most reassuring smile and said, "I'll be fine." I shook out my legs and resumed jogging to prove the point. She stayed put, looking unconvinced, but I simply said, "You coming?" and kept moving.

Over the following days, I found myself distracted thinking about the pain. I mostly felt it when I was running, but I was starting to get the occasional twinge when I was walking, and now sometimes that ache came on even when I was sitting still. In English, with Smilla, I smiled and pretended everything was fine, but I let my face go slack when she wasn't looking. In geometry, I worked out problems with Kristi as she continued to mostly ignore me. I had gotten used to holding up both ends of the conversation with her, but now I was growing quieter as the aches drew my attention and energy. And in my last-period biology class, I sat there before practice began and tried to will the pain away, doodling furiously in the margin of my notebook to have something else to focus on.

I didn't say anything else to Smilla about it, and so far, she hadn't asked. Cross-country practice happened five days a week, and on the weekends, she and I sometimes ran together or ran separately and met up in the middle. There was a long finger of forest that stretched from behind my backyard to the center of town, a secret passageway through the heart of suburbia. I knew each detail of that path, each crumbling section of stone wall, every initial carved inside every heart on the tall white pines. The path let out near the old-timey general store, where Smilla and I met to buy paper bags full of penny candy before crossing the road to the old cemetery, where we liked to hang out. The cemetery sat between the town hall and the First Church of Callington, and its rows of flat headstones poked out of the earth at uneven angles like crooked teeth, their inscriptions worn to whispers by two hundred years of New England weather.

It was late September now, the weather grown cool and the leaves turning scarlet and fiery gold. On the last Sunday afternoon of the month, Smilla and I had plans to meet up at our usual spot, but I was still feeling achy and tired. I visualized running quickly and painlessly, matching my old speeds, but it was hard to ignore that my body didn't feel right. It was less than a month since my victory at the cross-country meet, but I felt so different.

Smilla was waiting for me at the store, and we got our candy and went over to the cemetery. We ate licorice whips and caramel bull's-eyes as we stretched along the mossy earth between the graves, the compelling abstract that was death safely insulated from us by the hard-packed dirt below. Each time I tried to get comfortable sitting, my ankles and knees protested, and so, finally, I lay down on the worn grass and stared up at the overcast sky, wishing I had more candy. "Did you write your English paper yet?" Smilla asked me.

"No," I said. "You?"

"I'm still deciding which story to write about. I was thinking about the one with the little girl and the balloon. It reminded me of that time we went to the carnival in Haywood. Do you remember that creepy guy running the Ferris wheel?"

"Oh, yeah," I said, trying to make it sound like my heart was in it. "They had the best fried dough at that one."

"Yeah, they really did," she said. "So anyway, maybe that

one. Or maybe the one about the family in the mountains."
She kept talking, but I grew too distracted by my ankles to
listen. I was starting to feel scared. I ran my hands along
the solid earth and watched a few leaves flutter down from
the trees that swayed overhead in the chilly breeze. My running times had been getting slower and slower, and there
was another meet coming up in a week. I had to get better
before then.

Smilla must have noticed my attention drifting off,
because she asked, "Are you okay?"

"Oh, yeah," I said. "Sorry, just thinking about that
assignment."

She looked dubious. "Are you sure? I was worried about
your feet. Are you feeling better?"

I didn't want to lie to her. But I couldn't bring myself to
tell her the truth either. "I'm okay," I said, trying to sound
reassuring. "I should probably head back soon. You know
how my mom gets if I'm not home in time for dinner."

When we stood to leave, I waved goodbye as Smilla
turned and ran toward her house, making sure she wasn't
watching before I headed for mine. The thought of running
the whole length of the trail home made me feel exhausted.

Though I left myself plenty of time to get there, it still
took much longer than it should have, and my mother was
already setting the table when I arrived. She had her hair
pulled back in a ponytail, but standing over the boiling pots
had made a few wisps frizz their way out. "I asked you not to
stay out too long," she said. "Remember?"

"Sorry," I said, trying to sound casual. She probably thought I had lingered talking to Smilla. The truth was worse, so I didn't argue.

She sighed and turned back to the stove. "How's Smilla?"

"She's okay." By this point, my feet were throbbing and my hands were trembling again, and all I wanted was to go upstairs and take a quick shower.

But my mother must have sensed something off in my tone, because she looked over her shoulder at me. "Is something going on?"

"Nope. Just tired."

She looked unconvinced, but before she could ask any follow-up questions, the oven timer went off, drawing her attention. "All right, well, go get cleaned up. Dinner's almost done."

In the shower, I tried to relax my sore feet and settle my trembling hands. And at the table, I told myself to calm down and act normal, but I was focusing so hard on not shaking the spaghetti on my fork that I didn't hear my father addressing me until he said, "Anna? You okay, honey?"

"Hmm?" I said.

"I asked how Smilla's doing."

"Oh. She's fine."

My mother raised an eyebrow.

"Are you sure everything's all right?" asked my father.

I looked at him and then at my mother. They had both put their forks down and were studying my face. I mustered a shrug. "I was just thinking about this bio test I have coming up. It's no big deal."

My father was a worrier, and he panicked whenever I had so much as a sniffle. I couldn't imagine how he'd react to my nagging pain, fatigue, and shaking. My mother was calmer, stoic in the extreme, but she was a pragmatist, and if she knew I was having unusual aches and twitches, I'd be at the doctor's office before I could blink.

My mother resumed eating but kept a skeptical eye on me. My father watched me for another long minute, his face scrunched up like he didn't believe me, but I shrugged at him again and didn't give him any more information, so what else could he do?

I barely slept that night. The low, slow thrum of the throbbing pulsed through my feet and ankles, and it seemed to be spreading to my calves too. I flipped onto my side and then onto my stomach, but nothing helped me fall asleep. The numbers on my clock radio progressed onward, burning a hole in the night with their red glow. Eventually, hours after my parents went to bed, I got up and rustled through the bathroom medicine chest for a pain reliever. I hadn't taken anything up to that point, stubbornly refusing to acknowledge the pain. But now I just wanted to sleep. I swallowed a couple pills and headed back to my room, but when I got there, I went and stood by the window instead of getting in bed.

Through the blinds, the full harvest moon shone in at me, and I couldn't look away. I pulled up the shade and stared at the hypnotic glowing sphere hanging like a magnet on the sky. Its textures and shades, its slow procession through the tree branches and over the yard. I watched until it was out of sight and then collapsed into a restless sleep.

BY THE BEGINNING of October, cross-country practice was excruciating. Smilla and my parents were asking more frequently if I was okay, and my lies were becoming less convincing. I made up some excuses for Coach Antee about pulled muscles and twisted ankles, and it was a huge relief when all he did was give me a lecture about following his guidance and have the trainer tape up my ankles.

I kept forcing myself to go to practice, though now I was consistently at the back of the pack. So I mostly found myself alone as I ran, trying to focus on my surroundings instead of the pain.

On one chilly afternoon, the aches were especially bad, and they kept growing. And there was something else, too, something new. My feet felt uneasy, foreign, as though the arches were twisting, the muscle memory of running fading from my body. My toes curled the wrong way; my heels flexed. I felt the shock of the ground each time one of my feet landed, and though I tried to control my stride and keep it tight, I found myself bouncing much more than I meant to between steps. My feet searched for the ground, but it was like walking on the moon, my skittering skips not quite in my control.

Before long, the pain began to rise from my toes, fizzing upward through my legs like bubbles through a soda straw. I stumbled forward, trying to shake it off, but it kept growing. It singed me from the depths of my tendons and bones, all the way out to my skin. It traveled through my ankles and calves, my knees and thighs, and as it overtook my waist, it felled me like an old tree. I remember falling, a slow, endless descent in some direction I couldn't name, but I have no memory of hitting the ground.

TWO

I WAS MOVING through space in an unsettling way, twirling and flailing, my arms and legs reaching out for something solid but finding nothing. There was noise, somebody shouting my name, and a blur of branches and fallen leaves as I whipped my head around, trying to return to consciousness and orient myself. It grew hard to breathe, and I became dizzy, and then the sensation came back to me, that tearing pain through my lower legs, its tendrils constricting around my muscles. I tried to cry out, but no sound came. Faces appeared around me, and then there were hands holding my arms and legs, straightening me out.

Still dizzy, I finally brought the scene around me into focus. I was upright, and Coach Antee was standing in front of me, his hands on my shoulders. I had never seen him look worried like that, even when other kids on the team had been injured. A small crowd of my teammates gathered around us, and Coach called out for them to stand back and give me room. They did, all but Smilla, who pushed closer, coming up to one side of me and taking my left arm so that Coach could take my right. The two of them held me steady as I took one harrowing step after another through the woods and back out onto the field.

Jennie, ever the helper, sprinted over to us just as Coach and Smilla were settling me onto the bench by the soccer field. "I called her mom," Jennie told Coach, setting down my backpack, which she must have retrieved from the locker room. "She said she'll be here in ten." The concern on Jennie's face was unsettling, and I looked away.

"All right, everybody, back to the track. Do relays until I get there," he said, and everyone but Smilla jogged away, casting a few glances over their shoulders at me.

The sharp pain in my legs had subsided to a low, persistent throbbing, and I felt shaky and weak all over. "Are you okay?" Smilla asked, even though we both knew I wasn't. She sat next to me. "What happened?"

"I—I don't know." It was still hard to get enough air into my lungs to push out words. "My legs started hurting, and"—I took a deep breath—"I just passed out, I guess."

She swallowed, as if scared to say what was on her mind. "You know you weren't . . . on the ground, right?"

"What?" I tried to make sense of what she was saying, to stitch it together with my own experience.

Her face looked pained, as if about to break the news that a loved one had died. "You were floating."

"Floating."

She nodded and reached one hand out in front of her, holding it three feet above the ground. "About this high."

I studied her face to see if she was kidding. She wasn't, of course. I tried to remember what happened, tried to picture myself hanging in the air like she said, but it was hard to imagine. Had I been floating faceup or facedown? Vertical or sideways? Moving or still? A wave of dizziness swelled in my head, and I swayed. Smilla grabbed my arm and clutched it tightly. It must have been true that I'd been floating, because she seemed worried I might do it again.

"I . . . I didn't know . . ." I looked back toward the woods, which seemed more ominous now.

Smilla was quiet for a minute. "It was worse than you said, wasn't it?" she said softly. "How you've been feeling?"

I let out a long breath. "I guess."

"Why didn't you tell me?"

She was still holding on to my arm, pressed in close. I leaned my head against hers. "I'm sorry." It was all I could think to say.

Coach Antee came back over to me and put a hand on my shoulder. "Your mom should be here soon. You ready to try walking?"

I nodded, though I was unsure whether or not I was. Either way, he and Smilla helped me to my feet, and we began our long, slow trek across the fields to get to the front of the school. With each step, the knives grew sharper in my joints and muscles.

My mother pulled the car up to the curb and jumped

out just as we reached her. She gave me a quick once-over with her laser-focused mom vision before all three of them loaded me into the front passenger seat.

After he shut the door, Coach talked to my mother for a minute, and I leaned my head against the cool window to catch my breath. The pain in my legs simmered down to a dull ache again. I still felt confused as I tried to piece together what was happening. The pain, the woods, Smilla's description of my floating body. She waved when she saw me looking, and I mustered a nod in return. Then my mother was back in the car and we were driving away.

She gave me a brief minute of peace and then started with the questions—slow, deliberate, and persistent: *What happened? Were you feeling bad before this? For how long? What do you feel like now?* I answered as best I could, given my confusion and fatigue. At the emergency room, the nurses and doctors asked the same questions, and I repeated the answers I'd given my mom: *I can't remember. A little bit. I'm not sure. My legs still hurt, and I feel tired and dizzy.*

A nurse took my temperature, pulse, and blood pressure. I tried to read some clue from her about what was going on, but her expressionless face and tight white curls made her look like an old Greek statue. Someone else came in to draw my blood, and she lined up a baker's dozen of vials along the counter. The room went gray around the edges as I contemplated that much blood leaving my body. I must have wobbled, because my mother reached out and steadied me from her seat at my side. Her expression was calm, but a heartbeat of panic flashed like a pulsar just beneath her skin.

As the needle pierced my arm, pain radiated out from the pale underside of my elbow, which swelled below the border of the tourniquet. I felt another bout of dizziness and tried to stay grounded by focusing on the objects around me: A privacy curtain the pale green of a bar of soap. The pain chart on the wall with its ten round faces, a smile at one end gradually shifting to a look of anguish at the other. The phlebotomist dressed in scrubs festooned with teddy bears in baseball uniforms, her face pale and middle-aged but not as pale or middle-aged as my mother's face at that moment. And the vials, of course, filling with blood that flowed as slowly as lava inching down the side of a volcano.

My father arrived a few minutes after the blood draw. My mother and I had been there for almost an hour, the amount of time it took for him to speed from his office in the city out to the small hospital a town over from where we lived. His face was flushed, and he was out of breath, as if he had run the entire way. He looked around, his eyes wild, until he saw me in the corner, and then he nearly crushed me in a tight hug.

"Gentle," admonished my mother.

My father let go but kept his hands on my arms to anchor me. Or himself. I wasn't sure. "Are you okay?" he asked.

I gave a weak nod.

"I'm going to find the ladies' room," said my mother. She looked a bit dazed, but she nodded at me and put her hand on my father's back before disappearing into the hallway.

My father took her seat. "So, what happened?"

I was certain my mother had already explained things

when she called his office, but I told him anyway about cross-country practice, about blacking out. About floating. It had only been, what, two hours since it happened, and already I was tired of telling the story.

As he listened, his face burned red as it often did when he was upset. "What did the doctor say?"

"Nothing yet. They just took my blood." I held up my arm to show him the bandage, and when I let the arm drop, it took several long seconds for it to fall back to my lap, like a feather drifting toward the ground. He watched with worried fascination, and so did I, as if the arm belonged to someone else.

My mother returned, and then the doctor came in and gave me a brisk physical exam. He tapped my knees with a rubber hammer, and my legs kicked up in reflex like they were supposed to, but then fell slowly, slowly down like a gentle snow. He felt my pulse and ran his fingertips quickly along the tops and undersides of my forearms. "Okay," he said. "I'm going to send you home, but we'll want to get you in with a specialist as soon as we can. Tomorrow if possible."

A specialist? Why would I need to see a specialist unless it was something serious? But, no, I tried to convince myself, maybe it was just something unusual. I mean, floating? That was pretty unusual, right? But then I remembered the "as soon as we can" part. Tomorrow. Why so soon if it wasn't serious? I gripped the edge of the exam table, my fingernails digging into the vinyl.

"The front desk will call and get you an appointment," the doctor continued. "Dr. Liffey is the best in the area for these conditions. She's in the city, at Glenhorn Hospital. She'll take good care of you, okay?"

He was halfway out the door when my mother cried, "Wait!" The doctor paused in the doorway. "What kind of specialist?"

"She's a manifestologist. She'll be able to help you figure out what's going on."

And then he was gone. The three of us looked at one another. "What's a manifestologist?" asked my father.

My mother huffed toward the doorway. "Well, I guess we'll find out tomorrow." It was too late to go to the library, so there wasn't much else to do at that point if the runaway doctor wasn't going to help us.

We caravanned home, where despite it being dinner-time, I fell into a deep sleep for several hours. I woke in the dark, disoriented, and wandered downstairs, where my father was getting an orange from the refrigerator. "We just had sandwiches," he said. "Do you want one?"

I shrugged. I wasn't very hungry. But my father looked so tense that I finally let him make me a peanut butter and jelly. As he handed me a glass of milk, he said, "Oh, I almost forgot. Smilla called to see how you were doing."

I called back as soon as I finished my sandwich.

"How *are* you?" asked Smilla, with a heavy, inflected "are" instead of the normal bounced "you."

"I'm fine," I said. Reflex.

"Are you sure you're okay? I've been so worried about you!"

I didn't know if I was okay. It didn't seem like I was, but

I didn't have any answers. "I have to see a specialist tomorrow. Hopefully, they can figure it out."

There was a silence as Smilla searched for the right thing to say. "So they don't know what's wrong?"

"If they know, they didn't tell me." I picked at the edge of the bandage where they'd drawn my blood.

"Are you coming to school tomorrow?"

"I don't know. The appointment is first thing in the morning, so maybe after that."

"What about the meet on Saturday?"

"I don't know," I said again. It was Thursday now. I hadn't thought about the meet since practice that day, before everything happened, but I had a bad feeling about it.

She was quiet for a minute. "Do you need anything?"

I hesitated. "Maybe you can get the homework for my early classes tomorrow? I have some quizzes and stuff coming up, and I want to make sure I don't miss anything important."

"Yeah, of course. Hey, I'm sure you're going to be fine. It's probably just a little blip or something, you know?"

"Right," I said. Was she truly optimistic enough to believe that? What kind of blip made you lift off the ground and hang in the air? What kind of blip made people look at you the way everyone had looked at me that day? I pictured the faces of Coach and my teammates, the looks of shock or horror or whatever it was. I couldn't get them out of my head. Deep down, I knew this was serious, even if I didn't know how serious, or what kind of serious it was.

Normally, I was happy to talk to Smilla on the phone

for hours, but I was tired. I couldn't make words form sentences in my mind. "I guess I should probably get to bed."

"Yeah, okay," she said. "Call me tomorrow and let me know how you're doing?"

"Of course." I tried to push a smile into my voice so she wouldn't worry too much. "I'll talk to you later, okay?"

"Okay," she said. She sounded like she was trying her hardest to sound cheerful too.

When we hung up, I pulled the dictionary off my bookshelf and flipped to the *M* section. *Manifestology: a medical discipline focused on manifestological diseases and disorders.* Wow, super helpful. I scanned up to *Manifestological: of or relating to a family of diseases in which cells defy one or more laws of nature.* Defy laws of nature? How could the laws of nature not apply? But I had been floating. Defying the law of gravity. I still didn't understand how any of it was possible. Yet I didn't remember floating, so couldn't it be that everyone else had been mistaken? That this was all a big misunderstanding?

I was about to shut the book when my eyes landed on the word *diseases* in the middle of the definition. Sure, I had been feeling bad, but thinking of it as a disease made it seem so much more serious. *But, no,* I told myself, *that doesn't mean anything. The flu is a disease. Strep throat is a disease.* I'd had those before. Whatever this was, I would get over it. Still, even after I set the dictionary back on the shelf and tried to put the thought out of my mind, I couldn't tamp down the flicker of worry deep inside me.

IN THE MORNING, I woke feeling groggy and light-headed. I hadn't expected to sleep much after taking that long nap the previous afternoon, but I'd passed out and didn't regain awareness until my father nudged me awake just after six thirty. "Anna," I heard him saying on the edge of my consciousness. "Anna, wake up. We have to leave soon."

I pulled on a pair of jeans and a ragged sweatshirt and trundled off to the kitchen. My mother slid a plate of eggs and toast across the counter, but I was too nervous and disoriented to be hungry. She put the scrambled eggs between the two slices of toast, then put the sandwich into a baggie. "I'll bring it in case you change your mind."

It took almost an hour to drive into the city. On the way there, I leaned my head against the window and watched the sun lifting through the trees. Mist rose from the fields and marshes, the night's moisture coalescing in the cool autumn air. Soon, we were on the highway, and I looked into the windows of the passing cars. A woman in a passenger seat put on lipstick. A driver ate a bagel as he tore past us. A mother kept one hand on the wheel and waved her other arm at the back seat as three small children flailed about. Normally, I was in school at this time, and I had never thought about the details of other people's mornings. I had never thought about these strangers at all, their multitudinous presence on the highway. I had entered a world that had been going on without me for all these years, and now that I had been there and seen it, I would always be a part of it.

45

We exited the highway and entered a section of the city I'd never seen before. I mostly went to the lively university district, where Smilla and I looked around thrift shops and record stores and hung out at cafés. But this area might as well have belonged to a different city entirely. The buildings were gray and seemed to merge into one another, an endless row of concrete slabs. My father circled the block until he found the garage where we'd been instructed to park.

Each of my parents rested a hand on one of my arms and guided me toward a door marked 2 to indicate our garage level. Through the door was a half flight of stairs to the main hallway, and my feet, still sore, throbbed as I climbed. My mother took a small notebook out of her purse and looked up the directions she'd been given when the appointment was scheduled. "This way," she said. "I think." We walked along a windowless hallway hung with plaques commemorating the hospital's founders and prominent doctors through the years. At the end of the hallway was an elevator, which we took to the third floor, where another hallway led us to a skybridge that crossed over the street to an identical building on the opposite side.

We exited the skybridge to find ourselves in yet another hallway. My mother looked at the notebook. "Left," she said. This hallway had a long mural on one side and an atrium full of artificial plants on the other. At the end was another elevator. We got in, and my mother pushed the button for the floor below us. With each turn on this complicated path, the pain increased its grip on my legs, and I worried I was going to pass out again. We went down another hallway, and just when I thought we would be wandering forever, we turned a corner, and a sign ahead of us read MANIFESTOLOGY. Here we were.

My father led me to a seat in the waiting area while my mother checked me in at the reception desk. It was early; we were the only ones there, and it took just a few minutes for my name to be called. The nurse had me change into a thin fabric gown and then sat me on the edge of a paper-covered exam table to take my blood pressure and temperature. "Dr. Liffey will be in shortly," she said, making a few notes inside a folder that she then slipped into a slot outside the exam room door. My parents trailed into the room and lingered beside me while we waited for the doctor.

Dr. Liffey was a petite woman somewhere in her late forties. She had a head full of salt-and-pepper curls and a neat navy dress under her white lab coat. She shook my hand and my parents' hands, then got straight to business. "So, I understand you had a levitative incident yesterday? You were floating?"

Even though they hadn't been there, I glanced at my parents as if for confirmation, but they looked just as helpless as I felt. I could hardly stand to see them like that, and I quickly turned back to the doctor.

"I don't really remember it. But that's what they told me." This whole thing was so outlandish. Here in a new day, after a full night's sleep, I found myself wondering even more if it had truly happened. But if not, how could I explain the rest of the symptoms, the passing out, the way my legs hadn't fallen like they were supposed to after being hit with a reflex hammer in the emergency room?

"What do you remember?"

I described the scene, but it felt like describing a movie, as though I had observed it happening to someone else: running along the trail, falling, blacking out.

Dr. Liffey nodded. None of what I said seemed to shock or startle her. "And was that the first time, or has it happened before?"

"It was the first time," I said, although I immediately thought about that lightness I'd experienced while running.

She jotted some notes on her pad. "Okay. Was there a lot of pain?"

"Yes," I told her. "At first, it was just a little, just in my feet. But then it got bad and came all the way up my legs."

"Any other symptoms?" she asked. "Have you had any trouble sleeping lately?"

"Sort of," I said. I had thought it was worry keeping me up, but maybe it had been something else all along.

"And how long has that been happening?"

"A couple weeks, I guess. Maybe a month?"

"Any shaking or trembling in your hands or feet?"

It was getting harder to speak, so I just nodded.

She scribbled more notes. "What about cravings? Particularly for candy or sweet liquids?"

I thought about the soda at Cheryl's party and the milkshake at the diner after the cross-country meet. "A little, I guess." I couldn't bear to turn around and look at my parents, to see their reactions to everything I'd been hiding from them.

Dr. Liffey put her pad on the counter behind her. "I'd like to check your skin." She took my left arm and looked it over from top to bottom, and then she did that same thing as the emergency room doctor, running her fingertips along the top of my forearm. It tickled, and I had to try hard not to pull away. She repeated the process on my right arm, and then on each of my legs. "You haven't noticed any scaliness or discoloration?"

"No." I felt dizzy again, thinking about all these questions, all these ways my body might be betraying me. It wasn't until Dr. Liffey stepped back a couple feet and looked at me that I realized I couldn't feel the exam table under my butt anymore.

She came toward me, put her hands on my shoulders, and gently pushed until I was again seated on the table, which I'd been hovering several inches above. My legs ached. "Hold out your hands," she said, demonstrating with her own hands held out, palms-down, in front of her. She observed mine for ten or twenty seconds, and as she did, I noticed that they were shaking again, a tiny bit. "You do have a slight flutter," she said, but before I could ask her about it, she said, "Okay, let's check your eyes," and she fished a penlight out of her lab coat pocket and switched off the exam room light.

Switching on the penlight and pointing it at the floor, she put one hand on my head to steady me and then said,

"Close your eyes." After a moment, she lifted her hand away and said, "Okay, now put your hands out again like I showed you before. Good. Keep sitting as still as you can, and open your eyes."

I opened them. She was standing a few feet away from me and holding the penlight above her head, shining it at the ceiling. I did my best to keep still, but my eyes wanted to look at the light, that round circle like a moon on the acoustic tile. My head tilted backward all on its own, vibrating a bit as it went. My hands were fluttering again too, I realized, and I wished the doctor would turn the regular light back on. The longer the penlight shone on the ceiling, the harder it became to stay still, and soon I was hovering over the table again, my throbbing legs dangling beneath me.

She turned the room light on and the penlight off, then helped me back down. "Okay. There's one other test I want to do. What it does is measure your levitative sensitivity—in other words, how much your body wants to float. It's very simple: You'll be enclosed in a clear tube, and you'll breathe in some gas that triggers floating. The less gas it takes to make you float, the higher your levitative sensitivity. It's painless, and it just takes a few minutes." She circled a location on a paper map of the hospital and handed it to my mother. "After you're done, come back and we'll talk about the results."

Tears pushed up behind my eyes for the first time since the whole thing started. Whatever this was, it was serious. And what was it anyway? The doctor seemed to know already, so why wasn't she telling me? I looked at my parents to find their faces full of terror as they looked back at me.

"Why didn't you tell us?" asked my mother, but I had no answer.

The nurse found a wheelchair for me, since my legs were still so sore, and my parents and I tried to gather our wits so we could go down to the lab. The hospital, as we had seen on the way in, was large and difficult to navigate. Crammed as it was into a busy part of a major city, it encompassed multiple buildings situated on neighboring blocks or built into the narrow crannies between existing structures and connected by enclosed bridges over the street and by underground tunnels and parking garages.

We wound our way through the labyrinth to find the spot Dr. Liffey had circled on the map. My father pushed my wheelchair past reception desks for departments whose specialties I had never heard of and laboratories marked with biohazard and radioactive-materials signs. There were echoing basement hallways filled with enigmatic unmarked doors, punctuated by occasional cafeterias serving up red plastic trays full of foods I couldn't identify, the scent of deep-fried mysteries trailing us as we passed.

Finally, we found the lab we were looking for. My father wheeled me in. It was mostly dark, and there appeared not to be anyone there. In the middle of the room stood a large plexiglass tube almost as tall as the ceiling. The cylinder was notched on three sides with cross marks inside circles, like targets for shooting practice. The fourth side offered an opening, an arched doorway cut into the tube, with the cut-out piece hinged at the edge. At the top was a large metallic cylinder like the lid of a mason jar.

"Hello?" called my father.

A voice came through a speaker, deep and full of static, like a radio transmission from space. "Can you stand?"

I looked around and noticed a shadowy figure in a booth by the back wall.

"Can you stand?" the voice repeated.

My father helped me push myself out of the chair, my legs wobbling and fizzing with another wave of pain, and he walked me over to the tube. "You okay?" he asked. I nodded, and he joined my mother in the hallway, shutting the door behind him.

"Step into the cylinder, please," the voice said.

Dr. Liffey's words echoed in my head, that it would be painless and fast, but still I hesitated. Whomever that voice belonged to didn't even want to come out of his protective booth. But I knew he was waiting, and my parents were waiting in the hall for me, and my doctor was waiting for my test results, and another patient was probably waiting for their turn in the lab, and the birds were waiting for morning, and the trees were waiting for spring, and the stars were waiting for the universe to complete its great cooling expansion, and all of it seemed to depend on my walking through that doorway.

I took a very deep breath and slowly walked into the tube. "Keep your hands in," the voice directed as the door eased itself shut behind me and sealed with a low mechanical click. "Stand as still as you can and breathe normally," said the voice.

I did my best, but I felt claustrophobic in there. I breathed. I waited. After a moment, a quiet hissing noise began, and I felt a breeze come through the tube. A faint aroma wafted around me—lilac? My feet pulsated with pain, and then my ankles and then my calves, and then I felt air between the floor and me.

"Stay still," said the voice again.

I tried to breathe normally, but anxiety was burning brighter and brighter at my core. I was full-on floating now, drifting upward and lingering around the center of the tube, the thin hospital gown hanging off me like a curtain.

It was really true. I was floating. Even though I had hovered in Dr. Liffey's exam room just a few minutes earlier, that was only a couple inches above the table. I was close enough that I could have pulled myself back down, close enough that I could almost convince myself it wasn't happening. But now I was in midair, several feet off the ground, and there was no denying it. My instinct was to reach out and brace myself against the walls, but I didn't want to ruin the test by moving. So I hovered for what felt like hours, inhaling that synthetic flowery air.

The sound hissed to silence, and a few seconds later, I drifted back down, my legs crumpling in slow motion upon impact with the ground. The voice came over the speaker again. "You're finished." The side hatch clicked as it unlatched and cracked open.

Someone must have alerted my parents that I was done, because my father returned to the room. With his help, I wobbled to my feet and limped, stiff-legged and weak, the few steps to the wheelchair. He rolled me out, my lungs still full of mysterious gas, and the voice didn't say anything else.

In the corridor, I looked around for my mother. When I spotted her, she seemed like a stranger, blank and haggard, but then she saw me and came back to herself. "Ready?" she asked.

I blinked. "I was floating."

My mother let out a long, slow breath. "I know, honey." My father put his hand on my shoulder and squeezed. We sat there for another minute until I nodded, and we retraced our steps to the doctor's office. I was grateful to have my father pushing the wheelchair, as all the energy seemed to have drained out of my body. My mother kept fiddling with the map and disappearing around corners in front of us, and my father rolled me faster to keep up, my joints jarring against the frame of the wheelchair and sending tendrils of burning pain around my knees and hips.

By the time we reached the manifestology department, my test results had been phoned to Dr. Liffey. She called my parents and me into her office and slid behind a large desk. "Have a seat," she said to my parents. My father rolled me between the two chairs on the near side of the desk, and then he and my mother sat down. They looked somewhere between anxious to know what was going on and anxious not to know. Or maybe that was just me.

"So we have your test results," said the doctor. "Between the blood tests yesterday and the pressure-tube test we just ran, we can confirm a diagnosis of lepidopsy."

Lepidopsy. Lepid. Opsy. Leh. Pih. Dop. See. The word bounced around my head a few dozen times in the breath between the pronouncement and the explanation.

"It's a chronic manifestational disease," said Dr. Liffey. "Floating is one of the common symptoms, and so is fluttering." She reached into a drawer and pulled out a photocopied sheet of paper, the not-quite-saturated letters leaning at a slight angle against the edge of the page. "As I said, it's a chronic disease, which means we don't have a cure, but there are treatment options. With careful management, the majority of patients live a normal life span."

Normal life span. Nor. Mal. Life. Span.

She handed me the paper. LEPIDOPSY FACTS, it said in large letters at the top.

The disease gets its name from Lepidoptera, the order of insects that includes butterflies and moths, on account of the common symptoms of floating, fluttering, and discoloration or scaling of the skin on the limbs. Many patients also experience nocturnalism, often with a draw toward bright light sources, and a craving for sweet liquids. Unchecked floating is the leading cause of complications and death. The disease is most common among young women, though some males, children, and older women also develop it.

Light-headed, I gripped the armrests of the wheel-chair. I looked around, unsure of how to react. My parents were frozen in their seats. It was as though all the color had drained from my mother's face, which had gone as gray as the cement of the building we were in, and been poured into my father's, which glowed as red as a stoplight.

"I know this is a lot to take in," said Dr. Liffey. "I want to get you admitted and start you on a course of treatment right away. We'll keep you in for observation for several days to make sure everything's working."

I swallowed hard and tried to blink back my tears. I had never stayed in the hospital before.

"But," said my father, "how did she get this?"

"We're still not entirely sure what causes lepidopsy. There may be environmental factors or an underlying pre-disposition, possibly a hereditary component, activated by an infection or some other trigger."

My parents glanced at each other. Which one had the bomb living inside of them?

"It isn't contagious, and it isn't terminal. It just needs careful attention to keep it under control. And I want to emphasize," said Dr. Liffey, "that we're continuing to research this condition. We know so much more about it now than we did twenty years ago, and the treatments and prognosis are vastly improved."

That's good, I told myself. *Right?*

My father and mother stood. They stayed where they were for a moment, as if waiting for the doctor to say something that would make it all better, take it all back.

Oh, wait. There's been a mistake. This wasn't in your plans. It's impossible. But there was nothing else. My mother picked up her map, my father turned my wheelchair to face the door, and we marched slowly down the hall like a funeral procession.

THERE WAS PAPERWORK, which my mother took care of. There was my wheelchair to push, which my father did until we arrived in admitting. Without something to hold on to, he started growing lines on his forehead, his mouth tightening, his eyebrows scrunching, as if having his hands full was the only thing keeping him from imploding. He took the plastic bag that contained my sweatshirt and jeans from my mother and gripped it so hard, his thumb punched a hole through it.

As I sat there waiting for whatever came next, the word *lepidopsy* still echoed in my head. From somewhere in the deep recesses of my mind, I vaguely recalled seeing a public service announcement about it on TV. A close-up shot of a woman talking directly into the camera: "Lepidopsy is rare, but it's real. I should know—I have it." I hadn't paid much attention at the time, so I couldn't recall any details. But I was pretty sure I would have remembered if she had talked about floating. Maybe I should have paid more attention.

Finally, an orderly came and wheeled me into a room with two empty beds, and I chose the one by the window. A nurse who looked like my school librarian—silver bob, big brown eyes, a no-nonsense walk, and glasses on a lanyard around her neck—came in to start an IV. My mother sat in a chair next to the bed and made occasional remarks designed to reassure me—*It's going to be okay; we'll get this under control*—but I think we both felt better when she was silent.

My father paced and fiddled with everything in the room: the curtains, the rolling bedside tray table, the wires connected to the wall behind the bed. My mother was giving him a look, but he couldn't seem to calm down. "Would you like your dad to go pick up some of your things at home?" she asked me. None of us had anticipated an overnight stay.

"Oh," he said. "I can do that." He seemed grateful for the task.

While he was gone getting my pajamas and my toothbrush and my Walkman, my mother vanished down the hall for a cup of coffee, but only after asking me about fifteen times if I was sure I'd be okay on my own for a few minutes. Once she was gone, I played with the controller for the bed, adjusting myself up and down and up and down until the novelty was replaced by a dizzy, buzzy feeling in my head and gut that I feared meant I was about to lift off again. I left the bed alone and switched on the TV instead. It was only midday at this point, and the standard game show rotation was rolling through. "You've won . . . a new car!" shouted the announcer on *Name Your Price!*, and the audience broke out in shrieks and raucous applause.

All alone in the room, I felt something unexpected come over me: a sense of relief. To have a name for this thing that was happening to me. To have something to do about it. My mother came back and my father came back, and the nurse came and started medicine through the IV line, and as the game shows gave way to the talk shows and the evening news, we all relaxed some. My mother's cheeks were pink again, and my father stopped fidgeting. It was going to be okay, I told myself. It was.

BY THE NEXT morning, the dull pain in my legs had subsided almost completely. The nurse let me get up and walk around a bit, and even then, the pain stayed gone. The medication was working. I really was going to be okay.

Around midday, a new nurse walked in with a girl a few years younger than me, maybe eleven or twelve. She had just been diagnosed with diabetes after going into hyper-glycemic shock at school. They stabilized her blood sugar and set her up in the empty bed by the door for a few days of observation. Diabetes. A disease I had actually heard of. Her mother had it, too, and the two of them practiced insulin shots on oranges until the cool hospital room smelled like I imagined it did in the tropics. I suppose she saw it coming, knew just what to do when the fainting began, the ketoacidosis. She must have seen her mother's needles go in each day, as routine as toast. When the girl's symptoms came around and rang the doorbell like an old familiar uncle who repeats his stories and smells of mothballs, she opened the door and offered up fruit. Unlike me, watching from the next bed, who looked through my own front door only to find a stranger waiting.

The roommate seemed entirely unfazed by her diagnosis.

While I was relieved to know what I had and to have a plan for treating it, it still felt foreign to me, the idea of having a disease. The roommate discussed blood monitoring and insulin shots and glucose numbers with her mother and the nurses as though they were talking about the weather. I, on the other hand, barely had a grip on what was happening. I woke from a nap to the feeling of someone standing next to me and taking my temperature, and I expected to see my mother when I opened my eyes, but it was the nurse. When I turned on the television after dinner to watch my favorite comedy shows, there were news specials on instead. And as the medicine dripped through my veins, I dreamed I was walking through a fragrant grove of citrus trees in perfect rows. Everything was as neat as can be, but I woke up sweating, my hair plastered to the side of my face and the sheets disheveled, unsure which was my waking life and which was the dream.

The roommate arrived on Saturday, the day of the cross-country meet I was missing, so I was glad to have the distraction. I didn't want to think about Smilla and the others having fun without me. Still, I couldn't help picturing them all cheering one another on and celebrating their victories at the diner afterward. Hopefully, I'd be back for the next meet and we could pick up where we left off.

On Sunday afternoon, there was a knock at the door, and I turned to see Smilla standing there. "Oh!" I said. "Hi, come in!" She dashed over and gave me a big hug, but I could feel it was tempered with caution, as though she were afraid of breaking me.

"Here," she said, handing me a bright pink-and-yellow

gift bag with three orange gerbera daisies poking out the top.

"I can't believe you're here!" I had called her briefly to tell her what was going on after I first got checked in, but the days since I'd last seen her felt like a lifetime.

"Yeah. My dad talked to your mom, but I wanted to keep it a surprise."

Something about that made me feel weird, the idea of the three of them talking about me behind my back, deciding when I would have visitors. But I pushed the feeling down, put the gift bag on the tray table, and raised the head of the bed so I was sitting up. I was wearing pajamas, and my hair was all rumpled, and though I'd looked just like that a million times in the morning after a sleepover with Smilla, being in the hospital somehow made me feel self-conscious about it. "Ugh, I look like such a mess."

She waved me off. "You look great. How are you feeling?"

"Better. The medicine is working, I think. I walked around a bunch yesterday, and it didn't hurt at all."

"And you haven't . . . ?"

"Floated?" I thought about how I'd lifted off in the exam room and during the tube test. "Not since I started the medicine."

"Oh, I'm so glad." She beamed at me. "You want to open your present?"

"Of course!" I opened the bag. Inside was a glass soda bottle with the daisies in it, a card, a mixtape, and a bag of peppermint meltaway candies, my favorite.

"The girls slept over last night, and we made the card

together. We even got an olive pizza in your honor!"

The card was collaged with magazine cutouts and paper flowers. "It's great," I said, opening it up to read their well wishes. I felt that same twinge I'd had the day before when I'd thought about them hanging out at the meet without me, but again, I pushed the feelings away. "Hey, maybe we can all get together when I get home."

"Definitely!"

I set the card on the table next to the flowers and reached into the bag for the mixtape. "That's just from me," Smilla said with a sly smile.

I grinned back and looked over the song list she had written out in her careful cursive on a yellow strip of construction paper inside the plastic case. It featured lots of our favorite bands: The Barneys. Tween Murderino. Little Kathy and the Shakes. "I can't wait to listen to this," I said, which seemed to please her.

Last, I pulled out the bag of peppermints and opened it. I hesitated, thinking of Dr. Liffey's question about craving sweets. Was it bad to have them? Or just a symptom of the disease to *want* them? I wasn't sure whether I should eat any, but I didn't want to hurt Smilla's feelings. I took a single green mint out of the bag and placed it in my mouth, trying to ignore the pang of nervousness that hit me as the peppermint melted on my tongue. I held the bag out to her.

She slid her chair closer to the bedside and popped a pink mint into her mouth. "So what do you have to do while you're here?"

"Tests, mostly."

"Like, blood tests?"

"Yeah," I said, thinking of the plastic tube. "And other stuff. And they want to make sure the medicine is working before I go home."

"But you said it *is* working, right?"

"Yeah, I mean, I feel better. Hopefully, it'll just be another couple days." I chuckled. "I never thought I'd be this excited to go back to school."

She relaxed again. "I'm glad they figured it out. Like, can life just be normal again, please?"

"Seriously." There was a pause, and I sensed Smilla gearing up to ask me more about the hospital, the disease, all of it, but I didn't want to talk about it anymore. "So how was the meet?" I asked.

"The four of us came in top seven again!" she said, and then caught herself. "Of course, if you were there, I'm sure it would have been five out of seven."

She obviously wasn't taking my recent performance into account, but it was nice of her to say. "Wish I could have been there."

"Me too," she said. "It's not the same without you. And school isn't the same either. Oh, Ms. Meadows said to tell you she's thinking of you and hopes you're feeling better."

"Aw, that's sweet." Ms. Meadows was the kind of teacher who randomly brought in homemade snacks for everyone or let us watch movies during class, just because she thought we needed a break. The kind of person you could actually talk to, unlike some of our other teachers.

"Let's see, what else . . . ? There was a fire drill yesterday, and Harry Vanderberg was running through the halls yodeling, and all the teachers were trying to catch him. He's ridiculous." She chuckled and shook her head. "Oh, and the guys on the soccer team stood on the tables during lunch and did a musical number. I can't even explain it, but it was hilarious."

I smiled, pretending I thought the idea was hilarious too. Guess you had to be there.

"I got your homework," she said. "Including the geometry homework from Kristi. The girls told me she was weird, and they weren't kidding."

"Oh, what'd she do now?"

Smilla hesitated, like she regretted saying anything.

"What?" I asked, more serious.

She sighed and shrugged, trying to make light of what she was saying. "When I asked her for your assignment, she was like, 'Is it true that Anna can fly?' That's all. It's so silly. Like, who would even say that?"

I felt a bit queasy. The only people who had seen me floating were my teammates. And Kristi didn't seem to have many friends. If word had already made it to her, then the whole school must know. "So everyone's talking about what happened?"

"What? No! That's not what I meant," insisted Smilla, but she used the same tone as when she was pretending the team would have done better with me at the meet.

Several figures appeared in the doorway. "Knock, knock," said my father. My mother was standing behind him with a paper cup of coffee, and Smilla's dad was there too.

"How are you feeling, Anna?" he asked in his lightly accented voice. He was tall and slim, with wispy blond hair just like Smilla's.

"I'm okay, thanks." I sat a little straighter in my bed. He wasn't quite as strict as Smilla's mom, but he was so smart and serious that I always felt like I had to be on my best behavior around him.

"Glad to hear it." He smiled, but his face looked tense as he eyed the IV bag and the medical equipment on the wall. I tried to ignore his unease.

The roommate's mother came back and chatted with all the other parents while Smilla and I talked about TV shows and school gossip for the next hour or so, but I couldn't shake the sense that my floating was this week's real school gossip. And then, though it wasn't even five yet, the meal cart approached, and a scrawny guy in scrubs, who looked so young he could have been our age, brought in my tray.

"Well," said Mr. Jorgensen, "we should probably get going. Let you eat."

Smilla stood up and hugged me again.

"Thanks for visiting," I said. I was glad she came, but I was looking forward to getting out of the hospital and back to school so that everyone could see I was fine. That they could stop speculating about me flying.

"Of course! I can't wait until you're back at school. It's so boring without you." She gave me a little wave and a smile, and then she was gone.

That night, when I was getting ready to sleep, I put the mixtape Smilla had given me into my Walkman. One of my favorite songs by Poor Sylvia came on first, jangly guitars filling my ears. With all the visitors gone, I felt a stew of emotions catching up with me. Worry and sadness, and then annoyance with myself for feeling bad when things would obviously be better now that I was getting treated.

And then some other emotion came over me, one I couldn't name, something like the feeling of waving to someone while driving away from them. I let the tape keep running, and at the end of the first side was a melancholy love song by Hoover Snog, which made me cry, though I couldn't say exactly why. Something about the chords hit a tender nerve inside me. My roommate was quiet in her bed, but I didn't think she was asleep yet, and I didn't want her watching me. I turned toward the window and pulled the sheet to my face, and I rewound the tape and played that sad song over and over again.

THEY KEPT ME in the hospital for five days. On the morning of the day they released me, Dr. Liffey came by one last time to check in. "Good morning," she said, knocking on the door frame before stepping into the room. As before, she had on a white lab coat over a simple but smart ensemble, this time a tailored red top, a straight black skirt, and sensible but stylish black flats. "How are you feeling?" she asked me.

"Much better." My legs didn't hurt anymore, and my body felt nice and solid against the bed. I'd even changed out of pajamas and into normal clothes.

"Great," she said. "I'm writing you a script for the pill

form of the Coronide we've been giving you. It's a high dose, but we should be able to taper you down over time."

My mother, who was sitting in the chair next to me, took the prescription slip and added it to the sheaf of medical papers in her purse.

"Thank you for everything," said my father, who seemed relieved to have the worst behind us.

Dr. Liffey gave him a warm but matter-of-fact smile. "You're welcome." She turned back to me. "Now, this medicine can have some side effects. The most common ones are increased hunger and thirst. Most people get that, though part of it may be from the disease itself, particularly if you're craving candy or sweet liquids. Try to stay away from sweets—you'll feel much better." I thought of the peppermint candies Smilla had given me, and my face grew hot, but I didn't say anything. The doctor continued. "This drug can also cause a mild vibration of the bones, which might make you feel a little wired. It can also make you give off a slight high-pitched noise."

As she went down the list, I assessed whether I felt each symptom. Increased hunger? Not really, although the bland hospital food may have contributed to my flat appetite. Increased thirst, especially for sweet things? The milkshake incident, of course, but that was from the disease itself, before the medication started. What about the vibration and the noise? Not yet, but were the seeds of these annoyances already germinating somewhere in the deep darkness of my body?

"There are other side effects that aren't as common,"

said the doctor. "Numbness or difficulty moving the extremities . . ."

I curled my toes and balled my hands into fists to be sure I still could.

". . . a rattling feeling when you breathe . . ."

I inhaled and exhaled deeply, the air smooth into and out of my lungs.

". . . or possible mood changes."

Was there anything strange about the moods I had experienced after the diagnosis, anything that anyone wouldn't experience in this situation? It was impossible to say. All of this was new territory. A new planet. Maybe even a new dimension.

"Side effects may not kick in for a few weeks, but you should be aware of them. If any of them get especially bad, let me know. I'll want to see you every week for the time being."

"Every week?" my father asked, his calm demeanor crumbling and his eyebrows shooting up to his hairline, just as I could feel my own doing.

"To check in," she said, "get blood work done, make sure everything's going okay with the treatment. We hold a clinic every Wednesday afternoon for kids with manifestational diseases. You can come right after school."

My stomach swirled. Go into the city every week? Would Coach Antee be okay with me missing practice that often?

"Do you have other questions for me?" she asked.

"Can you tell us if we should be limiting her activities?"

my mother asked. "Going to school, exercising, anything?"

"Going to school is fine, though you might need to take the occasional sick day if you're experiencing symptoms. As far as exercise, it can be helpful for reducing symptoms. Generally, we prefer you try something on the slower side. Walking is good, swimming is good, even some light strength training. Anything too fast can make you feel worse: running, bike racing, that sort of thing."

I froze. "So I can't run at all?" What about cross-country? When would I ever get to see Smilla?

"It's not a good idea," said Dr. Liffey. "Especially right now, as we're just getting your illness under control. Try walking and see how you do with that first, okay?"

She stood, shook my parents' hands, patted me on the shoulder, and said she would see me next week. Even though I no longer felt like I needed one, a wheelchair came, and I was wheeled to the main entrance, where my mother waited with me for my father to pull the car around. I sat watching the big sliding glass doors open and close as people went in and out.

When the car arrived, I stood and walked through those doors. Despite the fact that I was leaving the hospital, the doors felt like the entrance to something, a world I had to face whether I was ready or not.

THREE

I WOKE UP at my regular time the next morning, and although I felt a tiny bit stiff and shaky, I insisted on going to school. My parents drove me in themselves, because they had scheduled a meeting with the principal, Mr. Halsing, along with all my teachers before classes started for the day.

In the car, I stared out the window at autumn overtaking the town, the colors of fire dripping over the trees, and the leaves dropping over everything. I thought about what people might say to me and how they might act, and what I might say or do in response. The best approach seemed to be not to make a big deal about it. If people stared or made weird comments, I would just ignore them. I braced myself as my father pulled up in front of the building and let my mother and me out before going to park the car. I took a deep breath, and we walked inside.

The principal's office was close to the main entrance, so there wasn't far to go. The hall was mostly empty this early in the morning, so there wasn't really anyone there to notice me anyway. I guess I'd been expecting something momentous to happen when I entered the building: some big record-scratch moment, a crowd of people stopping in their tracks and turning to look at me in unison. Somehow, the anticlimax was even more unnerving.

While my parents had their conference, I sat in the suite that held the principal's office, just outside the office door, listening as best I could. My father said I might be tired or have a hard time getting around, so I might be late to class sometimes and I'd need to skip phys ed for a while. My mother said there might be more days I was out sick and would need a friend to bring work home. Smilla Jorgensen had already agreed to help, she said. I hadn't heard Smilla agree to that. My mother must have asked her when she wasn't in my room. The thought of them talking about me outside my presence again tied a knot in my gut, and I hoped that the homework question was all there was to it.

My teachers yes-yessed and of-coursed and said they were glad to accommodate me and happy to have me in their classes. They discussed lesson plans and homework assignments and individual tutoring. They went on and on with my parents, but when the office door opened and they tried to talk to me, they couldn't seem to figure out what to say. Mr. Zayne, my history teacher, nodded and smiled but was silent, possibly the first time that had ever happened.

Mrs. Pozorski from biology opened her mouth to speak, then waved at someone down the hall, excused herself, and ran off. Ms. Meadows, the most reasonable of my teachers, wasn't able to make the meeting, and it was decided I would meet with her one-on-one after class in the time slot I was supposed to have phys ed, which was now off the table.

My parents hugged me goodbye and lingered before leaving, as if I might change my mind and decide to go home with them.

"I'm *fine*," I said in response to the question not asked aloud. I wanted them to leave, but when they did, I felt exposed and vulnerable.

As I walked to French, I tried to keep looking at the path ahead of me and not worry about anyone's reactions. Still, my eyes drifted to a few faces here and there. Was I being self-conscious, or were people staring at me? I braced myself for their commentary, but nobody said anything at all. Not until I got to the classroom and saw Jennie.

She waved me over to sit next to her. "How *are* you?"

It felt like a relief that someone had finally spoken to me and that it wasn't unkind, but at the same time, it made me uncomfortable, feeling so visible. I smiled at Jennie and responded quietly, hoping she would lower her voice so people wouldn't stare. "I'm okay. So what did I miss?"

She flipped through her ultra-organized notebook, back to the date I'd gone into the hospital. It seemed like such a long time ago already, but it wasn't even a full week. "I gave Smilla the assignments you missed while you were in the hospital," she said at full volume. "Did you get them?"

"Yep. Thanks! How are you?" All I wanted was to change the subject, but she couldn't seem to take the hint.

"I'm fine. Just been worried about you! I'm really glad you're feeling better. Is there anything I can do to help?"

She was looking at me so earnestly, and I thought if I just gave her a job already she might move on. "Maybe I can call you if I have questions about the homework?"

"Of course!" She beamed, delighted to be of use, and then, mercifully, we all fell silent as class began.

I saw Smilla at the door to third-period English. "Hey!" she said, and gave me a huge hug. We walked in and were, as usual, the first ones in the room. We were about to sit in our regular seats up front when Ms. Meadows, who had been writing something on the board, turned toward us. As soon as she saw me, the pleasant expression on her face clouded, and she burst into tears. She marched over and enveloped me in a tight hug before I could react, and I froze, arms pinned at my sides, while she wept.

When she finally let go, she shook her head, tears still streaming down her face. "Oh, Anna, I heard about what happened. Are you all right?"

I stood there awkwardly as Ms. M's face warped with worry. "I'm okay," I said. It was weird to feel like I had to reassure her. Shouldn't it be the other way around? "So," I said slowly, "Smilla gave me the homework, but Mr. Halsing said I should check in with you about anything else I missed." Technically, he'd said that I should meet with her the following period to get help catching up, but I didn't think I could take fifty full minutes of this.

She pulled a tissue from the box on her desk and dabbed at her eyes, took a deep breath, and tried to pull herself together. "Yes. Right. Just read those stories and write a one-page reaction paper to each. If you need a little more time or you need help with anything," she said, clasping my hand in hers, "I am here for you."

She looked like she might start crying again, so I sat down as quickly as I could, turning to Smilla so I could escape the conversation. As soon as Ms. M turned back to the board, I gave Smilla a wide-eyed *What the hell?* look.

Smilla smiled and shrugged. "She was just worried."

"I guess," I said, but I still felt unsettled. And it felt even weirder that Smilla had defended such strange behavior.

I made it through class without any further incidents and then headed to the library. Tucking myself into a carrel along the back wall to hide away for a little while, I let out a long breath. It was barely halfway through the day, and I was already exhausted. Emotionally, mostly, but I was physically tired too. I hadn't expected that. I thought that once I got back to school, with the medication working and my feet on the ground, I'd feel normal. But then again, I always felt a little tired getting back to my routine after being sick. I just needed to give myself a few days to get back in the swing of things.

At lunch, Smilla and Jennie fawned over me, constantly asking how was I doing, where did I want to sit, did I need help carrying my tray, what could they do to help? I told myself they would chill out soon and tried to change the subject. But it was the first real chance we'd had to catch up, and they were curious about everything: What was it like? What kind of tests did they do? And most of all: What *was* lepidopsy anyway?

I gave the briefest answers I possibly could, then steered the conversation to the TV shows everyone was watching. I had to take my scheduled pill with food, and I waited until Jennie started talking before swallowing it as discreetly as possible. But Min noticed. "What's that?" she asked.

"Medicine," I said.

Min, Smilla, and Jennie looked at me with concern. Cheryl, on the other hand, seemed to be having a hard time making eye contact. Her face was calm and pleasant, but she was looking everywhere except at me. I wanted to tell them to knock it off. But when the conversation turned back to classes and clothes and Min's ongoing boy drama instead of my illness, I felt invisible again. I didn't know what I wanted.

After lunch, I headed off to geometry and parked myself at a desk along the side of the room. As I unloaded my notebook and pen, Kristi dropped her backpack by the chair next to mine and said hi.

I actually looked around to make sure I was the one she was talking to. "Hey. Um, thanks for getting the homework to Smilla for me."

"No problem. So how are you feeling?"

I thought about what Smilla had said, that Kristi asked her if I'd been flying. That was weird for sure, but Kristi was actually being pretty nice to me right now.

"I'm okay," I said. Maybe she'd heard some gossip

about me that had gotten twisted, and she was just trying to straighten it out. Besides, was flying really that much stranger than floating?

Mr. Takahashi came over to my desk. He had nodded at me on the way out of that morning's conference but hadn't said anything beyond "See you in class." "Hello, Anna," he said now, fumbling with a piece of chalk. "How is your . . . How are you?"

"I'm fine," I said, smiling at him.

"Well, we're all glad you're . . . glad to have you back. Did you get the assignments from when you were in—sorry, from while you were out?"

I nodded. He lingered awkwardly for a moment, trying to think of something else to say, but eventually he just nodded back and returned to the front of the room.

As he walked away, Kristi turned to me and rolled her eyes. I snickered, and she gave me the faintest hint of a smile. In a day full of strange happenings, Kristi smiling at me, however subtly, had to be the strangest.

OVER THE COURSE of that first week back at school, I felt odd and self-conscious as the reactions kept coming. One of the girls from the team, a freshman, caught me in the hall, leaned close, and said in a hushed and dramatic tone, "Oh my *god*, that was so scary when you were floating. I was like, what is going on? It was bizarre."

"Oh," I said. "Yeah." When she continued standing there,

waiting for me to say something else, I added, "I have to get to class." As I walked away, I glanced backward and saw her watching me go. Other than feeling a little low-energy, I was fine. When were people going to let this go?

On Friday, I sat in the back corner in biology, more tired than I wanted to admit, and caught the cluster of boys on the opposite side of the room staring. When I noticed them, they turned to one another, muttered something, and laughed. I tried not to pay attention, but I felt their eyes on me all through class, and I could see their looks of disgust in my peripheral vision.

As the final bell rang and school let out, relief washed over me. I had made it. I shuffled to the bus and sat in an empty row halfway down, leaning my head back against the torn vinyl seat. The sports teams were gathering on the fields around the school: the soccer players bouncing balls on their knees, the lacrosse players swinging their sticks. Off in the distance, I could see my teammates stretching at the track. Smilla was out there somewhere, and here I was, sitting in a bus seat by myself.

The next Wednesday afternoon, I skipped the bus so my mom could drive me to the city for the pediatric manifestology clinic, where we met up with my father. Dr. Liffey's office was much busier than it had been during my initial visit. Several other teenage girls were sitting in the waiting room with their mothers, some with younger siblings in tow. A few other stray parents were there as well, flipping through ragged magazines as their kids were examined elsewhere. Almost everyone in the room was dressed in comfortable, unremarkable clothing: worn-in jeans and big sweaters, knit pants and turtlenecks. I felt out of place in my jean shorts over bright-green tights and vintage peasant blouse, but I wasn't sure how much I wanted to fit in here.

We settled in. I half-heartedly skimmed my history textbook while my father went through work papers. Meanwhile, my mother pulled out a book I hadn't seen before. It looked brand-new, and the title on the spine was *Searching for Gravity*.

"What's that?" I said.

She held it up for me to see. The front cover sported a design featuring the abstract shapes of moths, and under the main title was a subtitle: *A Patient's Guide to Managing Lepidopsy*. "They special-ordered it for me at the bookstore. You want to take a look?"

I shook my head. "That's okay." I was a little annoyed that she was reading a book that was supposed to be for people who had the disease, not their parents. But I didn't want to read it myself either. It felt embarrassing to show that much interest in it, at least in front of other people. Instead, I turned back to my textbook and tried not to let my mother notice the looks I kept sneaking at her.

After half an hour or so, a nurse came out and called me into an exam room. My parents waited outside while the nurse brought me in, checked my blood pressure, and had me change into a gown. I sat on the exam table and waited for Dr. Liffey.

But it was a stranger, not Dr. Liffey, who led my parents into the room. He was short, maybe an inch or two above my five foot four. "I'm Dr. Shiel," he said, offering me a limp handshake.

"Where's Dr. Liffey?" It was disorienting to have to come to this clinic and then not even see the doctor I thought I was here to see.

"She'll be in soon. I'm the resident here in manifestology. I'm going to do the initial exam with you."

"Oh," I said, suddenly feeling exposed in my thin cloth gown. "Okay." Wasn't a resident still a medical student or something? Was he even qualified to do the exam? I glanced at my parents, and they both looked a little surprised but not alarmed, so we proceeded.

Dr. Shiel checked my eyes and hands and skin just as Dr. Liffey had, but with a touch as weak as his handshake. Plus, he narrated the whole thing with medical jargon I didn't understand, which seemed to be solely for his own benefit. "No sign of squama on the brachium. That's good." He had me hold out my hands so he could check my flutter, which had all but disappeared. "Excellent," he said. "Only minimal *manus tremens*."

"What does that mean?" asked my mother, a subtle irritation creeping into her voice.

"Just the technical term for 'fluttering.' Nothing to worry about!"

So just say "fluttering," I thought. My mother and I looked at each other, unimpressed.

He finished the exam and made some final notes in my

chart. "Dr. Liffey will be right in," he said, slipping through the door. I was glad I'd be seeing Dr. Liffey. Even though I hadn't known her that long, I already trusted her opinion more than Dr. Shiel's. The door opened again, and Dr. Liffey came in, but Dr. Shiel was right behind her like a puppy. Between the two of them, my parents standing in the corner, and me, the tiny exam room felt very crowded.

"How are you doing?" asked Dr. Liffey. "You're looking good!" She skimmed Dr. Shiel's notes and then checked my arms herself, then did the whole penlight on the ceiling routine. "Much better," she said as I held my hands out nearly steady before me. "Any side effects at this point?"

"I don't think so. A little tired."

"Great," she said, examining my chart again. She looked back at me and smiled. "I'm pleased to see the medication working well. We'll get your blood tests next, and then we'll introduce you to our social worker, who runs the support group."

Support group? No one had mentioned that before. I wasn't sure how much I wanted to talk about my problems in front of a bunch of strangers. Besides, what was there to talk about? The treatment was working, and I was moving on with my life.

As everyone filed out of the room so I could change back into my clothes, I looked at my forearms. My skin looked normal, as far as I could tell. There were the same wispy light-brown hairs on the same backdrop of tan skin that there had always been. I brushed the fingertips of my right hand over my left arm, and vice versa. Everything felt okay.

I got dressed and went down the hall to get my blood taken, parents in tow, and sat in the waiting area for another half hour. There were parents with kids from toddler to teenager, most of whom I didn't recognize from my own clinic's waiting room. I wondered about the other departments they had come from, the other diseases they were dealing with. For a long time, a child wailed behind the closed lab door. Finally, she emerged, covered in tears and rainbow bandages, carried in her shaken mother's arms.

When the phlebotomist called me in, my mother asked if I wanted her to come. She was already starting to get up, but I shook my head and marched into the lab alone. I situated myself in the chair, watching as the phlebotomist read my lab slip and grabbed test tube after test tube out of the drawer. All the rubber tops sealing the tubes were different colors, and I wondered what they meant. Better to focus on that than on the volume of blood this woman would have to pull out of me to fill the dozen vials. There was a spring-green top and a lavender top. There were brown and pink and white tops. Some were variegated with different colors, like the orange-and-black tiger stripes, or the green and yellow of daffodil blossoms and leaves.

Although I still felt a little woozy thinking about all the vials, I was relieved that I remained solidly in my seat. I took a deep breath as the phlebotomist said, "Just a little pinch," and as the needle stabbed the inside of my arm, I stared at the anatomy poster on the wall showing the veins of the hand and arm that traveled beyond the shoulder, all the way into the heart.

The rubber tourniquet around my upper arm snapped as the phlebotomist pulled it off. She put a square of gauze against the spot where the needle was inserted and pulled it out, instructing me to press the gauze down tightly on the puncture. "Do you want a rainbow bandage?" she asked as she disposed of the needle and began labeling the vials.

Somehow, opting for the rainbow bandage felt like a defeat, as though by choosing the decorative option over the utilitarian one, I would be accepting an unacceptable fate. That I would be giving in to the permanence of my situation. "No, thanks," I said, and she gave me a plain beige one instead.

Back at the manifestology department, patients, nurses, and parents were still milling around. One of the nurses called me, and I followed her, my parents trailing behind me like comet dust. It must have been nearly five at that point, and the day was catching up with me. I still wanted to believe I was simply readjusting to my normal schedule after being in the hospital, but it had been a week already. Plus, the weariness I felt wasn't like the worn-out but satisfied feeling I used to get after a long run, the kind of tiredness that felt earned. I hoped it was only a passing side effect of my medication.

My feet shuffled as the nurse led me into a small office with a compact sofa and a couple of chairs around a shabby coffee table. "This is Lisa, our social worker," said the nurse.

Lisa appeared close to forty and sported a short and

funky haircut that was a not-quite-natural shade of red. She wore big hoop earrings and frosted lipstick. She shook my hand and then my parents' and offered us seats.

"So basically," she said, "I'm here for you to talk about anything you may be feeling or thinking about. If you're stressed, if you're sad or worried, you can talk to me. It's pretty normal to feel overwhelmed when you get this kind of diagnosis."

Part of me appreciated her saying so. Nobody else had acknowledged that I might be feeling anything beyond physical symptoms. But talking about it would only make the disease seem more real, and I did not want to do that.

After getting the introductions out of the way, Lisa sent my parents back to the waiting area and brought me into a small conference room down the hall past the exam rooms. "Here's where we have our group," she said. Three other kids, all girls, sat around a table and waved at me. "We're small today," said Lisa. "Not everyone comes in every week, so the group's different each time."

The others introduced themselves. Carrie was sixteen and had a disease that stretched and warped her limbs and organs. I wasn't sure exactly how it worked, but since it was manifestological, her cells must have been defying some law of nature. She had been mildly sick for three years before they diagnosed her. She was tall and thin and pretty, and I wondered how much of her height came from the disease.

Elaine was thirteen, short and round with shiny

auburn curls. She reminded me of a porcelain doll. She had been diagnosed the year before with a disease so rare there were currently only five other known cases in the country. It had something to do with the transfer of energy and resulted in an excess of heat building up in various parts of her body. I imagined her lungs glowing like embers inside her. The doctors had her condition under control with medications used for other disorders, but it was hard to know the best treatment for a disease that unusual. There just wasn't enough research. Although I felt a little ashamed for thinking it, I was glad I didn't have what she had.

And last, there was Pam. "I have lepidopsy too!" she said, sounding way too excited about it. Pam had a cane hooked over the arm of her chair, and she had clearly used it for a while: it was painted a metallic turquoise, with a row of silver rhinestones glued to the side. It seemed like she had accepted her defeat and accessorized accordingly. "The cane is to help me walk, because I have chrysalization around some of my joints. It's a sort of rare complication."

Revulsion and curiosity competed in my mind. I didn't want to be like that, with a cane and an attitude of casual acceptance. I couldn't. How long ago had she been diagnosed? How long had it taken her to get to this point? How old was she anyway? From the businesslike way she talked about her illness, it seemed like she was seventeen or eighteen and had had it for a while. Did she feel pity for me, knowing what might be in store?

Lisa and the four of us sat around the table for about half an hour. After the initial questions about my illness and diagnosis, I mostly listened. They talked about school, about grades and missed classes, about the frustration of dealing with teachers who didn't want to help them and the appreciation they felt for those who did. They talked about their homes and how far they had to come to get here (Pam lived just outside the city; Carrie was a little over an hour's drive south; and Elaine lived two and a half hours away, in a different state). They talked about boys and feeling self-conscious about their bodies, their scars and defects. I was at once fascinated and desperate to be anywhere else. It felt like I was being sucked into a pit from which escape seemed less and less likely, but soon enough, Lisa was opening the door again and releasing us back to the normal lives we were attempting to live.

Pam walked next to me as we went down the hall to the waiting area, leaning lightly on her cane. She had a slight limp. "Did you have all your checks yet?"

"I think so." I couldn't imagine what else there would be to check after my blood had been drawn and two doctors, a nurse, and a social worker had seen me.

"I still have to see Dr. Liffey," she said.

I nodded at her and turned toward where my parents were sitting so I could get my stuff and leave.

"Hey, Anna!" called Pam from behind me. I turned back to her, and she said, "We should exchange phone numbers in case you want to talk sometime."

"Oh," I said. The last thing I wanted was for this place to spill over into my regular life, but I didn't want to be rude. "Okay."

I pulled a page out of my notebook, tore it in half, and wrote my number on one piece. She wrote hers on the other, and we traded. "Great!" she said. "Well, see you next time!"

She parked herself in a chair in the corner next to a woman I presumed was her mother. As my parents and I put our coats on, I watched Pam take out a thick book and start reading. A little girl toddled over to her and climbed into her lap. Pam caught me looking and smiled, and gave a sort of fake-exasperated big-sister shake of the head. The girl curled up on Pam's lap and started sucking her thumb, and Pam went on reading, only now she read aloud. I caught bits of her narration as my parents and I gathered our things. The story was about life on another planet. About a queen who lived in an interstellar castle and looked through the windows at her airless world each day, wishing she could go out and walk around.

MY MOTHER FINISHED the lepidopsy book a few days later and left it on the living room coffee table. I kept seeing it there and ignoring it while my parents were in the room, but on Saturday afternoon while I was waiting for Smilla to come over, I had my opportunity. My father was outside raking leaves, and my mother was upstairs somewhere, so I parked myself on the couch and flipped the book open.

I skimmed through the introductory section about the author, a manifestologist who had interviewed dozens of patients and conferred with some of the leading doctors in the field to write the book. I was more interested in the chapter titled "What Is Lepidopsy?" It started with the basics that I already knew but went into much greater detail than the information sheet Dr. Liffey had given me.

> Lepidopsy is a systemic manifestological disease. Like all manifestological diseases, it is rare, and it stems from the body's cells defying a physical law. In the case of lepidopsy, that law is gravity. This disease strikes females more frequently than males, and its onset occurs most often in young adulthood.
>
> Floating (levitative activity) is the most common symptom of lepidopsy, and the most characteristic. Approximately 80 percent of all patients will experience floating at some point in the course of their illness. In most instances, this floating is mild and takes place a few inches to a few feet above the ground; patients can easily pull themselves or be pulled back down, and they may be held in place with gentle force.

I thought about Coach holding my shoulders at practice, about Dr. Liffey pushing me back to the exam table. Once they got me down, I was able to stay down, at least for a while. And since I'd started taking the medication, I hadn't floated at all.

In rare instances, floating may be more forceful or may carry the patient to greater heights. Greater force and higher altitude are not necessarily linked, though it is dangerous when they coincide. It is important that all floating activity receive prompt treatment, as unchecked floating, even at low heights, can cause significant cellular damage over time, resulting in permanent physical impairment or even death.

I looked up from the book and took a deep breath. *Normal life span,* I repeated to myself. *Normal life span, normal life span.* I was seeing Dr. Liffey all the time, and she would take care of it. Everything was under control.

Other common symptoms of lepidopsy include:

- Pain, particularly in the extremities, often preceding or coincident with levitative activity
- Fluttering of the hands
- Intense cravings for sweet liquids and foods
- Nocturnalism (insomnia and the drive to be more active at night), which may lead to daytime fatigue
- Light sensitivity (being drawn to sources of light, particularly in an otherwise-dark setting)
- Scale formation on the forearms or calves
- Light-headedness and difficulty focusing ("brain fog")

Each patient with lepidopsy is unique and may experience these symptoms in any combination or pattern. The disease may have active periods alternating with periods of remission, or mild disease activity continuing for a longer duration.

In other words, nobody had any idea what was going to happen to me. But I saw the word *remission* and held on to it. I already felt better, and I would continue feeling fine. I was determined for it to be true.

I flipped past a section of technical scientific explanations I didn't understand and landed on a section called "Managing Disease Activity."

While it is uncertain what causes lepidopsy or triggers flare-ups of disease activity, there are steps patients can take to improve their overall health and manage their symptoms.

- Get adequate rest, and try to keep a regular schedule. Although nocturnalism can make it difficult to keep to a normal daytime routine, doing so as much as possible can help reduce symptoms of fatigue. Being well rested may also help reduce disease activity, according to some studies. Working brief naps into your daily schedule at the times when your energy runs low may be helpful.

- Maintain a healthy, balanced diet focused on fresh fruits and vegetables, whole grains, low-fat dairy products, and small amounts of lean proteins. Although sugar cravings are both a common symptom of lepidopsy and a side effect of some drugs used to treat it, sugary foods and drinks are best avoided. For some patients, they may exacerbate symptoms, and a patient's nutritional needs may not be met if their diet is too heavily based on sugar and processed foods.

- Get exercise on a regular basis. Talk to your doctor about which forms of exercise are most suitable for you based on your symptoms and state of health. In general, slow, low-impact activities, such as swimming, walking, or stretching, may be helpful. Faster motion, such as running, heavy aerobics, or high-speed bicycling, may be dangerous and induce symptoms. If you are considering—

The doorbell rang, and I startled so hard, I almost fell off the couch. I took a deep breath. *Calm down,* I told myself. *It's just Smilla.* I didn't want her to see the book and start asking questions, so I shoved it under a couch cushion.

I let her in, and we wandered into the kitchen. "You want anything to drink?" I asked. I opened the refrigerator, and we both looked inside. My mother had cleared out all the sodas and juices after Dr. Liffey mentioned avoiding sweets, so the only options were seltzer and milk.

"I could make tea," I said.

"Sure!"

I handed Smilla a mug. "Do you have any honey?" she asked.

I dug the small jar out of the pantry and handed it to her. She spooned some into her mug and then offered it to me. I hadn't mentioned that I was supposed to be avoiding sweets, and I tried to appear nonchalant as I buried the jar back in the pantry even though I would have liked some.

In the living room, I grabbed the sofa where I'd hidden the book, and Smilla sprawled across the love seat, sighing. "I can't believe I even made it out of the house. My mother has been on me nonstop about essay topics for college applications. We're *sophomores.*"

"So how'd you bust out?"

Her eyes went wide and guilty. "I *may* have told her you and I had an English assignment to work on."

I laughed and shook my head. It was hardly the first time she'd used homework as an excuse to come over. "Whatever it takes. I'm just glad you're here."

"Besides, you know how my parents are about *building character.* Helping a friend get back on track with schoolwork after being sick is kind of catnip to them."

"Right," I said, but I could feel my face tensing into an uneasy smile.

She caught herself then. "I hope that's okay. I mean, I'm happy to actually help you if you need it. You know that, right?"

"Yeah, of course," I said, but she still looked worried. I didn't want to dwell on the illness or anything related to it, so I steered the conversation back to where it had begun. "Why is your mom so worried about college anyway? You have good grades, extracurriculars, all of that stuff."

She went on about her mom, but the mention of my being sick had distracted me, and I became overly aware of the book hiding under the couch cushion. I kept worrying that it would shift and fall out onto the floor, and that Smilla would not only see it and want to talk about my health, but that she'd know I'd been hiding it from her and get upset. It stayed where it was, but the whole time we sat there, I could sense it beneath me, as though it were vibrating or giving off heat. And soon, my thoughts shifted from the physical object to the information I'd read inside it. That last bit, about how running could be dangerous . . . Had I brought this on myself by running too much? Or by letting myself give in to that wild speed my body had been feeling recently?

"Are you okay?" Smilla asked.

"Oh, yeah, sorry. I got a little distracted."

"You sure?"

"I'm fine." I wanted her to stop giving me that look. That *You poor, delicate thing* look. "So, what does your dad say about it?" I asked.

She hesitated, but then she continued her story, and I breathed again.

From the kitchen, the telephone rang, and my mother answered it. A moment later, she came to the doorway. "It's Min," she said.

I looked at Smilla. Min didn't usually call me unless she needed a homework assignment or something. "Oh, yeah," said Smilla. "I told the girls I was coming over."

I felt something shift uncomfortably, some fault line deep in my soul. Smilla and I hadn't been alone in almost two weeks, not since she'd come to see me in the hospital.

I took the cordless phone from my mother. "Hello?"

"Hey!" said Min. I could hear voices in the background,

and I knew without asking that they were Cheryl's and Jennie's. "What are you guys up to?"

We were doing nothing, and I wanted us to keep doing nothing without interference. "Oh, this and that."

"Come over! We're hanging out." A burst of laughter bubbled up in the background.

Min's house was all the way across town. Plus, Smilla had just arrived. "I don't know," I said.

"What's going on?" asked Smilla.

I put my hand over the receiver. "Min asked if we want to go to her house." I scrunched my face and shrugged.

"They could come here if you don't feel like going out," said Smilla. She seemed to think I wanted to find a way to make this happen.

"Um, maybe. I don't know."

"Here, let me talk to her." Smilla took the phone and made her suggestion to Min. There was a pause, presumably while Min asked the others, and then Smilla laughed. "Cool," she said finally. "See you in twenty." She hung up and turned to me. "Her brother's driving them. It's no problem!"

"Great." I tried not to sound sarcastic.

When the others arrived, they came and sat in the living room with us. Min and Jennie were on the couch with me, and again, I worried about the book sliding out from under the cushion. But I probably didn't need to. No one was paying much attention to me anyway.

"Did you guys hear what Coach said about getting ice cream after the meet in Beckford?" Min asked the others.

"They have that amazing sundae bar at the Beckford Inn!"

Cheryl laughed. "You and your sweet tooth."

"Oh, you'll probably get strawberry ice cream with nothing on top, huh?" Min replied. "You're so *sophisticated.*"

"And you'll probably get something gross like gummy bears all over yours!"

"That's right. I'm getting my money's worth!"

They all laughed. Smilla turned to me. "You should come watch the meet! Then you can get ice cream with us!"

I felt left out enough sitting in the same room as them. Watching them from a distance as they ran sounded terrible. And watching them celebrate afterward over ice cream that I wasn't supposed to eat sounded even worse. "Maybe."

"Oh, you totally should!" said Jennie.

"You know," said Smilla, "maybe you could be the team manager or something. Then you could come to the meets with us and still be part of the team!"

A *manager*? What, like I was supposed to start timing the runners and handing out cups of water?

The others nodded. "That's a good idea," said Jennie.

"Maybe," I said again.

Smilla beamed at me, happy to help. This time, she didn't seem to notice how bad I felt. Maybe I was getting better at hiding it. Or maybe she was too distracted by the fun she was having with the others.

"Let's do something," said Cheryl. "Go for a walk or whatever."

"We could go by the elementary school playground," said Smilla, as though she were the host instead of me. "It's only a few blocks away. If you don't mind walking," she said, turning to me again. The others turned to me too.

"Um, sure, I guess." Dr. Liffey had said that walking was good for me, right? Maybe it would help me feel better. And at that point, I preferred to find out rather than continuing to sit around listening to them talk.

I went to get my coat from the front closet and then shuffled upstairs to tell my mother where we were going. I found her doing some of her freelance editing work at her desk, and she frowned when I told her.

"Are you sure you're up to it?" She put down her pen and peered at me over her reading glasses.

"It's fine," I said. "I'm fine."

She took off her glasses and set them on the desk, which I knew meant I was in danger of getting into a longer conversation.

"I'm *fine*," I said again, growing more emphatic but less convinced with each repetition.

"Well, if you start to feel bad, even a little, I want you to turn around and come home. Or send one of the girls to get me. And there's a pay phone at the school, right?" She grabbed a handful of change from the small dish on her desk and thrust it at me before I could answer.

I pocketed the dimes and quarters and fought the urge to roll my eyes. She wasn't usually this overprotective, but I was glad to have an escape route if I needed one. I thanked her and went back downstairs.

My street was pretty quiet, so the five of us spread out as we walked. Cheryl was talking about this trip she and her parents were planning to London over Christmas break. The others kept bursting in with questions and comments, and they were all so into the conversation that they were walking very slowly, for which I was glad. I was also glad that I could tune out the conversation without them noticing, because it allowed me to focus on how I felt physically. I had done plenty of walking around school since I got out of the hospital, but that was spread throughout the day. This was the first time I had walked so far in one stretch.

My hands were a tiny bit fluttery by the time we got to the elementary school, but that could have just been from the chilly October weather. I stuffed my hands in my pockets and followed the others onto the school grounds.

"So you two both went here?" Min asked Smilla and me. Just as the town had two small middle schools, it had three even smaller elementary schools.

"Yep!" said Smilla. "We met right there." She pointed to the spot on the playground where, in kindergarten, Todd Parrell stole my glove and laughed, and Smilla grabbed it back from him and comforted me. Then we gleefully and sloppily painted each other's nails with the bright-pink polish I'd smuggled out of my mom's makeup drawer and carried to school in my pocket. We had been best friends ever since.

We walked over to the swing set, where four swings swayed slightly in the breeze. Cheryl leaned against the pole on one side, and Min took the end swing next to her, Jennie and Smilla took the next two, and the last one was open for me. I sat on it motionlessly while the others got up to speed, sailing higher and higher. The thought of whipping through the air like that made me uneasy as I imagined myself being launched skyward and unable to come back down. So I just dangled there, kicking at the dirt below me.

We stayed for what felt like hours but was probably no more than forty-five minutes, wandering around the playground. I was pretty tired by the time we headed back toward my house, but I didn't want to make a big deal about it by calling my mom to come get me.

"So, Anna," said Jennie as we strolled along the road, "when do you think you'll be able to start running again?"

The question caught me totally off guard. I hadn't mentioned that I wasn't supposed to run anymore, but I was only realizing that now. "I don't know," I said. A reflex. But I honestly didn't know when—or if—Dr. Liffey would let me do it again.

"You could always try out for winter track if you're ready by then," said Min. "Or track and field in the spring."

"Yeah!" said Jennie. "Cheryl, Min, and I are doing all three again this year."

"And Smilla!" said Cheryl, turning to smile at her.

I looked over at Smilla, trying to contain my surprise. "You are?" This meant she'd be busy almost every afternoon year-round, not just in the fall. And that she'd be hanging out with the three of them constantly. But, mostly, I couldn't believe that they knew about her plans before I did.

"Well . . . yeah!" Her tone seemed overly bright and cheery, like she was trying to make me believe this was a good idea. "I really like running, and I want to keep it up."

"Your mom's not going to make you do all those other classes?"

"Well, it was hard to convince her, but then Coach said I might be good enough to get a college scholarship."

"Yes, because you are the most amazing!" said Cheryl, and the others echoed her sentiment. And then they were back to talking about cross-country, the upcoming meets, things that had happened at practice, the new running shoes they wanted, and so on, the entire way back to my house.

Min's brother came to pick the three of them up, and then it was just Smilla and me again. It was what I'd been wanting the whole afternoon, but now it felt soured. Still, Smilla was planning to stay for dinner, so she and I flipped on the TV to an old movie in the living room while my father cooked. He was making vegetarian enchiladas, since Smilla was joining us, and something about that made me want to cry.

I lay on the couch, watching people talk and argue and kiss in black and white, all the while sensing the lepidopsy book underneath the cushion below me like a time bomb. A commercial came on, and Smilla said, "You should ask your doctor when she thinks you'll be able to run again. You should totally do winter track and spring track and field with us! I didn't mean to leave you out or anything."

"Um, yeah." I paused for a minute, considering how much to tell her. "I'm not supposed to run anymore."

Smilla sat up straight on the love seat. "Like, ever?"

"I don't think so." Maybe it was possible I could run again at some point, but after what Dr. Liffey and the book had said, it seemed like pushing my luck to try.

"But I thought you'd be coming back!" Now she seemed on the verge of tears. "Well . . . maybe you still can. People beat the odds all the time! I was just watching this show about a marathon runner who got into a car accident and was paralyzed from the waist down. The doctors said he'd never be able to walk again, but he worked really hard, and now he's walking *and* winning races!"

I suddenly felt even more tired. "I'm not sure. I only know what my doctor told me."

"But sometimes doctors are wrong. You said yourself they don't even know what causes lepidopsy. They don't have all the answers. You can totally prove them wrong."

I wasn't sure how to make her stop. She probably thought she was giving me a pep talk, but it didn't feel that way to me. Mercifully, my father called us into the kitchen for dinner, and she let it go.

That evening, after Smilla left, my parents asked if I wanted to watch TV with them, but I just wanted to be alone. I went to my room, shut the door, and breathed for what felt like the first time all day. I kept thinking of what Smilla had said, about beating the odds. Was she right? Should I be working harder to get myself better and get back to running? The book said running *might* be dangerous, but maybe it wouldn't be. As tired as I was, I cranked up some music and jogged in place in my room for a few minutes, just to see what would happen.

It didn't take long. Traces of the dull ache I had felt that last day at practice flickered in my feet, and then my ankles. I pushed through it. My pace was way slower than usual, but it was harder to get air into my lungs. The pain began to rise into my calves, and the flutter grew stronger in my hands. My limbs still felt uncoordinated—not as bad as they had that day at practice, but they weren't working right. The fatigue was heavier now. The room started spinning, and I decided I'd better stop before I made myself float.

I sat down in my desk chair, grabbing the arms and trying to focus on one spot on my desk so that space would steady itself around me. It eventually did, but breathing was still an effort, and I kept feeling like I needed to cough but couldn't. I remembered then that one of the side effects Dr. Liffey had mentioned was a rattling feeling while breathing. Great. Now I felt even worse than I had before, and it was my own fault.

That night, I couldn't sleep. I kept thinking about the day, about the distance growing between Smilla and me. And words from the book echoed in my mind. *Permanent physical impairment. Death.*

No, I thought. *No, no, no.*

I finally got up and tiptoed downstairs. It was after two. My parents were asleep in their room, and the house was dark and quiet. I pulled the book from under the cushion and carried it back to my room.

When I turned on my bedside lamp, the light shocked my eyes. Was I more sensitive to it than I should have been? I couldn't tell. I flipped through the book again and came upon the heading "Complications." I felt a little nauseated looking at it, uncertain whether I really wanted to know what might lie ahead.

The primary risks from lepidopsy lie in the potential cellular damage and dangerous physical situations resulting from floating. However, there are a few rare complications that can lead to physical deformities and may potentially be fatal.

Thoraxing, or thoracic constriction, is when narrowing occurs around the central organs of the body. Symptoms of this condition include nausea, vomiting, shortness of breath, heart palpitations, and pain in the midsection. Some medications, particularly nadir-class drugs, may also contribute to this condition. Although uncommon, thoraxing is the second leading cause of death among people with lepidopsy.

Chrysalization is the formation of a webbed coating around one or more areas of the body, which can harden and restrict movement. This complication may occur externally, on the skin, or internally, around various joints or, more rarely, vital organs. Chrysalization is difficult to treat, though it is typically not dangerous unless the chrysalis forms over the face, restricting breathing, or around the heart or lungs.

Chrysalization. That was what Pam had. How uncommon could it be if the only other person I knew with lepidopsy had it? These descriptions made me feel even queasier, and then I worried that I felt nauseated because of thoraxing. I closed the book.

Shutting off the light and trying to get to back to sleep felt impossible, so I went into the bathroom and stared at myself in the mirror. *You look fine,* I told myself. *You feel fine, mostly. You will be fine.* I repeated the words over and over in my head, and even whispered them out loud a few times. As the book suggested, I balanced against the counter as I gently stretched my quads and calves like I used to do at practice. I reached my arms up toward the ceiling, and then down to the floor. *I am on the ground,* I repeated in my mind. *I am healthy. My cells obey the law of gravity.*

I got back into bed and closed my eyes, repeating the positive affirmations until I dozed off. It felt like no time had passed when I woke to the sounds of my parents moving around the house, but according to my clock, it was already eleven thirty. I thought again about the book, its suggestion to try and keep a regular schedule, but at the moment, I was too tired to do anything but fall right back to sleep.

ON HALLOWEEN, I chose what I thought was the eeriest item of clothing I owned: a long-sleeve T-shirt from the ethereal postpunk band Cimarron. The shirt was black and had the band logo in the middle, with creepy glowing eyes around it. But I arrived at school to find all the girls on the cross-country team wearing cat-ear headbands, with cat noses and whiskers painted onto their faces, since our school mascot was the Wildcats. At lunch, Cheryl said, "We look more like the Callington Calicos than anything wild." But her cat ears rode high atop her smooth hair, and she had even added a perfectly executed cat eye in smoky gray liner to complete the effect. If it wasn't official before that I was no longer a member of the team, it felt official now.

"You're hanging out with us tonight, right?" asked Smilla.

She and I had spent every Halloween since kinder-garten together, whether trick-or-treating, going to a Hal-loween party, or watching scary movies at my place. Last year, it was just the two of us, but now, it looked like it would be a crowd.

"Sure," I said.

"You have to!" said Smilla, even though I had already agreed. "It's a tradition!"

I had clinic after school that day and would be exhausted by the time I got to Smilla's, but I figured it was okay as long as we just hung around her house. But as soon as that thought entered my mind, Min said, "We should go trick-or-treating!"

"Aren't we a little old for that?" asked Cheryl.

Jennie smiled. "Could be fun." She was rarely the one to suggest such an escapade, but she often went along with Min's ideas.

Smilla looked at me.

"Oh, I don't know," I said. I'd had only a few clinic visits so far, but after each one, all I felt like doing was vegging out.

She turned back to the others. "Let's just stay at my house and hand out candy like we planned." She gave me a little smile.

I was grateful, yet I couldn't shake the feeling that I was holding them back, that she was babying me somehow.

"Fine," said Min, pouting. "But you can't stop me from dressing up."

Throughout the day, I saw kids dressed as ghouls and zombies, and the occasional teacher with vampire teeth. The costumes all seemed a little less creepy than usual. Now that I knew things like spontaneous floating and body-stretching conditions were possible, it was the real world that seemed scary.

When I got to geometry, I sat in my usual seat and was surprised to see a stranger next to me, where Kristi usually sat. "Hey," said the stranger in a familiar voice.

I turned and looked the person over: blond hair cut in a bob, neat makeup, a pale-pink sweater set. "Hi," I said, before realizing who I was talking to. "Kristi?"

She smirked at me. "I became the scariest thing I could think of: my mother."

I laughed. Now I could see a few strands of black hair poking out from under her wig. "What did she say about your costume?"

"Who cares? I guess her scares come later when I take it off and turn back into myself." Kristi pulled out her notebook. "So anyway, what are you doing tonight? Hanging out with the track cats?" She hissed a little on the *s*.

"I guess," I said, feeling a little embarrassed. It wasn't just Smilla and me anymore. The trio was part of my group now, even if I wasn't really part of theirs. "After I get back from the doctor."

I wasn't sure why I said it. Maybe to make myself seem more interesting to Kristi, less frivolous. In any case, her eyes lit up. "Do you have to go a lot? What happens there?"

It seemed a little personal, but it was nice to have someone care about what I was actually going through instead of talking about themselves. "Once a week. They check me out, take my blood and stuff. I guess sucking my blood is sort of Halloween-themed."

Her eyes widened. "Totally."

"Anyway. What are your plans?"

"Oh, whatever. I'll probably just eat candy in my room and work on my drawings. Or, who knows, maybe I'll dress up as a ghost and wander around the neighborhood, freak out Boone and his friends. He lives on my block, and they always get drunk and obnoxious on Halloween. Just hope I don't get egged." It was more words at once than she'd ever said to me.

I smiled, and class started. Kristi doodled ghosts and witches in her notebook all through class. When the bell rang, she said, "Have fun getting your blood sucked." She even gave me a little wave as she left the room.

My mother picked me up after school, and we headed for the city. The receptionist at the clinic was wearing a pair of sparkly antennae on her head, and the nurses wore hot-pink feather boas. Orange paper jack-o'-lanterns dangled from the walls around the waiting area. Some of the other kids and parents clearly got a kick out of all of it, but I still felt like a foreigner in this place. An outsider here; an outsider in the real world.

The nurse brought me into an exam room and took my blood pressure. Dr. Shiel checked me, and Dr. Liffey checked me. The phlebotomist took my blood, and I thought of Kristi. I followed Lisa into the conference room and listened to Pam and the others talk about their day, their week, their families, their health. I kept glancing at the clock on the wall as it ticked toward and beyond five, thinking about the others hanging out at Smilla's house without me and waiting for when I could leave and go join them.

As my mother finally drove me back toward home, I tried to gather my energy and pump myself up to hang out. Still, my mom was pretty intuitive, and she asked, "Are you sure you're feeling up to going out tonight?"

"Yes, I'm sure."

"Your dad or I will come get you at nine, okay? I don't want you staying out too late."

I thought about fighting her for a later curfew, but there was no way she'd give in, so it wasn't worth wasting my precious energy.

"And listen," she said after a beat, "I know you want everything to be normal, but just be careful, okay? Don't go running around outside or anything. And," she said, sounding tired herself, "maybe one or two small pieces of candy, but that's it. All right?"

"Mom, I get it. I'll be careful. Relax."

She made a soft snorting sound but didn't say anything else.

It was after six when I arrived at Smilla's, and everyone else was already there. "Yay, you made it!" said Smilla, and the others smiled and called out their hellos. They acted like they'd been waiting for me, but there was already an empty pizza box in the middle of the table, with bits of crust dotting everyone's plates. "I saved you some," Smilla said, and she retrieved a foil-wrapped plate from the counter. "You want me to heat it up?"

"That's okay," I said, taking the plate and joining everyone at the table.

"Sorry we didn't wait," said Jennie. "We were starving after practice."

"It's fine."

"There's soda in the fridge," said Smilla. "And not that weird all-natural stuff my parents usually get."

"Okay, cool," I said, though a knot was forming in my gut. I still hadn't mentioned my dietary restrictions to Smilla. "Maybe later." I tried to act nonchalant as I got a glass of water instead, but I could feel their eyes on me.

We sat around as Smilla carefully assembled a perfect bowl of candy from a half dozen bags of miniature bars and assorted other pieces. I was relieved that the girls had removed their cat ears and looked normal again. All except for Min, who had wrapped herself in a puffy brown sleeping bag and put on an oversized baby bonnet. "Get it?" she asked, pointing first to the sleeping bag and then to the bonnet. "I'm a tater . . . tot!" Min kept picking candies out of the bowl, with Smilla yelping at her to stop until she finally put the bowl on the counter to keep it out of reach.

It was probably better that she did, because I was tempted to grab a piece and shove it in my mouth before I could stop myself. Dr. Liffey had mentioned that these cravings for sweets could be either a symptom of the disease or a side effect of Coronide. I wanted all the symptoms of the disease to be gone, and it seemed like the cravings got better after I started on the medication. But now they were starting to feel worse, and I couldn't stop staring at the Halloween candy.

"How have you been feeling?" Jennie asked me, seemingly out of nowhere. "You were at the doctor today, right?"

I looked over at Smilla, who shot a guilty look back.

"You have to go every *week*?" asked Cheryl. She tucked a lock of shiny brown hair behind her ear and folded her long legs beneath her.

My cheeks burned. "For now."

Jennie went on. "It's a manifestological disease, right? I read an article about those a while back." She'd aced biology as a freshman while I was just plodding along in it as a sophomore. It wouldn't have surprised me if she ended up going into medicine herself. "Have you floated any more since practice?"

So many questions. "Nope, everything's good." People kept asking me how I was feeling, and it was getting annoying. Couldn't they see I was fine?

"That's good," said Jennie.

We moved to the living room when little kids started ringing the doorbell. Smilla put on the TV and flipped until she found a cheesy old black-and-white B movie about vampires, which she played loudly in the background, and everyone yelled out their favorite lines, since we'd seen it a bunch of times. The raucous noise was punctuated by the doorbell ringing every few minutes, and the girls all took turns giving out candy and cooing over the costumes.

Cheryl liked the princesses best; Jennie, the ninjas. Smilla couldn't stop going on about one particular infant dressed as the president, in a tiny suit and tie, sleeping in his father's arms. I didn't get up to open the door, but I watched from the couch. The costume *I* couldn't forget was the girl, maybe seven or eight years old, dressed as a butterfly. Large, elaborate wings bloomed out behind her, painted in blue and silver. Tiny sparkles glittered as she turned under the porch light, and before she left, she looked at me as though she knew me.

After my mother picked me up that night, I went straight to my room and lay down without brushing my teeth or taking off my makeup. School was tiring, and going to clinic was tiring, but the most tiring thing was trying to figure out how to be around other people. Trying to show them everything was fine and get them to act normal with me. I fell asleep in my regular clothes, which now felt like the weirdest costume of all.

FOUR

IN EARLY NOVEMBER, a month after being admitted to the hospital, I woke up with a bit of a headache. It was hard to focus in school, but mostly, I just felt weird. Like my skin didn't fit right and my body couldn't relax, no matter what position it was in. The pain relievers I took when I got home didn't help, nor did the soft blanket I wrapped myself in, nor the relaxing herbal tea I sipped on.

When I went to bed, I tossed for a while before falling asleep, and then I found myself wide-awake in the middle of the night. The numbers on my clock burned like candles for the dead—2:32 a.m. As I gained consciousness, I became aware of it: a thin, high-pitched noise.

I sat up and turned my head left, then right, trying to find the source of the sound. I got out of bed and opened the door, and the noise got louder for a moment, then quieted down again. It wasn't coming from the hallway. I went to my window, and as I approached, the sound again grew slightly louder. But when I cracked the window open, letting in a frigid breeze, it quieted back down. A light snow was falling, just enough to coat the ground. The world out there was silent and dark.

I shut the window and stood in the middle of my bedroom, turning and cocking my head, and that was when I remembered Dr. Liffey saying that this could be a side effect of the medication: the vibration of my bones making my body hum. It was like the whine of a television set left on mute, but louder. I had a tendency to hear those sorts of noises when others around me couldn't; my mother always said I had bat hearing. I hoped my perception of this sound was because of that bat hearing combined with my incurable proximity to myself. I held my forearm a few inches from my ear, which didn't make much of a difference. But when I pressed my hand against my ear, the noise resonated through my flesh and bone and blasted directly into my head. *Hummmmm.*

As this was a Monday night (or rather, a Tuesday morning), I had school the next day, so I returned to bed and tried to go back to sleep. But I kept hearing it. I tossed. I turned. I got cotton balls from the bathroom and stuffed them in my ears, but that made the noise worse. My only hope was to try and drown it out. I turned the radio to the classical station. Something slow and orchestral was playing in a minor key. Perfect.

I lay down and tried to focus on the sound of the symphony. I couldn't hear the hum anymore, but I could still feel a faint vibration. The numbers on the clock kept flicking by:

2:48 and 2:49 and 2:50, 3:13, 3:29, 3:47. After an hour had passed, the radio's sleep timer switched itself off, and the room went silent, except for the hum. *Hummmmm.*

In the morning, I could barely peel myself out of bed. I was starting to notice a pattern: When I had insomnia, I always managed to fall into the deepest, most cavernous sleep shortly before I was supposed to wake up. In my flailing, I had wrestled the blankets off, and woke up cold and shivering. I pulled them into a cocoon around me and smacked the snooze bar repeatedly. Eventually, my mother came in. "You're going to be late for school," she said. And then, "Are you feeling okay?"

I mumbled nonsense in reply. She was about to say something else, but then she stopped, her face pensive. She squinted and looked around. "Do you hear something?"

I didn't answer.

My mother leaned down toward me, ear first, and then stood up again. I watched as understanding came over her: that I was the source of the noise, and why.

"Do you need to stay home today?" she asked softly.

"I don't know," I muttered. The vague discomfort I had felt the day before had crested and broken into this vibration and sound. I had a geometry quiz and an English paper due that day, but maybe I could make up the quiz and hand in the paper late. These were not the sorts of things ordinary students got away with, but my teachers had promised to do whatever they could to help me out.

So I stayed home and dozed on and off throughout the day. By the afternoon, the temperature had rocketed into the fifties, melting all the snow. I opened my windows for a while and let the whispering of the wind in the trees wash through the noise coming from my body. But as much as I tried to will it away, the hum remained steady through that night and into the following morning. If anything, it got stronger.

My mother came in to wake me up for school on Wednesday, so I got out of bed and pulled on a giant gray-and-white sweater, the thickest one I owned, in order to muffle myself. Still, the vibration made me feel as though I were sitting in an idling car or leaning against an old refrigerator.

In first period, I slid into one of the plastic chairs in the back corner and tried to make myself invisible. When Jennie arrived, she came over and sat next to me. "Hey! Were you sick yesterday?"

"Oh," I said. "Yeah." It was easier than explaining. Besides, technically I was sick every day now.

The teacher shut the door to begin class, and everyone around us quit talking as she got into her lesson about irregular French verbs. As the classroom noise faded down to nothing but the teacher's voice and chalk against the blackboard, the hum made its presence known again, at least in our little corner of the room. I watched Jennie in my peripheral vision, waiting for the look to come over her face, and soon enough, it did. Her brow scrunched up, and she twisted her head this way and that, trying to zero in on the sound.

She caught my eye and must have seen my expression— what was it? sorrow? resignation? anguish?—because her face flashed with recognition. *You?* she mouthed, and I nodded. She put her hand on my arm in sympathy, but then stiffened. The vibration. She felt it. She pulled her hands into her lap, but from the way she was studying me, it seemed she wanted to keep examining this strange new phenomenon. For the rest of the class, I tried to pretend I didn't notice her glancing over at me every so often.

Second period was study hall, and on the way there, I stopped in the music room to see Smilla, who was getting ready for chorus rehearsal. Even though I had felt a little disconnected from her lately, she was still the first person I wanted to talk to when anything big or sad or difficult happened.

She was standing by the baby grand piano, arranging some sheet music, and she looked up as I approached. "Hey!" she said. "You okay?"

I shrugged. "I guess."

"Not feeling well yesterday?"

"I couldn't really sleep the night before. I have this side effect from my medicine."

"It keeps you up at night?"

"No, it's . . . I mean, I couldn't sleep because of this vibration. From the medicine. It creates this hum."

She squinted a little, trying to understand. "Like a ringing in your ears?"

I was getting frustrated trying to figure out how to explain it. The music room was full of kids talking and milling around before practice started, so Smilla couldn't hear the hum for herself. "No, it's in my actual body," I said, but she still looked confused, and I leaned against the piano to think for a second.

A high hum filled the room. The baby grand was doing exactly what it was designed to do: amplify a quiet vibration into a loud one. The entire chorus fell silent and looked toward the source of the sound. Their eyes traveled from the piano to me, and I jumped backward, nearly tripping over a music stand, my face burning. Smilla's mouth hung open. Now she got it.

"I have to go," I breathed, and darted out into the hallway as quickly as I could.

I ran for the bathroom. Running even that short distance made my feet ache, but I needed to get out of sight. I shut myself in a stall, trying to catch my ragged breath. The piano. My body was like one of its strings, striking a note that filled the wooden case, and the room. I tried to relax, to breathe deeply, but all that did was accentuate the rattling feeling in my lungs. The side effects were starting to pile up.

The bell rang in the hallway as second period started. The bathroom was empty. I touched one fingertip to the stall door to see what would happen, and the hum increased in volume, though not as much as it had with the piano. This sound was thin, tinny, not like the piano's rich, full version. I would have to be cautious. Avoid hollow, resonant objects. The desks in some of my classes were those old wooden ones with tops that lifted to reveal a compartment inside. I would take care not to lean on them.

I skipped study hall and wandered the building instead, darting around corners when I saw teachers coming and pulling my hands into my sleeves to mask the vibration, for as much good as that did. I had never cut class before. But study hall didn't matter as much as a real class, and the teacher would probably assume I was out sick or had gone to the nurse.

When the bell rang for third period, I slipped into my English classroom, the first one to arrive. Instead of sitting in the front like Smilla and I usually did, I took a seat in the back corner. When Smilla walked in, she looked to our usual spots and then scanned the classroom until she saw me.

She rushed over and sat next to me. "Hey, are you all right?"

I nodded, but I still felt shaky from the shock of embarrassing myself in front of the entire chorus.

"Oh, Anna. Is there anything I can do?"

I wished there were. "I don't think so." I swallowed hard to keep from crying.

At the front of the room, Ms. Meadows looked around. I hoped with everything I had that she was just taking attendance and that she wasn't able to hear me from all the way over there.

I looked back at Smilla, who seemed to be trying to figure out what to say. She fumbled for a minute, and then said, "It's not that loud. People probably won't even notice."

But Smilla had seen everyone staring at me in the music room, and I was sure they'd talked about me after I ran out. How could she pretend like this, when it was so obvious what was really going on?

As class began, I started to wonder if she had always done

that and I just hadn't noticed before. Those times I'd tripped or discovered toilet paper on my shoe and she'd assured me no one had seen it, was she lying then too? And what about the times I had asked what she thought of an outfit I put together or an album I liked, or had expressed any thought at all? Had she always been sparing my feelings?

As class ended and we walked out, I thought about asking her. But I couldn't bring myself to say anything. She was my only real friend, and I needed her more than ever.

I skipped my usual library time the following period, shuddering at the thought of being the main source of noise in that quiet space. I thought about skipping lunch, too, but I was starving, and besides, there should be enough noise in the cafeteria to drown me out. When I got there, no one said anything about the hum. Jennie and Smilla already knew about it, which meant that Cheryl and Min almost certainly did by now too. I ate my lunch quietly while the four of them talked, and I tried to let go of my worries about Smilla and just relax for a little while.

Even though I had a full lunch, I still felt unsatisfied. Not for more food, but for candy, for soda, for milkshakes, for the butterscotch chip cookies my mother used to make before she rid the house of all the sweets I wasn't supposed to have. The cravings had gotten worse since Halloween—and, really, the word *cravings* didn't do justice to the way I felt. Wanting sugar was like wanting sleep after being awake for two days. As the girls talked, I gazed across the cafeteria to the soda fountain, relieved when it was finally time to get up and go to my next class.

In geometry, Kristi plopped into the seat next to me and was still for a moment. Then she turned to me, wide-eyed. "Oh my god," she said quietly. "I *can* hear it."

"Great to know the news is out." The only thing more supernatural than my health was the speed at which gossip traveled through school.

But Kristi didn't appear sheepish, and she didn't back down. "So what if it is? You're never going to get people to stop talking."

"Well, I mean, it's none of their business," I insisted. "And it's not like I need another reason for everyone to look at me like I'm an alien or something."

She leaned toward me, her voice insistent. "Listen. If people give you a hard time about it, they can go screw themselves. Besides, I think it's interesting."

I slouched in my chair. I wasn't sure I wanted to be interesting. Not like that.

She went on, scowling at the other kids making their way into class. "Look at all these people. They're all trying to look perfect, but they're not." She pointed to one kid, then another, then another. "Pill problem, police record, gets blackout drunk every weekend." She looked at me again. "I think it's more honest not to hide it. Just be who you are. What's wrong with that?"

I didn't have an answer. Maybe she was right, but I still tried to keep my hum to myself as much as I could. I crossed my arms over my chest and stayed like that until my muscles started to cramp, and then I sat on my hands instead. But three-quarters of the way into class, I began thinking about Smilla again, about how she wanted to hide everything and pretend it was okay even when it wasn't. She couldn't have been more different than Kristi. And I thought again of what Smilla had said to me in the hospital about Kristi acting weird. But Kristi hadn't been weird to *me* since I got out of the hospital. She'd actually been really decent. Had Smilla lied about Kristi too?

Lost in thought, I slipped up and accidentally rested my elbows on my desk. The hum resonated through it, and in the split second before I caught myself, everyone in the class, including Mr. Takahashi, turned and looked at me. I yanked my hands off the desk as though it were burning and tucked them under my thighs, but people were already murmuring to one another about it, and I wanted to vanish.

"Okay, let's focus now," said Mr. Takahashi, turning back to the board, but not everyone went along with him, at least not right away.

When class ended and I was gathering my things into my backpack, Betty Bittman turned around from the seat in front of me and looked me up and down. "You sound like a mosquito or something," she said.

Before I could react, Kristi leaned toward her and said, "Oh, you don't like the way she sounds, *Bertha*?"

"Shut up!" hissed Betty.

"You got it, *Bertha*."

Betty grabbed her stuff and stomped out of the room before Kristi could say it again.

Kristi turned back to me. "See? You just have to stand up to people when they give you crap."

I didn't know what to say. I was shocked, but not in a bad way. I wanted to thank her. I wanted to applaud her. "Betty's real name is *Bertha*?"

Kristi gave a dramatic sigh and nodded. "We were friends once, a million years ago. Sad how things go sometimes. Anyway. Let's get out of here."

"Okay," I said, and followed her out of the room. As we went our separate ways in the hall and I headed to my next class, I felt 1 percent less self-conscious as my body buzzed along.

ALTHOUGH I'D NEVER heard a hum coming from anyone else at clinic, they were all familiar with the sound. "I had that when I was on a lot of Coronide too," said Pam, giving me a sympathetic smile. "It got better when they tapered me down."

It was cool that the other support group kids were nice to me, but despite the hum, despite everything, I still couldn't see myself as one of them. When Carrie talked about the stretched kidney that was causing her to retain fluid and the blood pressure medication the doctors had put her on because of it, she seemed so calm. "Dr. Liffey said she might want to do a biopsy at some point," she said, "but hopefully we'll see good results from the meds and we won't need to do that. And at least the water weight is going away. I have a school dance next week, and I was worried my dress wasn't going to fit!"

I listened to Elaine talk about the experimental new

drug Dr. Liffey was trying on her, and how she had volunteered to be part of a study with some researchers who were examining her disease. In her sweet singsong voice, she said, "It's a little bit risky, but it feels good to help with the research. And obviously, I hope the treatment will help."

And of course, I listened to Pam, who talked more about the chrysalization around her left knee joint, which was stiffening the leg and making it hard for her to walk. That, of course, made me think back to the book my mother had bought. It said that chrysalization was rare, so didn't that mean Pam's case was unusual? And if it was, I didn't have to worry about being like her, right? She clearly had it much worse than me.

Pam talked about other medications I hadn't tried yet, the way this one made her more sensitive to noise and that one made it harder to concentrate in class. Was it generous of these girls to share this information for everyone's benefit, or was it selfish of them to dump their feelings onto all of us? I didn't know, but it did get my attention when Pam said, "My friends at school just don't get it. Last Friday, we went out for pizza, and then they wanted to go to this coffee shop that was like a half mile away. It didn't even occur to them that I might not be able to walk that far." She sighed. "So I had to decide whether to push myself and be in massive pain or be a total downer."

"What did you do?" asked Elaine. Her cheeks blazed bright red against her pale complexion, a side effect of her new medication.

Pam looked off into the corner of the room, as if watching

the events of the night play out before her. "I told them a story." Her gaze snapped back to us, and she looked around at everyone as she spoke. "I told this silly story about one time when I was babysitting my brothers and they locked me out of the house. I just needed something to make everyone focus on me so I could walk really slowly and they'd have to go at my pace. No one would forget I was there and walk so fast they left me behind." Her voice got quieter. "I mean, it's happened before."

There was a long silence as we waited to see if she would continue, but her lips were pressed together and her eyes had drifted into the corner again.

After an appropriate amount of time had passed, Lisa turned to me. "And what about you, Anna? Would you like to talk about how you've been doing?"

I took a minute to consider the question. There'd been the whole chorus staring at me when I leaned on the piano. Betty freaking Bittman. And Smilla, all my questions and insecurities about Smilla. But I couldn't bring myself to say any of it. Besides, maybe Smilla was right that I could beat the odds—not the running part, but if I was really careful and followed all the rules and took good care of myself, maybe my symptoms would stay away and I could forget that any of this had happened.

"I'm okay," I said.

The support group, being held during regular clinic hours, was occasionally punctuated by a nurse coming in to retrieve one of us for Dr. Liffey and Dr. Shiel. One came in to fetch me just then, and I slipped out of the conference room as quickly as I could without making direct eye contact with anyone.

The nurse brought me into an exam room. I took off my clothes and piled them on one of the chairs, put on a gown, sat on the crinkly paper-covered exam table, and watched my stocking feet dangle over the edge. I kicked my feet up slightly to see if they would catch the air and float, but thankfully, they fell back toward the floor like normal.

When Dr. Shiel came in, I waited for him to notice my obvious hum, but he just muttered to himself in Latin until I brought it up. "I don't know if you can hear it," I said, though I knew he must, "but I have a pretty bad hum."

"That's standard with Coronide," he said without pausing the exam. He didn't seem to notice me glaring at him.

He finished his routine, and then Dr. Liffey came in. They tested my eyes, my skin, my reflexes. Fingertips over forearms, penlight on the ceiling. "You seem pretty steady at the moment," said Dr. Liffey, and I held on to her words for dear life.

THE CROSS-COUNTRY SEASON wound to a close in mid-November, and with the end of the season came the relief of not having the pressure to pretend to be happy for the runners anymore. Smilla had continued encouraging me to go to the meets and cheer on the team, saying, "It might make you feel more connected," and "It'll help you visualize being able to run again!" But each time she brought it up, I felt a little more frustrated that she kept pressing me about running even after I'd told her I wasn't supposed to.

Over Thanksgiving break, Smilla called and invited me to the movies. *It'll be good,* I thought, a chance to hang out with less pressure to make conversation. "Sure!" I said. "I think they're still playing some of the horror movies from Halloween. Or maybe the one about the time-traveling scientist guy."

Smilla didn't miss a beat. "We were talking about seeing *Wesley and Evelyn.* It looks pretty good!"

I didn't have to ask who "we" was. I had made the mistake of thinking that for once, Smilla wanted to hang out with *me.* And I didn't particularly *want* to see *Wesley and Evelyn.* It was historical romance, which I wasn't interested in. Also, I'd seen commercials for it, and it looked sad, which definitely wasn't what I was in the mood for. "I don't know," I said. "Are you sure you're not up for something else?"

"Oh, it's just that the girls really, really want to see it. Please come? We want you to!"

In other words, they were going whether I tagged along or not.

I thought about staying home. Watching TV with my parents again or listening to music in my room while thinking about the girls having a good time without me. "Okay. I guess."

"Oh, yay! We're meeting there at two. See you then!"

When I arrived in the theater lobby, right on time, the four of them were already there, and I wondered if they had come together. If Smilla had left out that part. When I reached them, they were talking about how sad they were that the cross-country season was over. I couldn't get away from the topic.

"But indoor track starts soon!" Cheryl reminded them.

"And we have the banquet in a couple weeks!" added Min.

Smilla turned to me. "Are you coming to the banquet?"

I hadn't even thought about it. I had gone the previous year, of course, but this year, Smilla hadn't mentioned it, and if she wasn't going to, it was unlikely anyone else would. "I don't know," I said.

"You're totally welcome to," said Jennie, as though it were her call to make. "You ran for part of the season."

"Yeah, coming in first at a meet definitely gets you invited!" said Min.

That meet felt like it had happened decades earlier, not months. "Maybe," I said. I didn't know exactly when or where the banquet was happening, and if I asked, I'd be letting on that no one had told me about it before today.

"You should!" said Smilla.

I was only saying maybe to get them off my back. What I really meant was no, but she no longer seemed able to pick up on those sorts of signals from me. In that moment, I leaned back and looked at the four of them looking at me. And it was the four of them now, wasn't it? It wasn't the three of them plus Smilla, and it certainly wasn't the three of them plus the separate pair of Smilla and me.

We got our tickets and headed over to the concessions counter. I got popcorn, but the rest of them went to the bulk candy area, where you could fill up a bag from bins of gummies, chocolates, and other assorted sweets. I still hadn't told them that I was avoiding sugar, and I didn't want any looks of pity, so I didn't say anything now. They cooed and laughed like little kids while I stayed in the main part of the lobby and waited. I picked at my popcorn, wishing it were strawberry chews, tart lemon drops, chocolate-covered caramels. My mouth watered. What was taking them so long?

Finally, they came out to find me, their clear plastic bags of sweets gleaming in the light, and we went to find seats. I entered the row first and tried to position myself next to Smilla, but then Min popped in ahead of her, so I wound up between Min and an empty seat. Cheryl, Smilla, and Jennie were talking at the far end, and Min listened in and interjected from time to time. It was hard to catch what they were saying from where I sat. I could faintly hear the sound of my own hum, but fortunately the space was large enough to mostly swallow it, and the padded seats absorbed a lot of the volume. I sat there, all alone with my supposed friends, stewing and waiting for the previews to start.

The movie told the tragic tale of a star-crossed couple in the nineteenth century, full of romantic tension and a few steamy love scenes. And then, about halfway through, the heroine coughed. Nobody coughs in a movie without dying before the credits roll. And sure enough, the latter part of the movie involved watching her waste away, eventually taking to her bed, where she received one last kiss from the hero before gracefully and beautifully expiring.

I wished I could teleport back to my room. I didn't want

to be there, with friends who barely noticed me, watching a tearjerker that only reminded me of my own situation. And maybe my situation was worse, because unlike the heroine, I didn't have a hero to declare that he loved me no matter what. My own friends couldn't even be there for me. And there was certainly nothing graceful or beautiful about my illness. I thought about walking out of the theater and calling my parents to come get me. Yet I stayed until the music swelled and the lights came on, until my sniffling friends stood to leave. "Oh my god," said Min. "Wasn't that good? It was so sad!"

"And romantic," said Jennie.

They went on and on about the movie as we walked down the aisle toward the exit. When we got back into the lobby, Smilla asked what I'd thought.

My body tensed. "It was okay. I don't know about the whole sickness story line, though." As soon as I said it, I wondered if I should have; they were going to realize that I felt bad, and then they'd feel bad for being thoughtless, and I would feel bad for making them feel bad.

"But she *had* to be sick," said Cheryl. "It's what made him realize he had to go back and confess his love!"

"And she was so brave," said Min.

I stood there in shock for a minute. They'd completely missed the point. They thought I was trying to debate the plot of the movie rather than expressing how it made me feel about my own life. "I'll be right back," I said, and walked as quickly as I could to the bathroom, hoping to get there before I started crying.

I sat in the stall and tried to let the tears out delicately, blotting them with a piece of toilet paper instead of ugly crying and letting my eyes and nose get all red and puffy. I didn't want to go back out there, but we still had an hour before Min's brother was supposed to pick us up. If I said I wanted to leave, everyone would want to know why, and I did *not* want to talk about it. So I sat there until I was able to steady my breathing, and then I gathered my courage and pushed through the door.

The lobby had mostly emptied out between features, so I had a clear view across to where the four of them were standing. They looked like such a complete group without me. I took a deep breath and tried to plaster a smile across my face as I approached.

"There you are," said Smilla. "You guys want to go over to Mangoes?" That was the chain music store at the other end of the mall. Everyone agreed, and we headed off.

They bounced around, hopped up on sugar and tragedy, talking about the boys they wanted as their romantic leads and pointing out things they liked in shop windows. I lagged slightly behind, feeling a tiny bit fluttery and not wanting to walk too quickly and make it worse. I paused to check out some earrings in one of the windows for what seemed like half a second, but when I turned around, the others were gone. My face grew hot. Had I really been left behind at the mall like a lost toddler? I wanted to cry again, but I bit my lip and swallowed hard.

As I peered into one shop after another, trying to find them, I started feeling overwhelmed by the fake-cinnamon scent from the cookie stand mixing with the cacophonous blend of perfumes from the bath-and-body product store and the music selections changing with each doorway. My flutter was getting worse, and I began to feel light-headed. My toes were starting to tingle, and my ankles were getting sore. *Calm down,* I told myself. *Calm down or you're going to start floating in the mall.* I looked beyond the upper story and into the tall skylight and felt woozy.

Not knowing what else to do, I made my way to Mangoes. There, by the bargain bin, I discovered Smilla looking through cassette tapes. "Hey," she said. "Where did you go?" She seemed genuinely curious.

Relief flooded through me, followed quickly by anger. "Nowhere," I mumbled.

"Is everything okay?" she asked.

"I'm fine."

She didn't look convinced. Now, suddenly, she was paying too much attention to me, giving me that ultra-concerned expression that I hated. I had nothing to say, so I wandered the store until I found an empty aisle where none of them could look at me.

I was quiet for the rest of the outing. I was quiet on the ride home, and at the dinner table with my parents. I didn't want to say anything to anybody, but when I lay in bed that night, I couldn't stop thinking about the day. I was so invisible to Smilla now that she didn't even notice my absence.

Out of nowhere, Pam popped into my mind. How she said she'd developed the habit of telling stories to keep her friends from leaving her behind. How they had done it before. Maybe I wasn't as different from her as I had imagined.

But I couldn't be like her, just another sick kid. I was doing better overall. Dr. Liffey had said so. I'd felt shaky at the mall because I'd pushed myself too hard, because my so-called friends made me. Smilla, who was so focused on making me do what *she* wanted that she couldn't accept that I probably wouldn't be able to run again. She and the others didn't get it, and they didn't seem interested in trying to get it. I tried to put them out of my head so I could get some sleep, but I couldn't get comfortable. I shifted from one side onto the other, onto my back, onto my belly, but I ached in every position. All I could do was lie awake watching the light of the nearly full moon creep across my bedroom floor.

IT WAS TOO early when I woke up again, just starting to get light out. I was still uncomfortable, but something was different now. It didn't hit me until I sat up and felt a hard, prickly surface beneath my hands and body where my bed was supposed to be. I wasn't in bed at all; I was above it, pressed against the rough popcorn ceiling.

I flailed and panicked, scraping my right palm against the plaster as I struggled to push myself back down to my bed, into normal gravity. But my body kept drifting up as soon as I stopped pushing.

I was floating. Again. Worse.

How could this be happening? I'd been doing everything

right. I was taking all my medications right on schedule, plus multivitamins, and eating as many fruits and vegetables as I could, trying to follow the advice of the lepidopsy book and my doctors. Also on the advice of the book, I'd been doing those gentle stretches in my room, and I was careful not to run or to walk too quickly. I'd even been saying those ludicrous positive affirmations. And yet here I was.

I crept across the ceiling until I reached the spot above my desk. Pushing myself to standing, I found myself subject to a reverse gravity that held me to the ceiling and let me limp around up there, upside down, the plaster prickling my feet. I reached over my head toward the room's floor and grabbed for the top of my desk chair, which hung there like a stalactite. But I couldn't get a good grip on it, and it toppled onto its side on the carpet over my head.

I needed something steadier. The desk would be, but it was just out of reach. I jumped to grab the edge of it and almost did, but I slipped and fell back up to the ceiling, scraping my knee in the landing. I pushed myself to my feet again, even sorer now than I was before. I thought about trying the bookshelf instead, using it as a ladder, but I figured the books and the shelf itself would likely tumble just like the chair. No, it had to be the desk. It was the only thing steady enough that was close to being within reach.

I took a deep breath and squatted, remembering how in gym class (before they'd given me the medical excuse to skip it), we had all been measured on how high we could jump. The trick was to get some spring into it. *Ready,* I told myself. *Set. Go!*

I leaped again and caught the edge of the desk drawer. I dangled there for a second, but was unable to hold on tightly enough, and I tumbled back to the ceiling again. This time, I didn't get up right away, instead lying on my side, defeated, my cheek pressed against the roughness just as it had been when I woke up. I didn't know what to do next. With each passing moment, the pain grew worse, and it got harder to think about trying to get down. I lay there remembering what the book said about unchecked floating causing cellular damage or worse, and I began to cry.

There was a soft tap at my door, which then opened to reveal my father, who stood there, sleepy-eyed, in his gray T-shirt and worn-out pajama bottoms until he saw me above him. "Anna!" he cried, running over to help. "Come on, grab my hand."

To do so, I would have to stand again, and I was so tired.

"Come on, honey," he said, stretching up to try and help me down.

I felt like my body was made of rock, some strange mineral from another planet. I didn't want to, but I pushed away from the ceiling, my skin scratched, my wrists and arms achy.

"That's it," he said.

I wobbled upright on my stiff legs, and he grabbed hold of my arms and pulled. It didn't take much effort for him to get me back into normal gravity, but it did to keep me down. My feet didn't want to stay on the ground, so I was hovering in midair, but my dad gently swung me toward my bed until I was in place over the mattress, where he pressed down on my shoulder and my knee, and then tucked the sheet in tightly around me. Once he was convinced I'd stay in place, he let out a deep breath, his cheeks burning with a combination of worry and exertion. "I heard a crashing sound, and I didn't know what was going on," he said.

"I'm sorry," I said.

"Oh, honey, no. You don't have to be sorry. I'm glad I was here to help you. I'm going to get your mother, and we'll take you to the doctor."

"Now?" I asked. It was five twenty in the morning, not even fully light outside yet. On a Saturday, no less.

My father glanced at the clock. "Oh," he said, like he hadn't realized what time it was in all the chaos. "Well, soon. Anyway, don't move." He padded off to get my mother.

"Can't," I muttered from my swaddled position under the sheet. I was out of energy.

My parents came into my room together a couple minutes later, my mother looking as sleepy as my father had before he'd found me on the ceiling. "Are you okay?" she rasped.

I pulled one scratched arm out from under the sheet and tried to let it drop onto the mattress, but instead it hovered, slowly but firmly rising toward the ceiling until my father helped me force it back under the covers. I looked at my mother, not needing to say anything. "Why don't you try and sleep for a little bit?" she said. "We'll stay with you."

I dozed for an hour or two, and then my father woke me with some toast and peanut butter, which I ate in bed. It was a strain just to pull my arm down to get the toast to my mouth. When he headed to the kitchen to get another cup of coffee, my mother helped me get dressed, keeping me half tucked into bed so I didn't lift off again.

Standing on either side of me, my parents walked me downstairs, each taking an arm to keep me upright and close to the ground until they could get me into the car and seat-belted in. After they secured me, I had to hold my arms and legs stiff to keep them where they were. If I relaxed at all, they drifted upward again. By the time we reached the highway, my muscles were shaking with exertion. I tucked my hands underneath me and my feet under the seat in front of me, which helped, but I still couldn't relax or else everything came loose again.

We arrived at the hospital just before eight o'clock. My mother had paged the doctor's office before we left home, and Dr. Shiel was waiting for us. He took us over to a special exam room that had straps attached to the table, and he and a nurse helped me get fastened down. The nurse took my blood, and Dr. Shiel did his standard exam with those creepy, limp hands of his.

"So what's going on?" asked my father. "I thought the medicine was working."

"Well, sometimes the dose needs to be adjusted or we need to try something else," said Dr. Shiel. "There can be a honeymoon period, where things get better for a little while before declining again."

So reassuring, I thought. We waited for the lab to rush my results back, which we were told would take about forty-five minutes. My parents and I hung around the exam room, waiting. My mother, as always, had a book in her purse, and she read as I flitted in and out of a light sleep, my muscles growing sore where the straps bound them. My father paced and fidgeted until my mother sent him out to the waiting area.

Dr. Shiel came back in with my chart, trailed by my father. "Dr. Liffey may want to start you on another drug," said Dr. Shiel. "We'll check with her when she gets in. Either way, she'll prescribe you a medical tether."

"A what?" I asked.

"Here, I'll grab one and show you." Dr. Shiel zipped out of the room and came back a moment later with a piece of beige rubber tubing six or eight feet long. At one end was a small clip, and at the other end, a series of three thick metallic discs, like an ellipsis, leading up to a larger metal clip. He held up the end with the small clip. "You wrap this part around your waist and hook it." He demonstrated, using the small clip to secure the tubing around his own waist. "And then this end," he said, now holding up the side with the ellipsis and the big clip, "you can hook on to your chair or some other heavy object." He attached the loose end to the arm of one of the exam room chairs. "If you're walking around, you unclip and just wrap the rest of it around your waist." He looped the tubing around his midsection and then went around once more, hooking it into place with the big clip. I thought about the bulk of all that rubber and metal and tried to imagine an outfit the tether wouldn't ruin.

"The other neat thing about it," he said, as though this

were all a fun experiment as opposed to my actual horrifying life, "is that the loose end has a couple of weighted and magnetized pieces, so if you start to float, you can toss this end and try to catch it on something." He unhooked the big clip and unwrapped most of the tubing. He flung the end of the tether toward the sink, where it wrapped and wrapped its length around the long pipe of the faucet until its magnets snapped together with a metallic clunk.

He removed the tether from his body and unwrapped the other end from the sink, then handed me the whole contraption. The tubing was stretchy and about the diameter of a thick drinking straw, and the magnets were heavier than I would have guessed. There was an expectant smile on Dr. Shiel's dorky little face, as though he thought I would be excited to get this ball and chain.

He gawked at me until I said, "Do I have to put it on now?" I was still securely strapped to the table, so it seemed redundant.

"No, I suppose not," said Dr. Shiel, his smile fading a tad. "Dr. Liffey will be in soon."

Had I been harsh with him? Ungrateful? In that moment, I was too tired, achy, and upset to care. Was my mother giving me a disapproving look for being so rude? Or was she glaring at him instead of me? I closed my eyes so I didn't have to find out.

Dr. Liffey arrived about twenty minutes later. "So what's going on?"

"I woke up on the ceiling," I told her.

She nodded and looked at the lab results that had just

been added to my chart. "Some of your levels are running a little high today," she said. "Have you been having any other symptoms?"

"I don't know . . . Maybe the fluttering is worse."

"Okay." She put the chart on the counter. "I see Dr. Shiel gave you a tether. Did he show you how to use it?"

"Yes," my father said.

"Do I really have to?" I asked.

The doctor parked herself on a rolling stool and slid toward me. "It's important to be able to get back down when you're having spontaneous floating events. They can be especially dangerous outside, but inside's not great either. Ceilings aren't designed to be good to walk on, as you probably discovered. So anyone with a history of floating more than a few feet off the ground gets one of these."

"I have to wear it . . . all the time?"

"Better safe than sorry," she said. "You can sleep without it if you want, as long as you have your sheets tucked in nice and tight. And you don't have to wear it in the shower unless you're feeling unstable." She unstrapped my forearms and legs, leaving my torso and waist attached to the exam table. "Okay. Let's check you out."

She did the usual skin-eyes-flutter check. As tired as I was, I anticipated each request, holding my arms out or my hands palms-down in front of me when I knew she wanted me to. Only today, instead of lifting my hands up to hold them in front of me, I had to pull them down to get them there.

"Well," she said finally, "you look okay otherwise. I think

what we'll do is try another medication to help get things back under control."

"Instead of the Coronide?" asked my mother.

"I think we'll use both at once for the time being." Dr. Liffey pulled a pad out of her lab coat pocket and scribbled a prescription. As she handed the slip to my mother, I saw the name Gravanil written on it. *Like gravity?* I wondered. *Or like grave?*

I kept waiting for Dr. Liffey to tell me I needed to be admitted, so when she got up to leave the room, I had to ask. "Do I have to stay? Overnight?"

"No," she said. "Let's just try this medication. It should kick in within twenty-four hours. It might make you a little sleepy, give you some sound sensitivity, but other than that, the side effects aren't bad. You have the tether, so start using that right away. You want to give it a try to make sure you're comfortable with it?"

It was too much information to process all at once. I clicked open the latches on the table straps, drifting halfway to the ceiling before I could get the tether fastened around my waist. "Just throw it anywhere?" I asked.

"Try for something nonbreakable," said Dr. Liffey. "But in a pinch, use whatever you can get."

I looked toward the chair where my father was sitting. "Look out."

He hopped out of his seat and went to stand behind my mother. I grabbed the heavy end of the tether and threw it toward the arm of the chair. It clunked off the corner but didn't attach.

"It helps if you grab it a foot or two from the end and just kind of swing it," said Dr. Liffey.

I reeled the line in and imagined I was fishing. For what, exactly? For myself? I swung the tether hard, nearly whacking my parents on the backswing, but I managed to get the thing to wrap around the chair's arm and the magnetic bits to connect.

"That's great," said Dr. Liffey. "Practice until you're confident you've got the hang of it. And keep it on until you're tucked into bed. You can hook it to your dad's belt loop while you walk to the parking garage."

The doctor and my parents helped me to the floor and onto my feet, and I retrieved the end of the tether from the chair. The heavy magnetized clip at the end was a large carabiner, and I handed it to my father, who clipped it to his belt loop as instructed. I linked arms with my parents—my father on my left and my mother on my right—and they walked out to the car with me hanging on tightly and gliding forward between them, my feet hovering just above the floor like a ghost.

On the car ride home, I stared out the window at the bare trees and the flat gray sky. I knew there was no cure for lepidopsy, but this was the first time I really felt like it was here to stay. I pictured months, years, a lifetime of being tied to the earth with an ugly rubber string, of trudging in and out of doctor's offices, of missing out on the things that the people around me got to enjoy.

And then Dr. Liffey's offhand words popped into my head: *Spontaneous floating events. They can be especially danger-*

ous outside. It was so casual, the way she'd said it. But it wasn't the sort of thing she would say without good reason. I imagined the girls before me who had lifted off into the sky and never come down. I hated the idea of wearing this anchor, but I was terrified at the idea of drifting up and up into thin air, growing ever thinner as the altitude grew higher and the chance of rescue grew lower.

MY PARENTS TUCKED me in on the living room couch for the rest of the day so I could watch TV, and they brought me food and drinks and my Walkman and anything else I asked for. By the time they transferred me back up to my bed to go to sleep that night, I was already feeling more solid on the ground, and by the following morning, I was able to walk on my own. Since I was due back at school the next day, I went to the basement to practice using the tether so I'd be prepared.

I stood five or six feet away from one of the basement's metal support posts and threw the heavy end toward it. The carabiner clanged loudly on the post the first few times I threw it, and I heard heavy footsteps overhead and then my father's voice shouting as he came down the stairs. "Honey? Are you okay?"

"I'm fine. I'm just practicing with the tether."

He reached the foot of the staircase and looked around to make sure I was really all right. "Oh, good. You want any help?"

"No, thanks." When he didn't move, I added, "Don't watch me!"

"Okay, okay. Call if you need me."

I waited until I heard the door shut at the top of the stairs before going back to practicing. I tried to remember how it had felt when I threw it correctly in the doctor's office. Maybe I was holding it too close to the end. I slid my hand up the cool rubber tubing, about a foot beyond the three magnetic dots, and, instead of throwing the clip directly at the post, swung the tether toward it from the side. It wrapped and clicked. With the end of the tubing attached successfully to the post, I gave the line a tug to see how strong it actually was. Pretty strong: I had to walk over and pull the clip and the magnets apart from each other by hand.

I kept practicing while my mind drifted back to the day before yesterday at the mall. I got mad all over again, thinking about being left behind, and I threw the tether clip so hard that it smacked against the post with an earsplitting crack. The footsteps overhead started up again, and when the door to the basement opened, I preemptively shouted, "I'm *fine!*"

There was still a small part of me that wanted to tell Smilla what was going on with my floating, with the tether, all of it. But I knew her reaction would only upset me more. She'd tell me she was glad I was okay, like everything was fine now, like I didn't still have a disease with no known cause or cure, and no idea what the future held. She'd tell me to just keep going, to keep pushing, to try and *beat the odds*.

I threw the tether enough times to feel confident that

it would hold me and reasonably confident that I could throw it correctly. But I kept throwing it after that, again and again, whipping the rubber tubing as hard as I could.

WHEN I GOT up on Monday, I peered into my closet for a while and sighed. What could I possibly wear that wouldn't look horrible with a gross rubber tube wrapped around it? Eventually, I pulled on some jeans and laced the tether through the belt loops, wrapped the remaining length around my waist several more times, and secured it in place with the clips. Over that, I wore a baggy T-shirt and the biggest flannel button-down I had. When I checked myself out in the mirror, the tether was fully hidden by my clothes, so much so that my mother asked where it was before I even sat down at the breakfast table.

No one at school said anything about it all morning, but I couldn't shake my awareness of it. I was supposed to clip it to the chair as soon as I sat down, but I waited until class began so I could hook it to the chair leg when no one was looking. I fiddled with the clip at my waist, unable to stop making sure it hadn't slipped, and hoping that everyone was so used to my hum by now that they wouldn't turn and look at me. My body was still a little sore after this last round of floating, and I sat through class after class wondering what the future held. I still wanted to believe everything was going to be normal again, but it was getting harder and harder to trust that that was true.

At lunch, I sat with Smilla and the others out of sheer

force of habit. None of them said anything about our trip to the mall.

"Oh my god," said Min, laughing, "Mr. Zayne kicked Kevin Halloway out of history, and then he wouldn't leave, he just kept staring in the window."

Cheryl laughed too. "Kevin is such a weirdo. He's in my algebra class, and he got detention for drawing all over his desk. It was all these sexy ladies but with animal heads, like ducks and stuff."

Everyone else laughed as well, but I couldn't even bring myself to smile. I knew it wasn't fair to expect them to ask how I was doing, since I hadn't told them about the latest floating incident. But it seemed like none of them had thought much about my health since shortly after I was diagnosed. As much as I didn't want to talk with them about being sick, I didn't understand how it was so easy for them to get past it.

I hurriedly finished my lunch and stood to leave. "I need to go to the library," I lied.

"Oh, okay," said Smilla. "See you later!"

The rest of them turned from me back to one another to continue their conversation, all except Min. "Hey, what's that?" she asked. She was looking toward my midsection.

In horror, I looked down and saw that the wrapped length of the tether had slid below the hem of my T-shirt. "Nothing," I said. "I have to go."

I slung my backpack over my shoulder and grabbed for the tether, gathering it up under my shirt. I made a beeline for the exit so I could get to the bathroom and fix it, but Smilla was right behind me. "Hey," she said. "What's going on?"

I stopped in the hallway just outside the cafeteria, looking at the kids coming and going around us. "It's to help me stay down. I was floating again," I said in a low voice. It felt like admitting failure.

"What? But I thought you were doing so well!"

I swallowed hard, trying not to get teary. "It can happen, I guess."

"So what happened? Are you okay? Was it like last time?"

I glanced around at the kids nearby, a few of whom were looking my way. "Can we not talk about this right now?" I started toward the bathroom again, but Smilla continued after me.

"You never want to talk about it," she said.

I stopped short and stared at her. I felt like I'd been slapped. "You never ask me about it. All you ever want to do is talk to Cheryl, Jennie, and Min about running and trips to Europe and depressing movies."

Smilla looked at me like I had two heads. "They're your friends too. And every time I try to ask how you're doing, you change the subject."

"It's because you keep pretending that it's all going to magically go away. But it's not!" As I said the words, I realized I was saying them as much to myself as to her. "This is how it is now, and I'm not going to have some miraculous recovery and be a champion runner again."

"Anna, you don't know that."

"This is what I'm talking about! You're not listening to me! I don't want to hang out with you guys and talk about running all the time, and I don't want to watch cheesy movies about sickness and death." I had kept everything bottled up for so long, and now I couldn't stop barfing it all over her. "I mean, look at this thing!" I held out the bunched-up tether I'd been white-knuckling. "Can't you see I'm not like you anymore?"

Smilla, who was standing there trying to take everything in, looked at the tether and said, "Come on, it's not that bad. You can hardly even notice it."

"Stop lying!"

The color left Smilla's face as she looked at me in shock. I'd shocked even myself by yelling at her. We had never had a real fight in ten years of being friends, and now I had screamed at her. In public. The people standing around us had faded into the background while I'd ranted, but now they were coming back into focus: dozens of kids standing within earshot at their lockers, up and down the hall, and others wandering our way to see what the commotion was about.

For a moment, I wondered if I had gone too far. But I didn't want to listen to her contradicting me anymore, about the girls being as much my friends as hers, about my potential to *beat the odds*, about how inconspicuous the ugly tether was. "I have to go," I said. Turning my back on her, I walked past the spectators as quickly as I could without getting shaky. I kept my hand on the tether and stayed close to the lockers along the wall in case I needed something metallic to clamp on to. My head felt full of lead and my feet felt full of air, and it seemed that I might turn upside down at any moment.

FIVE

I STORMED AWAY, my mind buzzing. I felt shaky inside, but I didn't know if I was fluttering from walking too fast or trembling from the shock of what had just happened. Not thinking about where I was or what time it was, I headed on autopilot toward geometry.

I was almost to the classroom when I heard a loud "Psst!" behind me, but I ignored it and kept walking. I heard it again, and then Kristi jumped into my path. "Hey!" she said. "I was calling you."

"I have to get to class," I said, trying to push past her.

But she grabbed my arms and said, more softly, "Hey, stop a second. It's fifteen minutes till class starts."

I looked around, as if just now realizing where I was. "Oh."

Kristi squinted at me for a second, then seemed to decide on something. "Come on." She turned to face the same direction as me, linked her arm through mine, and walked me past the classroom and down the hall.

We were headed toward a set of double doors that led outside, behind the building, and I was about to protest. I couldn't hang around outside right now, not when I felt this shaky, not when it was only a couple days since I would have floated who knows how high if it weren't for the ceiling catching me. But she turned at the last minute and opened an unmarked door I'd never gone into.

It was dark inside, a small, windowless space, and I started to panic as I heard Kristi rustling around. She flicked on a lighter and lit a half-used tea-light candle. "Have a seat," she said, parking herself on the floor and setting the candle in front of her. It illuminated what appeared to be a janitor's supply closet, with shelves full of paper towels and cleaning products all around us.

"Are you sure we should have an open flame in here?"

She gave me a crooked grin. "Ah, good, you're snapping out of your trance."

"I'm serious."

"Yeah, I do it all the time. Nobody ever comes in here, at least not during school hours. Sometimes I just can't deal, you know?"

I nodded. I did know.

"So, big fight with the BFF, huh?"

I shook my head. "How do you do that?"

"Do what?"

"How do you know everything that happens when you hardly talk to anyone?"

She shrugged and offered up a coy smile, which looked wicked in the candlelight. "I have my ways."

I was starting to wonder if some of those ways included a network of hiding places like this one throughout the school.

"Anyway, what happened?"

I sighed. "I should go get ready for class. I still have a couple problems on the homework I didn't finish yet."

"Anna. Are you seriously telling me you can think about polygons at a time like this?"

I looked down. "No."

"Then tell me."

I sighed and joined her on the floor. And why not? It seemed like she—unlike Smilla, unlike the other girls—actually wanted to hear what I had to say. That she could take it. So I told her about how it all started. The pain while I was running, how it grew and grew until that fateful day at practice. I told her about the hospital, about the weird plexiglass tube and the other kids at clinic and what lepidopsy was. How they didn't know what caused it, and they couldn't cure it.

The bell rang, and I kept talking. I told her about the most recent flare-up, about waking on the ceiling, my dad dragging me down, the tether, everything. And she listened, rapt, to every word, not contradicting me or pretending it was all going to be fine, just listening. It was such a relief to be honest that I found I couldn't stop.

"And Smilla," I said. "We've been best friends since kindergarten, but it's like there's this brick wall between us now and she can't see through it. And she's describing what's happening on *my* side of the wall—to me—and it makes no sense, because she's not here. And it's such a bunch of crap that she really wants to know how I'm doing! All she wants to do is hang out with Cheryl, Jennie, and Min, and I'm just this annoying sick girl who can't keep up with them."

Kristi shook her head. "I'm sorry, but those girls are the worst. They were really mean to me all through elementary and middle school."

I wasn't sure I could picture them being actual bullies, but maybe they were different when they were younger. And anyway, I was in a bad mood. "Yeah," I said. "They *are* the worst."

She clapped me on the knee. "That's the spirit!"

The candle was burning lower now, and with it, my anger, leaving a lingering sadness behind. "I did everything my doctors told me, and it's like it doesn't even matter. I stopped running, and I've been trying to eat right and get enough sleep and take my medicine on time and all that. But it just got worse." I shook my head. "I thought I could make it go away."

"But you can't. If a doctor can't cure it, why would you be able to?"

It was a good question. I hadn't thought about it that way before. "I don't know. I just thought I could. I mean, I stopped eating sugar because they told me to. And you have *no* idea how bad this thing makes you want sugar."

"Hold on a sec." She reached into her backpack and riffled around, and then pulled out a couple of lollipops. She pulled the wrapper off one and stuck it in her mouth, then handed the other one to me.

I stared at the candy. My mouth watered, but I hesitated.

"If it doesn't matter what you do," she said, "you might as well do what you want."

"I don't know."

"Life is short. That's the reality, whether people want to admit it or not."

I took a deep breath and slowly peeled back the wrapper. I looked at the lollipop. In the flickering light, it gleamed red like a jewel. Red like blood. I slid it into my mouth before I could think any more, and the intense sugary sweetness mixed with the tartness of artificial cherry flavoring made my mouth pucker. And some part of me deep inside finally relaxed.

We sat there eating our lollipops in silence. I kept waiting to see if something bad would happen, if I'd start floating or fluttering or be drawn to the dying flame, but there was nothing. Something shifted in my mind at that moment, some belief about the way I had to be.

The bell rang again, signaling the end of the geometry class we'd skipped. "I guess I better get to my next class," I said. "Thanks for listening. Most people just don't get it."

"Tell me about it," said Kristi, and we opened the door and walked back out into the light.

I MANAGED TO avoid seeing Smilla or the others for the rest of the day, and though I heard people murmuring about the fight, I tuned them out. I felt even more tired than usual by the time I got home, and I went directly to my room and took a nap. The metal clips of the tether dug into my back, but I was too exhausted to care.

The next morning, I dreaded going to school, and I thought about telling my mother I was sick and couldn't go. But I knew I'd have to deal with seeing Smilla sooner or later.

In first period, I took my regular spot in the back corner of the room, and when Jennie came in, she sat in the front row and didn't turn around once. I watched the back of her head all through class, wondering what she and the others had been saying about me and feeling gross about it.

I wondered if I had been too harsh with Smilla. But when I played the fight over in my mind—and everything that had led to it—I felt my anger bubbling up again. Picturing her face as she looked at me in Mangoes after they'd left me behind. Thinking of her taking the phone from me at my house to invite the other girls over when I'd thought she wanted to hang out with just me. That insistent tone in her voice when she told me I should keep fighting, keep trying to overcome, to beat the odds, to run again. What more could I possibly have done that I wasn't already doing to feel better? Why couldn't she see how hard I was already fighting just to keep my feet on the ground?

During study hall, I tried to focus on my geometry textbook to cover what I'd missed when I blew off class with Kristi the day before. I'd been trying to stay on top of all of my schoolwork over the previous month, but I still didn't feel like I had entirely caught up from the times I'd been absent. Technically, I was current on homework, but it felt like I was failing to grasp some of the concepts my classmates seemed to understand. And I was distracted now, too, because next period, I would have to see Smilla in English.

When the bell rang, I dragged my feet to Ms. Meadows's classroom. Smilla was already there, sitting in the middle of the front row, and when I came in, she locked eyes with me. I tried to read her face, and while it seemed as though she might want to talk, I didn't know what to say, so I made my way to my usual spot in the back.

Unlike Jennie, Smilla kept looking over her shoulder at me, but each time our eyes caught, I quickly looked away. She lingered after class, and while I wasn't certain whether she was waiting for me or it was just taking her a while to get packed up, I made sure to stay in my seat until she was gone.

At lunchtime, I went to the library and sat in a secluded corner of the stacks, nibbling the sandwich I'd brought. We weren't allowed to eat in the library, but I didn't want to go to the cafeteria and have to see the girls, to see their judgmental stares for how mean I'd been to Smilla. But it was hard to hide in the library. I was careful not to lean against the shelves, but my hum still gave me away when anyone got close enough to hear it.

"Hey," someone whispered, and I looked up to see Diana from the cross-country team coming around the corner of the row toward me. I only knew her from practice and meets, but I remembered she was kind of a busybody. "Are you and Smilla in a fight?"

"What?" I said, caught off guard by her question. She and I had never had a serious conversation about anything, and now she wanted me to confide the details of my personal life?

"I heard you guys had a huge blowup outside the caf. What happened?"

"Nothing," I said, willing her to leave.

Diana took a few steps closer and crouched down by a shelf of astronomy books. "Come on, you can tell me." Despite the low light, her eyes gleamed, an animal hungry for prey.

I thought about Kristi and how she would react in this kind of situation. "It's none of your *business*," I said, a thrill running through me.

Another figure emerged from a different row of shelves. It was one of the librarians, the one with the silver bob. "Shh," she said.

Diana scowled and disappeared, and I was relieved she'd gone until I remembered I was holding food and would probably get kicked out of the library for it. But the librarian only gave me a dirty look until I put it in my backpack, and then she left. And I was alone once again.

ON THE WAY to clinic that week, I actually thought about telling everyone at group what had happened with Smilla. Would they understand? Pam, at least, knew what it was like to be left behind by her friends. And the others had expressed frustrations with theirs too. But had any of them ever yelled at their best friend and made a scene like I had? I wasn't sure what the other kids would think if I told them how I'd acted. Also, I was worried that if I talked about the fight at clinic, it would get back to my parents, whom I still hadn't told.

When I arrived in the waiting area, I found it packed with people. It turned out that in addition to all the weeklies, most of the sometimes kids happened to be there: a bunch of every-other-weeklies, some monthlies, and even a few quarterlies. Pam, Carrie, and Elaine were regulars, and I still barely knew them. Talking about myself in front of this huge group of other kids, these strangers, was not going to happen.

As annoying as the visits to clinic were, they had already grown routine, and I had my own ways of killing time. I usually spent my hours in the waiting room listening to music or half-heartedly flipping through my homework. Today, the wait was so long that even after I'd finished listening to my Tails Will Tell tape and completed my French assignment, I was still waiting. It was taking forever to get everyone through their appointments.

Pam was over in the corner with her mother, who was trying to keep Pam's little sister Ashley's squirming to a minimum. Pam usually pitched in, but at the moment, she was buried deep in another thick book, its cover depicting a sweeping spiral galaxy in the background and a solo astronaut drifting through the vacuum of space in the foreground. She was too caught up in her reading to notice the other kids and parents jammed in around us, to hear the conversations and murmurs, or even to hear her own name being called.

"Pam?" the nurse said again, holding a chart in her hands.

Pam looked up, coming back to her surroundings from someplace far away. "Oh," she said. "Sorry."

I watched her go down the hall to the exam rooms. Her limp seemed a bit worse than I remembered.

I didn't feel great either. I hadn't actually floated since I started taking the new medication. But despite the late-autumn chill outside, it was stuffy in the waiting room, overheated, and I felt myself growing light-headed, and then a bit light in my seat. I didn't want to start floating, for the other kids to look at me with fear about what might happen to them—or worse, recognition of something that already had.

Finally, the nurse called me in. I stumbled getting out of my chair, tripping over my feet, which weren't quite flat on the ground. I tried not to make eye contact with anyone, not to let them notice me. "I'll join you in a minute," said my mother.

"That's okay. I got it." I could feel the heat of her concerned gaze, but I refused to look over. Instead, I shuffled toward the nurse with one hand resting above my tether clip, keeping my gait as normal as I could as we went into the exam room.

Dr. Shiel came in a few minutes later, and after his exam, I waited for Dr. Liffey to come in and do her check. My thoughts drifted to Pam's book cover, that lost, lonely astronaut. I thought of Smilla, and the time we went on the rickety old roller coaster at Weatherhill Park and screamed and screamed, half with laughter and excitement, and half out of the fear that the chipped wooden scaffolding might collapse under us and launch our car into the air to come crashing down among the rides and cotton candy stands. My mind swirled and dipped like that old coaster. I thought of Kristi and her candle in the supply closet, of Diana in the library asking gossipy questions. My mind couldn't seem to stay still.

Dr. Liffey came in and asked, "How are we doing today?"

"A little dizzy," I said.

"Hmm." She walked around to my side and pushed gently on the top of my shoulders. "You are floating just a tad." She looked over my chart, her brow lined with concentration. Or concern. I couldn't tell. "We'll want to keep an eye on this. Have you been floating at home or at school?"

I shook my head, but that made me dizzier, and I lifted off the table another inch or two. "No, not really."

"Easy." She pulled me back down again, and I stayed put for the moment. She checked my arms and my flutter. "All right," she said, as though she were leading into some new bit of advice or prescription she wanted to give me, but nothing followed. It didn't occur to me until right then that there might come a time when all the options were used up, that there would be no more treatments left to try. The end of the line.

After I got my blood drawn, the oversized group of patients, a dozen of us, crammed ourselves into the little conference room for our support group meeting. I wound up sitting between Pam and some boy, the only one I'd ever seen at clinic. Once everyone had settled in, Lisa shut the door and began the meeting. "Wow, big group today! Welcome, everybody." She stood in the corner of the room, as there were no chairs left. "Why don't we go around and do a quick check-in?"

Elaine started. "I'm still doing that research study," she said. "It's kind of annoying. They have to do a million tests to see how everything's working, but I think the medicine they're giving me is pretty good." She did look better, with less of a blazing flush and more of a healthy glow than she'd had before. She went on about her treatment for a minute, but my mind was drifting again. I tried to bring myself back, to focus on the people in the room.

The introductions went down the line and around to a girl I hadn't seen before. She was petite and very thin, startled-looking, with great big eyes and a huge red turtleneck sweater that seemed to be devouring her. "I'm Marina," she said, her voice soft enough that people had to lean in to hear her better. It turned out she had the same stretching disease as Carrie, and I wondered if she would stay short or if she'd wind up tall like Carrie too.

I checked Marina out, trying to seem like I wasn't staring. I wondered what else that oversized sweater might be hiding. She seemed hesitant to say anything else, but Lisa stepped in. "This is Marina's first time at clinic, so let's all welcome her." Everyone smiled and nodded, and she seemed to relax a degree or two. It occurred to me that I was no longer the most recent addition to the group, and the realization shook me. It was yet another sign that the disease wasn't going away. To Marina, I was just another one of the sick kids.

Carrie went next, and then a few others, and then Pam. "So, yeah, not much new with me. I have lepidopsy. I'm mostly okay, just a little internal chrysalization around a couple joints, but things are mostly under control, I guess. School's fine. My family worries, but they're fine." Pam was much less talkative than usual. Plus, I thought I remembered her saying she had chrysalization around one joint, not more than that. She shrugged. "That's about it, I think." She turned and looked at me, the next one in line.

I glanced around the room. Everyone was looking my way. "Um. I guess I'm a little dizzy today . . ."

"Can you say your name for everyone?" asked Lisa.

"Oh, sorry. Anna."

There was a silent moment, and then Lisa said, "Go on."

"Right. Just kind of dizzy, and floating a little, still. I'm on Coronide—sorry for the hum—and a new one. Gravanil . . . Anyway."

A couple kids chuckled, though I hadn't meant to be funny. Coronide was used for a lot of different manifestational diseases, and I knew the others were laughing in recognition, in solidarity with my side effects and my parade of pills, but I wasn't sure whether I felt comforted or self-conscious.

"I don't know, it's a little hard to focus today."

"That's fine," said Lisa. "We can go ahead and move on to Mikey."

Mikey, the boy, was the last one in the circle to take his

turn. He was sixteen, medium tall, and somewhat pale and pudgy, but it was hard to know if that was his natural state or if he had once been lean and athletic. He had a different disease, whose name was too complicated to remember even right after he said it, and it turned out he was one of the quarterlies. "Things are fine, basically. Dr. Liffey tapered me off Coronide, so I'm not taking any medicine right now."

"That's great," said Carrie. Marina smiled, like maybe there was a shred of hope for her after all. But Pam let out an exasperated little breath, which I probably only caught because I was sitting next to her.

After the group, Pam and I shuffled out last. "Boys," she said. "They never have it as bad as us."

"Really?" I said. Mikey was the only boy I'd met who had a manifestational disease.

"I've only known a few guys in the group, but yeah. They get, like, a teeny bit of fluttering or stretching or whatever, but that's it. And it clears up super fast."

"Huh."

"There are a couple guys who used to come to clinic, and now they don't even have to because it's so under control. They just see Dr. Liffey once or twice a year to get blood work done."

I was scared to ask, but I needed to know. "Have you been coming every week the whole time you've been sick?"

"I was on every other week for a little while, but mostly, yeah."

"Oh." I pictured a future of coming here every week for the rest of my life, and I let out a heavy breath.

"But it's only been like a year and a half. They say it takes a little while to figure out the best combo of treatments and everything, and then things usually settle down. If it weren't for the chrysalization, I probably could come less."

"Oh," I said again, surprised. I didn't want to admit that I'd thought she'd had lepidopsy for much longer, based on how she talked about it. "What grade are you in?" I asked.

"Sophomore. I'm fifteen too."

I didn't want to say "Oh" again, like a jerk, so I said, "Cool," though I had no idea what was supposed to be cool about it. I was in shock that she was the same age as me when she seemed like such an expert on all this. And that it hadn't taken very long for the chrysalization to affect her. It worried me how quickly things could go downhill. Like me winding up on my ceiling and needing a tether just when I'd thought things were going okay.

We arrived in the waiting room, which was clearing out. My mother looked up from her book and began gathering my belongings. Pam's mother was dozing in her chair, with Ashley curled up asleep in the seat next to her. "Mom," Pam said quietly, putting her hand on her mother's shoulder. "It's time to go."

They were still getting their things together when my mother and I put on our coats to leave. "See you next time," Pam called, and I looked back to see her smiling at me, a big genuine smile that surprised me for some reason.

"Bye," I said, and she waved at me, and then we were gone.

OVER THE NEXT week, I kept expecting something big to happen: that Smilla was going to confront me, or that I would float up to the ceiling in school. Anything. But things were mostly calm. Sure, Smilla and the girls were alternately ignoring me and giving me dirty looks when they saw me, and my feet weren't consistently staying all the way on the ground, but those things were becoming routine, and I almost began to get used to them.

In the meantime, Kristi seemed even more interested in me than before. In geometry, she occasionally slid her hand over my notebook and pulled it away again without a word, leaving a piece of candy behind. I was still hesitant about eating these offerings, but my cravings won out. And each time, when nothing terrible happened, it got easier to accept the next piece. Sometimes, I caught Kristi looking at my feet as they hovered just above the floor, but she seemed more interested than judgmental. I didn't have to be perfect around her.

I was spacing out one day during Mr. Takahashi's lecture when Kristi whispered, "Cool."

"Huh?"

She tilted her head toward my notebook, where I realized I'd been doodling again. Without even thinking about it, I had covered an entire page in a field of wildflowers, all different varieties, and a lone girl standing in the middle, facing away.

"Oh," I said, instinctively covering the drawing with my arm.

"Why are you covering it?"

"I don't know."

"Ladies," said Mr. Takahashi, looking our way, and I flipped to a clean notebook page and pretended to take notes.

After he resumed his lecture, Kristi turned to me once again. "You should come over this weekend. I have a ton of art supplies you should check out."

I was a little surprised. Even though we'd been getting along lately, I wasn't expecting her to extend our—was it an actual friendship now?—outside of school. But it wasn't like I had anything better to do. I was pretty sure this was the weekend of the cross-country banquet, and the last thing I wanted to do was sit around imagining the others in their nice dresses, having fun and talking trash about me.

So that Saturday, my father drove me over to Kristi's house. No one else appeared to be home, but I found clues about the other inhabitants as she walked me up to her bedroom. In the living room, there were cream-colored couches and a glass coffee table, all arranged at perfect angles to one another, like a fancy hotel lobby from a movie. There was a small bedroom full of pink frills and stuffed animals—probably a younger sister—and a larger bedroom with a floral-print bedspread and an unreasonable number of throw pillows.

Kristi's bedroom was the only one with a closed door, and when she opened it, it was like walking through a portal into another dimension. The walls were black, and when I stepped closer to them, I realized they were covered with hundreds of sheets of black paper, some of which were further covered by drawings and paintings. "My mother wouldn't let me paint it," said Kristi when she saw me looking. Her bed was unmade, and there were piles of things all over the floor: books, tapes, laundry, school supplies. The one section of the room that was pristine was by the window, where a small table sat with nothing on it, next to a bookshelf full of neatly organized pencils, pens, ink bottles, drawing pads, and all sorts of other art supplies. "Welcome to my studio. What do you want to try?"

I felt intimidated by the spread. I had always liked to doodle and play with color via the magazine collages I made, but these seemed like professional-grade art supplies. I had no idea what to do with them.

She must have sensed my discomfort, because she pulled out a notebook-sized sketch pad and a couple drawing pencils. "Here," she said, scribbling little swatches on the page with different pencils. "Maybe start with a lighter one, and then you can add shading." She drew a circle with a light pencil and shaded it in a bit, then a bit more with a darker pencil, to make it look like a three-dimensional sphere. "Just play with it."

She got out a set of charcoal sticks and a large sketch pad for herself and began drawing furiously. I hesitated, my mind suddenly blank. When I doodled, I never thought too much about what to draw. I just drew. But now, it felt like there was so much pressure to do something good, something real. I picked up one of the light pencils and scribbled to get a feel for it, then did the same thing with the others.

I turned to a clean page and began sketching a close-up of a face.

Kristi's drawing was really good, some kind of phoenix-type creature, wild yet controlled at the same time. "I've been working a lot in monochromatics lately."

I wondered if her new look this year was less about changing her personality and more about living out her art somehow.

"That's nice," she said, examining my drawing. "But true art has passion. It means something."

I looked down, embarrassed. The face on the page stared blankly back at me.

"See, the phoenix represents what I'm feeling. It has emotion. Just draw from your feelings."

"Like from my fight with Smilla," I said, though I had no idea how to draw that.

"Or your disease," said Kristi.

"Maybe."

"Sure. You must have a ton of emotions about that. You can tell me about it if you want. Maybe that will help unlock something."

I still wasn't sure, but I slowly drew the outline of a figure floating above a thin line. I filled in trees and rocks. It was what I imagined I'd looked like that day at cross-country when I'd floated for the first time.

"See, there you go!" said Kristi. "Come on, we've earned a break."

I followed her to the kitchen, where in contrast to her

dark room, everything was such a bright white that it almost made my eyes hurt. I stood by the counter and examined a white ceramic bowl full of plastic lemons while Kristi poked around for refreshments. "We have popcorn," she said.

"Sure."

She stuck the bag in the microwave and went to the refrigerator. "Can't have popcorn without soda," she said. "Ginger ale, root beer, or lemon-lime?"

"Oh, I don't know," I said. The occasional piece of candy was one thing, but an entire can of soda was another.

"Come on, live a little." She held a can of root beer in one hand and a can of lemon-lime in the other and danced them around on the counter.

I supposed if I started drinking the soda and felt bad that I could stop, right?

Kristi cracked a can of lemon-lime and started sipping it. "Ahh. Hits the spot."

The microwave beeped, and the smell of popcorn filled the air. I swallowed hard. "Root beer."

"Attagirl," said Kristi, handing me the can. She poured the popcorn into a large bowl and placed it on the kitchen table. "Nothing spillable in the studio," she said, parking herself in a chair and her soda on the table.

I sat across from her and took a sip. It really did hit the spot. I didn't know if there was an amount of sugar that would satisfy my gnawing hunger for it, but it felt incredible to stop fighting so hard and give in to it. At my house, I didn't even have the option. I had found myself awake in the middle of the night once in a while, contemplating eating straight sugar, right out of the bag, or swallowing honey by the spoonful—that was how bad it was. I took another sip of root beer and let out a long, slow breath.

I gazed out the picture window into a wooded backyard. When I turned around, Kristi was looking at me with a faint, enigmatic smile on her face. "What?" I asked.

"Nothing," she said, but she didn't look away.

My self-consciousness was growing and, with it, the urge to make some kind of small talk to break her out of whatever spell she was under. "So did you do the geometry homework yet?"

That seemed to work. She made a disgusted face. "Takahashi is a sadist. Giving us all those problems to do over the weekend."

"Yeah," I said, though she hadn't answered my question. "So . . . do you have siblings?"

Kristi rolled her eyes. "Just my stepsister. My mother's off having a *girls' day* with her." She made air quotes around "girls' day." "She's the perfect little doll my mother always wanted."

"Ah."

"How about you?" she asked.

"Nope, just me and my parents."

"Lucky."

"I guess." I didn't have to worry about my parents comparing me to another kid like Kristi did, but sometimes my house felt so quiet. I'd always wondered what it would be like to have an older sibling to help me figure things out, or a younger one who looked up to me.

"So, any word from the *runners*?" She said that last word like it was a curse.

I shook my head. I pictured Cheryl glaring at me silently, Jennie linking arms with Smilla and protectively turning her away from me. They'd been communicating what they were thinking, all right, but not in words. I imagined them eating shrimp cocktail in a banquet room somewhere.

"You're better off. Those three are a bunch of succubi."

"A bunch of what?"

"You know," she said. "Succubus, succubi. Demons. Sorry about your pal Smilla. Looks like they've got her now."

"Yeah." I looked back out the window into the woods. It seemed like both yesterday and forever ago that I had run with all those girls in the woods behind the school, back when the trees were full of leaves that were turning bright and colorful. Now the branches were bare.

"Listen." Kristi reached across the table and put her hand on my forearm. "Oh wow, I can feel it," she said, gazing at me with wide, bright eyes. My hum. "That's so wild." She snapped herself out of it but kept her hand on my arm. "Anyway. You're better off without them. They clearly don't get what you're going through. Did they even try to understand?"

"Not really."

"So forget about them! Life is too short to hang around with people who are terrible. And pretending everything is great when it's actually not is terrible too. Like, what, you were just supposed to ignore your disease so you could keep doing whatever they wanted?"

I gave her a sarcastic chuckle. "I tried. It didn't work."

"You need people who can see you for who you are. Now, come on, let's go put some more of who you really are down on paper." She led me back to her room, and I settled into its comforting darkness.

IN THE WEEKS that followed, Kristi and I hung out more and more. It was nice to have someone to sit with at lunch who I could actually talk to, especially when Cheryl and the others glared at me as I walked across the cafeteria. Kristi and I talked about art, about projects she had done or wanted to do, about materials she thought I should try or subjects she thought I should explore, usually related to my illness. "There's so much there," she said. "You're going through something really intense. You have to capture those emotions before they're gone."

I wasn't sure those difficult emotions would ever be gone: the sinking feeling I still got when I saw Smilla frowning at me from the other side of the classroom; the dread that I was becoming like the other sick kids at clinic, no matter how hard I tried not to; the loneliness of going through something that no one around me seemed to understand. And in that way, Kristi was a sort of optimist. But only in that way. In most other regards, she held a bleak view of life. She told me about how this girl was rude to her in the locker room before gym, or how that guy was being a total jerk on the bus, what horrible people all the other kids were, and how she couldn't wait to get out of this town. I got bits here and there about her parents' divorce, how her dad sent money but never called, how her stepsister could do no wrong while Kristi could do no right in her mother's eyes, and how it seemed like her stepfather didn't even notice her existence.

And the more she talked about people being awful, the more I noticed it myself. It was as though I'd had my eyes closed my whole life, just ignoring people's rudeness and inconsiderate behavior, but now it was all I could see. Girls whispering and glancing at me in the hallway. Teachers staring past me or through me instead of making eye contact. Jennie's and Min's faces going cold and turning away every time they saw me, while Cheryl looked disgusted and shook her head. Maybe Kristi was right. Maybe everyone really was terrible. Except for her, the only one who listened.

On the Friday before December break started, I woke up with a headache, but I took some pain relievers and went to school anyway. By third period, though, it had gotten worse. Smilla and I did our usual dance of ignoring each other in English class, with me waiting until she was gone to get up and leave, but that day, I found her lingering outside the door as I walked out. "Hey," she said.

"Hey." I kept walking toward my locker, but I didn't protest as she walked alongside me. The hall was pretty full, but people were moving along to get to class, and by the time I approached my locker, things had thinned out a bit. I figured Smilla would take off for class, too, but she didn't.

"Listen," she said, standing in a tight posture by the locker next to mine. "My parents and I are flying to Sweden tomorrow for break. I didn't want to leave with things like this between us."

As hurt as I still was by her actions, as pessimistic as I was becoming about humanity in general, something inside me melted a little. I looked at my shoes. I didn't know what to say, so I just let her talk.

"I'm sorry I made you feel like I wasn't listening. Or like I was lying to you. I didn't mean to do that—I just wanted you to feel better."

"Okay," I murmured.

"And I'm worried about you. You have that rope thing now." She gestured toward my tether. "I don't know if that means things have gotten worse or what." She paused and scrunched up her face. "Plus . . . I've noticed you spending a lot of time with Kristi lately . . ."

"So?"

Somewhere down the hall, someone slammed a locker shut, and it sounded like a cannon going off.

"The girls grew up with her—they've told me things." She shook her head, brow furrowed. "I really care about you, and I just think being around someone so negative might be bad for you." Her voice got a little bit louder and more emphatic with each sentence.

"What is that supposed to mean?" Now I was getting loud too.

She had this scared, hesitant look like she was afraid she

might shatter me with a single word. "You know, they say that keeping a positive attitude can be good for your health! Like, it helps your immune system and everything!"

She was shouting now, and the whole world seemed to be ringing as anger buzzed within me. She had no idea what my life had been like lately. How could she possibly think she knew what would help me? "So it's my fault that I'm sick. Because I'm being negative." My tone was cold and too aggressive.

"Anna," she said, her tone wounded. "No, that's not it. I just . . . I feel like maybe she only likes you for your illness. And I care about you, and—"

"You don't know anything," I said, my words coming out way louder than I meant them to, but I couldn't control myself now. "She listens to me! She cares about what I'm *actually* feeling instead of what she wants me to feel. *You're* the one who doesn't like me for who I am."

Smilla looked sadder and more wounded than I'd ever seen her before, but I was too worked up to calm down. "I feel like I don't even know you anymore," she said. Her tone was subdued, but her volume sounded like she was talking through a megaphone directly into my ear. How was she doing that?

"Well, I guess that's one thing we agree on," I said, trying to lower my voice from a yell to a normal volume as classroom doors shut around us and the period began.

"What?" she screamed.

I couldn't deal with her anymore. I shut my locker, and

though I hadn't slammed it, I still cringed and recoiled at the blast of sound. I began walking away, and even my footsteps were too loud. My head throbbed. What was going on?

"Anna?" Smilla called after me. I doubled over, holding my hands to my ears. But that only made things worse, amplifying my hum into a scream. I shuffled away, breaking into a jog as I headed for the nurse's office. As I ran, the shakiness started. My ankles throbbed. Every noise along the way was torture. The voices from surrounding classrooms, even with the doors closed, were overwhelming. I ran faster, and the tingling pain began climbing my calves. I was tripping over my own feet, my body slowly lifting off the ground. Fumbling for my tether clasp, I tried to slow down, but the screaming around me was getting worse.

Clumsily, I crashed through the door to the nurse's office, and the nurse turned abruptly and said, "Hey, slow down!" which was so loud, I shielded my head with my arms. Then she realized it was me, the person who'd been taking up space on one of her cots for all those hours over the last few months. "Are you okay?" she said in what must have been a normal tone, but her voice sounded like it was blasting at me through a speaker.

"It's too loud," I said, trying to keep my own voice quiet enough not to hurt my ears.

"I can't hear you, honey," the nurse said, and I shrank back from her in pain.

I swallowed, and the sound was like metal grinding against concrete. I took a deep breath, and it sounded like a jet engine. "It's too loud," I screamed in a low voice.

She looked worried, but she nodded at me and scribbled a note, the pen loudly scraping over the paper. She held it up: *I'll call your mom*. With her hand on the phone, she turned back and pointed at me, then at the small single-unit bathroom inside the office. It took me a second to realize she was trying to give me shelter from the noise of the conversation she was about to have.

Even from inside the bathroom, even though I could tell she was trying to keep it down, it sounded like she was screaming. What was happening to me?

Even after the nurse got off the phone, I stayed in the bathroom. With the drip of the faucet and the echoes of every movement I made amplified times one hundred, it was probably no better than being out in the main nurse's office, but at least I felt protected. After fifteen or twenty minutes, there were footsteps and a loud banging that was probably really a light tapping at the door. I opened it, and there was my mother.

She put her arm around me and ushered me out of the office and through the halls toward the front entrance. It was torture. I was glad it was the middle of the period and the halls were basically empty, not only because it was quieter but also because I couldn't keep the tears from running down my face.

When we got to the car, my mother opened her door and threw her purse on the seat, and then she took off her coat. It was cold enough to feel like it might snow, and mine was still in my locker. I started to put it on, but she tapped me on the shoulder and then gestured at me like she was putting on earmuffs. It wasn't for the cold; it was to muffle the sound. I got into the back and lay across the seat with her coat jammed around my head, though it only helped a little to dull the horrible roar of the engine, the rumbling of the tires over the road.

At home, my mother took me to my room and tucked me into bed. She left and shut the door behind her as quietly as she could. A few minutes later, I heard the phone ring half a time from down the hall. I let out a cry at its volume, which in turn pierced my eardrums and made me sob. A couple minutes after that, my mother appeared with a pill I recognized as an antihistamine and a glass of water. I didn't think this seemed like an allergic reaction, but I didn't care—I just wanted the misery to stop.

I sat up, shaky, and swallowed the pill and half the water, each gulp hammering inside my head. My mother covered me with my down comforter and left me in whatever silence could be achieved. A thin haze of drowsiness settled over the room, and I fell into a sleep like a black hole.

When I woke again, it was around five o'clock, and the daylight had faded from the sky. I got up and went to the bathroom, but the world was still screaming. My mother must have heard me moving, because her footsteps came booming toward me from downstairs. She held out a glass of water and a different pill than before, but like before, I took it without question. She nodded at me and helped me back to my room, where I again buried myself under the covers, the sound of the sheets rubbing together like ocean waves crashing around me.

But soon, the sounds began to fade, the edge came off, and I finally managed to relax. A few minutes later, my mother reappeared, and by then, things sounded almost normal again. At least until she spoke. "Feeling better?" she asked. Her voice was still a touch louder than it should have been, but her words seemed slightly muffled, as though my head were still wrapped in her coat.

"I think so," I said.

"Good," she said with a sigh. She sat down at the end of the bed. "I remembered Dr. Liffey saying sound sensitivity was a side effect from the Gravanil, but I didn't know it could be that bad. She called in those sound reliever pills to the pharmacy, and I got them while you were sleeping."

Great, I thought. *Even more pills.* "Thanks."

"Are you hungry?" she asked.

I nodded. I was starving, in fact. I hadn't eaten since breakfast. It was the period before lunch when everything had started, when I ran to the nurse's office.

When everything happened with Smilla.

That hurt look, even more hurt than she looked during our first fight, flashed back into my mind. But so did what she'd said about Kristi, and about how I needed to keep a positive attitude. I didn't even know what to feel about Smilla anymore. She didn't want to be the kind of friend I needed, but she didn't want me to be friends with anyone else either?

Fortunately, I didn't have to deal with Smilla for a while, as school vacation had officially, if unceremoniously, begun. A break was what I needed, I told myself. A real break, not a hospital stay or a day tucked tightly under my covers.

I hung out in my room as I waited for dinner to be ready, and I put on some music just to see how my body would react. It was an older album from the Frill, their second, and the first track started right up with a peppy drumbeat and a horn section. It no longer hurt, fortunately. Yet even though I pressed my headphones to my ears, the song was missing some of its texture. The drumbeats were less crisp than usual, the guitar notes less distinct. When the vocals started, the words were a little harder to distinguish than they should have been. The song was good, but not as good as it was supposed to be. It was the same with the next track, and the next. Tired as I was, I still listened to the whole tape, wondering all the while if anything would ever be right again.

SIX

WE HAD A typical quiet Christmas at home, just my parents and me. Typical except for my larger than average haul of presents: my parents' attempt to make things better in whatever way they could. They got me a stack of cassette tapes, some earrings, some sweaters. Unlike the previous year, they didn't get me any new running clothes or gear, and while nobody commented on the lack of it, I noticed. I suspect we all did.

Although it had only been a few months since my diagnosis, it felt like forever, and now I had all day and all of those long winter nights to contemplate things. I tried to remember what my life used to be like. Before the l-word. Before I lost Smilla. When I first started getting sick, I thought I was living a nightmare, but now, it seemed more and more like my life before, my healthy life, had been the dream.

My vacation days were punctuated by the occasional trip

out to dinner with my parents, and I hung out at Kristi's house a couple times to draw and sneak Christmas cookies and candy. But other than that, I was alone. I played tapes in my room until I grew too frustrated by the fuzziness of the sound, and then I sat in silence. I tried to read, but it was hard to focus. Mostly, I ended up flat on the couch in front of the TV, watching everything and nothing. I had wanted a break from life, a moment to relax and catch my breath, but now that I was in it, it didn't feel right either. All I was doing was lying around, thinking about my illness even more. It was sinking in finally that this was it. I had lepidopsy, and there was no escape.

When school began again after New Year's, I dragged myself through each day. I found myself numb as I went through the same routine over and over: get up, get dressed, get on the bus, go to class, tether myself to my seat, stare at the blackboard, untether myself, go to the next class, tether myself again, and so on. The days slogged by like that, one after another, blending into one another. Snow piled up and melted and piled up again on the frozen world. The iciness I felt from Smilla and company grew icier. The constant energy of my classmates—their exuberance, their enthusiasm for this or that movie or band or bit of gossip from school, their stories from the parties I wasn't invited to—all of it exhausted me and filled me with an angry sorrow.

The only break I had from the awful monotony of the school day was when I got to see Kristi during lunch and geometry, and during the class periods we occasionally cut to hang out in one of her secret hiding places. She was the one person I could talk to about how I really felt. I could say, "Ugh, I feel like garbage today," or "I was just thinking about how, if I die, they'll give me a page in the back of the yearbook, like they did when Ralph Jones died in that car crash last year. And everyone will pretend like they were my best friend and they're so sad."

And instead of contradicting me, like Smilla would, Kristi nodded, and she said things like "What does it feel like?" or "Oh my god, that is one hundred percent right."

After I drank the soda at her house that first time, I kept waiting for something bad to happen, but it didn't. Nor did anything bad happen after I ate the candy she gave me in class or the cookies we had at her place. And so, little by little, more and more, I tried breaking the rules, just to see what would happen. I got a grape soda out of the vending machine at school, and I drank it. And again, nothing bad. The next day, I bought a double chocolate chip cookie from the cafeteria. No one working there knew I wasn't supposed to have sweets, so they sold it to me without question. I felt watched, but I still slid my money across the counter, put my cookie in my backpack, and marched off, head held high.

I broke other rules too. My mother noticed if I didn't put my tether on for school, so I always started the day with it on. But I began taking it off and stuffing it into my backpack on the bus, only putting it on again on the way home. The floating seemed to be pretty much under control, so what difference did it make? What difference did any of it make, except that after all the junk food, all my great thrifted clothes were starting not to fit me as well anymore. But how much did it even matter? What was the point of having a sense of style when the world just saw a sick girl? No matter what I wore, I couldn't change that.

Even though people didn't always say things to me directly to indicate that that's how they saw me, the odd bit of gossip still occasionally found its way to me. "Is it true you have wings growing out of your back?" asked Lacey Davis as we washed our hands in the girls' room one day before class. She didn't sound the least bit hesitant about asking, as if she had the right to know anything she wanted about my body, and she leaned to the side as if to peek around and check me for wings herself.

I turned my body to keep myself facing her. "What? No."

She looked skeptical. "Come on, you can tell me."

I had no idea why she thought I would tell her anything. Lacey and I weren't friends, and I knew that anything I told her would immediately get back to all of her lacrosse team buddies. There was no way to convince her short of taking off my shirt, so I just slung my backpack over my shoulders and got out of there as quickly as I could.

Or then there was the time I was shuffling down the long hallway to biology one afternoon, and one of the band kids, cruising along with her saxophone case, paused to ask why I walked so slowly. She and I had never had an actual conversation in our lives.

When she kept looking at me and seemed to expect

an answer, I said, "What do you care anyway?" and she walked off in a huff, as if I were the one who had done something wrong.

Another day, when I was on my way to the nurse's office to rest instead of going to the library, a little freshman boy saw me and said, "You're *still* sick?"

I ignored him, but as I entered the office, I heard some unknown voice respond to him behind me. "She's probably faking it." And for the next forty minutes, I lay on my cot, seething.

I had almost no restraint with my parents. It was, of course, safest to yell at them, since I knew they had to forgive me. My mother mostly hinted, asking if I might like to get involved with some activities at school, join a club or something. I'm sure she was worried about my dwindling social life. I brushed off her suggestions and refused to discuss it. My father seemed to notice Smilla's absence all of a sudden, and asked one night at dinner how she was doing, said he hadn't seen her around in a while. "Ask her yourself," I snapped.

"Anna," my mother said sharply, and we all ate in silence for a little while. "You know," she said quietly after a few minutes, and I braced myself for a lecture, "I realize things haven't been easy lately. But that's no excuse for talking that way to your father and me."

"Oh, I'm sorry I haven't been reacting perfectly to having a life-threatening disease."

She closed her eyes for a second, then went on. "You've

been spending a lot of time lately with that Kristi girl. I'm not sure she's the best influence on your attitude. She's been a little rude when I've answered the phone."

I knew that I was probably proving her right, but I said, "Well, what am I supposed to do, not have any friends?"

"What about Smilla and your running friends? You never told me what happened with them, but I'm sure you can work things out."

"I agree, honey," added my father. "You two have been friends since you were tiny. You'll get over this bump in the road."

"I don't want to talk about it," I said in a low voice. "And I'm sure I *can't* just work things out."

"You could call Pam from clinic," said mom. "You two seem to get along pretty well."

I swallowed my last bite of food and stood up to leave. "I need to go do my homework." They didn't try to stop me.

In my room, I opened my history textbook but didn't even look at it. Call Pam? Was she serious? Was I nothing more than a sick kid to my mother now too? Some sad-sack hard-luck case with nothing else to talk about but the disease that was ruining my life? And why was the whole world trying to keep me from being friends with Kristi when she was the only person who even wanted to hang out with me?

ONE DAY IN early February, Kristi and I decided to meet up in the center of Hammond, the next town over. There was an art supply store she wanted to go to, and she promised I would like it. It took some convincing to get my parents to let me go, considering how they felt about Kristi. I also had a bunch of homework to do, but it was a Saturday, and I left the house so infrequently that I guess they felt like it was worth it for me to get out once in a while.

As my father drove me over, he asked, "So how are your classes going? Do you feel like you need any extra help or tutoring or anything?"

"I don't know. I'm okay." The truth was, my grades were starting to slip, and my parents probably had some clue about that, even if they didn't know the full extent. It felt impossible to focus on studying for quizzes and tests, on writing papers and doing homework. Some girl in the next row of the classroom would be wearing a new pair of high-performance running shoes strictly for fashion's sake, and I'd spend long stretches of class churning with anger about it. These girls didn't care about running, only about whether or not they looked good, about whether their sneakers matched their manicures. I didn't even *want* to run anymore, but at least they had the choice. I raged silently about how unfair it was that they still had their health and their looks and their freedom, that they still had everything but spent their time complaining about it. How could I focus on my teachers with such unfairness shoving itself in my face all day?

My father dropped me off in front of the café where Kristi and I had agreed to meet. "I'll pick you up at four. But if you need me sooner, call me. Okay, honey?"

"Okay," I said, climbing out of the car.

"I love you," he called.

"You too," I mumbled, but I didn't look back.

I went into the café and sat at a table by the window. He was slow to pull the car away from the curb and drive off, as if waiting for me to change my mind and go back to him. Although I could feel the cashier glaring at me from behind the counter for monopolizing one of the tables without buying anything, I waited until I was sure my dad was gone to go up and get a rocky road brownie and a strawberry Italian soda.

I had just finished gobbling the brownie when Kristi swooped in the door in a long black trench coat. It was too cold for it, but she didn't seem to care. "What'd you get?"

I looked at the crumbs still dotting my plate, feeling a little sick and somehow still not satisfied. "Brownie."

"Cool," she said, though she seemed a little distracted. I sucked down the rest of my soda, and now I was freezing on top of feeling nauseated, but I pulled on my jacket, and we headed around the corner to the art supply store.

The shop was fairly small, and only a few other people were there. I could feel the clerk watching us as we strolled the aisles. Despite the tight space, the shelves were packed with all sorts of inks, paints, papers, and clays just bursting with potential to become something beautiful. I felt a tiny spark of excitement, and the feeling almost shocked me. I hadn't felt that in a long time. I couldn't remember how long. Maybe I'd felt it on my last vintage store outing with Smilla over the summer, that sense of joy and potential as I flipped through the racks of clothing, the possibility of finding the perfect piece around every corner.

Kristi and I wandered up and down, and she pointed out different products and talked about what you could do with them. I had brought a little money with me, thinking I could maybe get some basic supplies to fool around with at home, but I was having trouble settling on anything, even after examining each display several times.

"I was thinking about what Lacey said to you," said Kristi, fingering some high-end pencils. "About growing wings. And I totally had this idea that you should draw all the bizarre things people have said to you. Like a series."

"Maybe," I said. I wasn't so sure I wanted to dwell on that stuff more than I already was.

"No, you should! And you could do a whole other series about all the kids you told me about from the clinic. Like, you could draw the girl with that heat disorder with flames shooting out of her body. That would be so cool."

The suggestion seemed odd to me. Their conditions didn't feel like my story to tell, my art to create. Instead of responding, I turned the corner and inspected a display of brightly colored acrylic paints, tubes of colors like a mountain of precious gems with magical-sounding names. Cadmium yellow and orange. Cobalt, crimson, viridian. Looking at those colors, I could almost feel something inside me waking up. Maybe this was what I needed. Some color in my life again.

I was checking prices on a couple of the smaller tubes when Kristi said, "Psst," and waved me over. She was standing in front of a rack of charcoals like the ones she had been using to draw her monochromatic phoenix the first time I went to her house. They didn't call to me like the paints did, but I looked at the set she was holding, figuring she wanted to tell me something about the materials. It was a high-quality, medium-sized set, with six or seven charcoal pencils in it, the metal case just big enough to hold in one hand.

Just small enough to slip into a pocket.

It was in hers before I could react. Kristi linked arms with me and tugged my tether down a bit so that with my coat open, the tubing was visible below the hem of my sweater. She jerked me out into the front of the store so quickly, I didn't even realize what was happening. "Are you okay?" she said loudly, but she didn't give me a chance to answer. "Can you make it out to the car? Come on, we better get you home." She pushed through the front door out to the street.

The clerk watched us leave but said nothing. Maybe my confusion played as disorientation and sold Kristi's act. We walked back toward the café, and I buttoned my jacket against the February chill as we went. "Hey," I said, "slow down!"

She stopped in front of a bench and grinned at me.

"Um, what just happened?" I asked.

"We got some great drawing supplies," she said, lifting the edges of her trench coat to curtsy at me.

"But why did you steal them?"

She widened her cool blue eyes at me. "Shut up, will you? Do you want to get caught or something?"

Get caught? *I* hadn't done anything. Not that the clerk

would necessarily see it that way. I lowered my voice. "Come on. Why did you do that?"

"Anna," she said as if I were asking the silliest question in the world. "I got them for you!" She looked around to make sure no one was watching, and then she pulled the case out of her pocket and handed it to me.

"I don't know."

"Do you know how expensive that shit is? Artists are supposed to be revolutionaries, not capitalists. Everybody takes what they need to get their work done." She looked at the charcoal set, which I was still gripping out in the open. "Put that away, will you?"

I wasn't sure what else to do, so I put the set in my coat pocket. But I didn't move, nor did I feel any less weird about it.

"Anna. Listen to me. You have so much promise as an artist, and you have so much subject matter to work from. You just need the right tools. And as your friend, I think you should take those charcoals, go home, and draw everything you can possibly think of about this disease. People are totally going to react to your art about it. You'll see."

I looked over toward the clock outside the bank on the corner. There were only a few minutes left before my dad was due to pick me up, and I sat on the bench to wait. I didn't know what else to say to Kristi. I just felt tired. The charcoals weren't even the materials I was interested in—they were what *Kristi* liked to use. And why was she so obsessed with the idea of me making art about my illness?

"You're not mad, are you?" asked Kristi. "You know I'm just looking out for you."

"Sure," I said, attempting a smile and a nod.

"So you want to hang out next weekend? The parents are going out of town if you want to sleep over. We could do an all-day drawing session."

"Maybe," I said, but then I caught myself. Why did I keep saying maybe when I really meant no?

"Why?" asked Kristi. "You have something better to do?" Her tone fell halfway between jealous and condescending.

Right on cue, my father's car pulled up. "Gotta go." I had never been more relieved to get in and drive away.

When I got home, I carefully extracted the charcoal set from my pocket so that my parents wouldn't see it, then I brought it to my room and buried it in a drawer. I felt gross about the whole encounter.

I went into the bathroom, stripped off all my clothes, and turned the shower up as hot as I could stand it. I let the water flow over me. Was it possible that Smilla had been right about Kristi? That my mother had been right? I hated the thought of admitting that either of those things could be true. But I didn't like what had happened.

And the worst part was how she'd used me to get away with it. Pretending I was having a flare-up, pulling at my tether. Like I was an object and not a person. A human shield.

Smilla's words rang in my head. *I feel like maybe she only likes you for your illness.* It was a horrible thing for Smilla to say. But what if it was true? I thought about how interested Kristi was in all things lepidopsy, and had been this whole time. When we first got paired together in geometry, she wanted nothing to do with me. And then as soon as I got sick, she was all buddy-buddy.

But wasn't she just trying to be nice? She did listen when I told her what was going on in my life, which was more than anyone else did. But she also kept pushing sugar on me. Was she actually trying to get me to float so she could see it happen? Was it possible that she was every bit as invested in my being sick as Smilla was in pretending I wasn't?

I scalded myself for a good long while before reaching for the soap. As I lathered my arms, my skin felt rough. Maybe I had broken out in some kind of stress rash because of the events of the afternoon, or a heat rash because of how long I'd been in the shower. I lathered and rinsed my arms three times, but still my forearms felt the same. I didn't see anything, red as I was from the heat of the water, but when I got out and dried off, I understood. The rest of my body returned to its normal skin tone, light tan and smooth, but my forearms bore the faint beginnings of scales, vaguely iridescent in the steamy light.

I almost laughed. If only Kristi could see this. But even these faintly purple scales defied her desire for me to express myself in black and white. My body resisted what she wanted, what Smilla wanted, what any of us wanted.

I DIDN'T SAY anything else to Kristi about the incident at the art supply store. For the next few days at school, we kept sitting together, but in geometry, I focused on the work, and at lunch, I just let her talk. If she noticed anything was wrong, she didn't let on. At one point, I looked across the cafeteria to where Smilla was sitting with Cheryl, Jennie, and Min, and I thought back on how invisible I had felt when I sat with them. How it seemed like the conversation would be exactly the same whether I was there or not. I hadn't thought I'd feel that way with Kristi, but I was starting to.

That Wednesday at clinic, everything was running ahead of schedule for once. Pam and I had both been seen early by the doctors, and when I got to the lab to get my blood drawn, she was just finishing up. I headed in next, and she said, "I'll wait for you!" and she parked herself in the sitting area before I could say anything about it.

When I emerged, drained and bandaged, she hoisted herself up with her cane. She seemed even stiffer than before, and our pace was slow as we walked back down the hall. I thought about my mother's suggestion that I call Pam, and how quickly I had dismissed it. Now I felt weirdly guilty, like Pam knew somehow what I'd been thinking, could tell that I wasn't interested in being friends.

There was a long moment of silence, and then Pam looked at me thoughtfully and said, "What do you think Dr. Shiel is like outside this place? I feel like maybe he goes home, powers down like a robot, and lies in a wooden crate until it's time to go to work again."

Despite myself, I laughed.

"If he goes home at all," she added. "He always seems to be around."

"That's true," I said. "Maybe he lives *here* and powers down in a supply closet or something."

We looked at each other and smiled. Huh.

"Hey, we have half an hour before group starts," she said. "You want to wander around a little?"

The question opened a door in my mind that I hadn't known was there. The idea that you could step outside the infinite loop of the same old doctor/lab/group routine and improvise for a bit. "Okay," I said. It was better than sitting around the waiting room and doing homework.

We strolled down the hall in the opposite direction from the manifestology department. As people passed going the other way, I kept expecting someone to stop us and tell us we didn't belong there. But no one did.

"What's this?" asked Pam, pausing in the doorway of a dimly lit room.

I stood next to her and peered inside. There was a large clear tank full of liquid, something like an aquarium but sized to fit a person.

"Fish tank?" I suggested. "Or a really weird bathtub?"

"Maybe that's the tank where they grew Dr. Shiel," she said, and we devolved into a fit of giggles. A nurse emerged from a nearby office and looked our way, so we scurried along before we got in trouble.

We peered into rooms full of wires and enclosures, full of large machines and shelves lined with small containers. As we walked through the unfamiliar corridor, there was a moment when I remembered what it was like to come to the hospital for the first time. Before I was so used to everything. Back then, it had scared me because of how strange it all was. Now what scared me was how familiar it had become.

We passed by a couple of vending machines, and I sighed and slowed a little as I looked at the soda and candy inside.

"Are you going to get something?" Pam asked.

"I want to, but I don't know if I should."

"I know what you mean," she said. "I miss candy. I mean, I sneak a little sometimes. But I'm pretty sensitive to sugar, so I try to avoid it. I won't rat you out, though, if you get something."

I stared through the glass at the packages. Even though I'd gotten into the habit of stealthily consuming baked goods and sodas, I could never completely enjoy sugar without worrying that it would send me smashing into the ceiling. "Nah, I'm okay."

We pushed on. Again, we were quiet, but after a few minutes, Pam said, "Can I ask you something?"

I expected her to ask something about me: about why I never talked much in group, or why I hadn't called her, or some other thing I was doing wrong. "Okay."

But she didn't look at me with accusation in her eyes. She just looked sad. "Do you ever feel like no matter how hard people try, they can't really understand what you're going through?"

I was so surprised by her question that I stopped short. She seemed to get along so well with her family and all the other kids in the support group. And even though she sometimes talked about friends who didn't get it, it seemed like she had good ones too. But even she felt like nobody understood her?

"Yeah," I said. "I do."

"Can we sit down for a minute?" she asked, and I noticed she was struggling even harder to walk now.

"Sure," I said, and we turned into a small alcove with a couple of chairs in it.

She parked herself, hooked her cane over the arm of the chair, and looked at her feet. "When I first got sick, my best friend, Katie, was totally there for me. She was amazing—she brought me presents, visited me in the hospital, you name it. And then after a while, she sort of faded away. I don't know. I guess I just figured she was busy, and I was so preoccupied that I didn't think too much about it. But lately, it's felt like she's just . . . gone. I kept calling her and trying to talk to her in school, and she kept ignoring me. So this past weekend, I told my mom I needed to get a home-work assignment so she would drive me to Katie's house, where she couldn't avoid me. I made her tell me what was going on, and she said it was just too much pressure. Every-thing I was going through was too hard on *her*. *She* couldn't handle it anymore."

"Wow," I said, shaking my head. Some of my less favor-able interactions with Smilla ran through my mind. "I thought my best friend would be there for me through any-thing too. She didn't actually go anywhere. She just kept doing all the same stuff as before and expecting me to keep up. But I can't."

"And then you start to feel invisible, right?" asked Pam.

"Yes! Exactly!" I felt shocked that Pam understood. And then I felt a little ridiculous for feeling shocked. She had experienced the same thing. "She was my best friend, and we'd been through everything together, but suddenly it was like she couldn't admit what was happening. She thought I was going to have some miraculous recovery and everything was just going to go back to how it was."

"Oh, boy, the miracle cures!" said Pam. "Suddenly, everyone's a doctor! 'Oh, have you tried this fitness regimen where you hang upside down like a bat for two hours a day?' 'Have you tried this magical diet where you only eat grapefruit and black olives?'"

"You're not serious."

Pam smiled and shrugged. "Well, okay, those *particular* examples are made up. But they're not that far off from what some people say. Like, okay, great, thanks—where did you get your MD?"

I gave her a smile, but it quickly faded. "It just seemed like she thought I wasn't trying hard enough to get better," I said.

Pam shook her head and frowned. "We come here every week and take a million pills and do everything the doctors tell us to. How are we not trying hard enough?"

I was quiet for another moment, and then I asked softly, "Do you remember that thing you said at group about your friends leaving you behind while you were hanging out?"

"Ugh," she said. "How could I forget?"

"Yeah, well, it happened to me too."

Her face turned serious. "Aw, man. I'm sorry."

I told her about that time at the movies, the mall, all of it. How Smilla didn't even realize what she and the others had done.

"Did you say anything?"

"No. They could tell I was annoyed, but they didn't know why."

"And then if you do explain it, you feel sort of pathetic," she said. "Like you're asking for something unreasonable, when, like, how do they not even notice what they're doing?"

We headed back toward clinic as the hour for the support group approached. I thought about how I'd been feeling lately about humanity, that everyone was terrible and nobody understood. But as I followed Pam into the conference room, I realized it might still be possible for people to surprise me in good ways.

OVER THE NEXT few weeks, the conversation with Pam kept echoing through my head. I thought about her question, about whether people really understood me, no matter how hard they tried. I thought about Smilla and the others: Kristi, my parents, the other kids at school. None of them seemed to understand what it was like to go through what I'd been through. And I wasn't sure how hard they had tried to.

But then I thought back on my first big fight with Smilla, how she said that I never wanted to talk about how I was feeling. I thought about how I never wanted to talk at the support group, or to my parents. Was it my fault for not letting people in?

With Kristi, I was growing increasingly uncertain about how much I wanted to let her in. Things mostly went back to normal with her: we worked on assignments together in geometry; we ate lunch together and talked about people and art and so forth. But I made excuses every time she asked me to get together after school or on the weekend, and I felt an uncomfortable sour sort of feeling underlying everything. Those charcoals were still sitting in my drawer at home, unopened.

On an unseasonably warm Monday at the end of February, I was on my way down the hall at the end of the day and saw Smilla standing up ahead at her locker. She didn't see me, and I could have walked right by, but something drew me toward her.

"Hey," I said.

She turned toward me, surprised. "Hey."

It had somehow been a couple months since we last spoke, and I wasn't sure how to start again. There was a feeling inside me that I couldn't quite put into words: Something about how hard it had been to sleep lately, something about how I missed her, but some version of her that I wasn't sure existed anymore. Something about how maybe she was right that I hadn't been open with her, and maybe I wanted to be more open, but that I needed more from her too.

"How are you?" I asked.

"I'm okay," she said quietly.

I nodded, searching my mind for what to say next. "Do you have practice today?"

"Yeah. Winter season's almost over."

It was almost spring. How had so much time passed since everything started, since I first got sick? Since we stopped talking?

She closed her locker and gestured toward the gym. "I should probably . . ."

"Yeah," I said. "Maybe sometime we could—"

Someone linked their arm through mine and yanked me away. I whipped my head around to see that it was Kristi, and she was giving Smilla a sappy smile. "Hi, Smilla," she said. "Aren't you supposed to be off running with your little friends?"

Smilla didn't say anything. She just stood there looking hurt, and Kristi yanked me down the hall before I could react. "You don't want to miss your bus, do you?" she asked.

She was walking too fast, and my feet were getting sore and shaky. I pulled my arm away from her and slowed down. "Ow," I said. I looked over my shoulder, wondering if I should go talk to Smilla again, but she had already disappeared into the crowd. I turned back toward the front entrance of the building, frowned, and kept walking.

"What is going on with you anyway?" demanded Kristi. "You've been super weird and quiet lately, and now you're talking to Smilla again? What's up?"

"Nothing." We were outside now, and I just wanted to get on my bus and go home.

She grabbed my arm again. "You're not lying to me, are you? You know how much I hate that."

I swallowed. "I'm just not feeling great. I need to get home, okay?"

She peered at me for a moment, scanning me to see if I was telling the truth. "Fine." She let go, and then her whole demeanor changed and lightened. "Call me later!"

I got on the bus and leaned my head against the window. My head hurt, my feet hurt, and there was a tightness in my stomach. The bus pulled out of the driveway, and I watched the world go by: bare trees; lonely-looking houses; patches of icy, dirty snow still lingering in the shadowy places.

THAT NIGHT, I lay in bed, replaying the scene with Smilla and Kristi over and over in my mind, wishing I hadn't let myself be pulled away like that. The bright numbers of my clock radio changed and changed, inching toward and past midnight, and I couldn't stop staring at them. But I couldn't keep lying in bed either.

I went into the bathroom, locked the door, stripped off my pajamas, and stared at my unfamiliar form in the mirror. I examined its hands and legs and wide stretches of skin until they became abstract pieces of sculpture, not anything connected with me. My stomach had become rounder, my legs softer. I tried flexing my calves and poking at them, but the hard, strong knots of muscle from my running days were no more. Were they still in there somewhere, underneath the layers of fat?

My arms, too, had grown softer, and the scales along the tops of my forearms had become more pronounced. Now, when I rotated my wrists under the bathroom light, I could see more than the faint, flashing hint of iridescence. Instead, full silvery purple scales shimmered there, each the diameter of a pencil eraser. Despite how warm the day had been, it was still winter and easy to keep my arms concealed under long sleeves, but what would happen when spring came? In the privacy of the bathroom, I stared at the scales, exposed them to the air and the light, rubbed at them until the flesh underneath was red. They appeared so delicate, yet they were more like a thin veneer of armor, unable to be broken or scratched away.

When I finally got dressed again and wandered back to my room, I circled around for a while, shuffling my feet on the carpet and touching the doorknob to make a spark. The light, I craved it like sugar, and I zapped my finger against the knob again and again. Sometime around two, the moon shifted its angle in the sky and began to shine in through the cracks between my window blinds, and I found myself mesmerized. It was full that night, its light blazing in through the slats and sliding across my floor as it lifted into the sky. I was so tired, but I couldn't get my body to stay in bed or my eyes to stay closed, so I went to the window, opened the blinds, and ran my fingers along the frame as I stared out at that silver orb. It glided in a slow loop across the sky. Eventually, it was directly above me, above the house, and I couldn't see it anymore. I got back in bed and tried going to sleep again, but I was even more restless than before.

I put on a pair of slippers and went out the back door into the yard in my pajamas, and I looked around. The grass was bathed in a faint blue glow from the moon, which seemed to grow brighter the higher it rose. A small patch of leftover snow gleamed in the corner of the yard. I stood there, breathing in the cool night air.

That moon. I stared at it, stretched my hand as if to reach up and touch it.

I didn't realize I was off the ground until I glanced around to find myself at eye level with the roof. A breeze picked up, making my hair flutter and pushing me toward the next-door neighbor's yard. I flailed and spun, grabbing at my waist for my tether before I remembered I had taken it off to sleep hours earlier, and I hadn't put it back on before I left the house. I flapped my arms, trying desperately to lower my altitude, but I just kept drifting. I crossed through one yard and into the next, and soon I was over the pond on the next block. My legs were throbbing now, and the pain was creeping through my thighs and toward my waist. *Breathe,* I told myself. *Try to calm down.* But nothing seemed to work. I flew beyond the pond and grabbed at the treetops on the other side, managing to pull myself down a little, but I was too panicked to maintain my grasp. I passed through another yard and across the street, seeing power lines ahead and gasping in terror. I pulled myself into a tight ball, and just barely flew over without grazing them. I could hardly breathe.

Now I was above an open field, the one behind the elementary school, and I was slowly rising again. What if this was it? The end? I looked at the moon and burst several feet upward. "Don't look, don't look!" I whispered, hysterical, focusing with all my might on the ground below. I stared at the playground equipment, miniaturized by the distance. I looked at the flagpole, foreshortened as I drifted above it, out of reach. Something moved across the ground, a flash of white like a waving handkerchief: the stripe of a skunk. I tensed instinctively, not wanting to be sprayed, but the skunk was calm, unafraid, rooting about without a worry, nothing and no one within reach of it.

I continued watching the skunk as I passed over and across the field. This was it. I was going to die. I was going to be one of those girls who just floated away. And it was my own fault. I should have stayed inside. I should have worn my tether. I was going to die, and the last memory Smilla had of me would be me leaving her to go with Kristi. She would hate me forever. I began to sob. I didn't want it to go like this. I didn't want this to be the end.

Something brushed my leg, and I whipped around to find myself drifting by the huge white pine tree that grew next to the school. It was taller than any other tree around, probably a hundred years old. Back in elementary school, some rowdy boy would occasionally break the rules to climb up into it, and at least one student had fallen from a high branch and broken a leg. At that height, he was lucky it had only been his leg.

Frantic, I grabbed at the branches. The first few I caught were thin and snapped off in my hands, but I kept grabbing, and I managed to get hold of a thicker branch. My hands trembled, the flutter starting up again as I carefully reached from branch to branch, still crying as I worked my way back to earth. Halfway there, an owl flew out of the tree, just inches away from me, startling me and making me lose my grip. *No, no, no.* I reached out with both arms and tried to hook myself on to a branch with both feet as well, and I caught myself again. I took a deep breath. More carefully now, I slowly climbed my way down the tree, twigs and pine needles getting caught in my long, tangled hair.

Finally, finally, my feet touched the ground. My slippers had come off at some point; I hadn't noticed when. There was a large tear in the side of my pajama top, and standing there, numerous blocks away from my house in the middle of the night, I felt very exposed. I didn't think I could make it home if I tried to walk—not with stocking feet and no tether and the impossibility of keeping myself on the ground. There was a pay phone in front of the school, I remembered, if I could make it there from the tree without floating away. I looked across to the building. Ever since going off to middle school, and especially high school, the elementary school had seemed so small. Yet now, the space I would have to cross—probably only a quarter the length of the high school track—seemed enormous. I was terrified to let go of the tree, but my arms were growing sore from trying to keep myself down, and I knew it was just a matter of time until my hold gave out and I began to drift up again.

Still grabbing the tree trunk, I lowered myself all the way to the ground. Maybe if I held on to the grass, I could crawl to the pay phone. I got on my hands and knees and tried to grab a fistful of grass in each hand. But it was dry and brittle, and it broke off in my fingers. I was already lifting off, and I knew I had to find another way. I grabbed on to the tree trunk again and thought it over.

With nothing but grass and pavement between the pay phone and me, all I had was speed. I had to get there as fast as I could, before I floated too high to reach the phone. It was one of those open ones on a pole with a little overhang, which would give me something to grab on to even if I was flying through the air. I just couldn't get too far up.

I took a deep breath, and with one arm still around the tree, I got as close as I could to the starting position for a sprint. Another deep breath. *Three, two, one.*

I ran. As fast as I could. I focused on the feeling of my feet hitting the ground: left, right, left, right. I couldn't go as fast as I once did, but the adrenaline rush helped me build up a decent burst of speed.

I was barreling straight for the pay phone, and I was almost there when I felt my feet scrambling to touch the earth. I was beginning to float again. Fortunately, I had enough momentum going from the run that I continued soaring toward the phone, and I grabbed on to the edge of it as I sailed through the air and almost past it. My arms were nearly yanked out of their sockets. Sideways and hovering, I clung for a good minute before pulling myself back around to the telephone side. I rotated my body so I was vertical again and my feet were touching the ground, even if they didn't want to stay there. I clutched the receiver, wrapped the cord tightly around my wrist, and called my house collect.

The phone rang four times and was just about to go to the answering machine when my mother picked up. "Hello," she said, her voice flattened by sleep.

The operator's voice came on the line. "You have a collect call from Anna. Will you accept the charges?"

"What?" said my mother. She sounded more awake now but still disoriented. "Yes, okay, yes."

"Mom, it's me," I said, even though she already knew that. My voice came out frenzied, cracked.

"Anna, what's going on? Where are you?"

"Come get me. Please. I'm at the elementary school. In the front." My hands were starting to flutter harder now.

"What? How— Okay, I'll be right there."

The phone clicked as my mother hung up, and I imagined her running for her shoes and keys. I wondered if she would wake my father or just go. My arms were getting tired from holding my body steady, and I was freezing cold. I tried to picture her movements to distract myself from the aching and shivering: *Now she's going downstairs. Now she's opening the garage door . . . pulling out of the driveway . . . stopping and turning left at the end of the street.* As I pictured her nearing the school, I heard a car approaching. It seemed to be going too fast, like it was going to speed right by me, and I worried that it wasn't her, but then it screeched into the circular driveway, and my mom came running out toward me.

I was crying again before she even got to me, before she helped me into the car and took me home and got me up the stairs and into my bedroom, before she tucked me securely back into bed. She was kind enough to wait until we got home to ask me what happened, and she sat next to me and petted my hair as I told her. "I don't even know how it happened," I sobbed. "I just went outside, and then I was up so high—" My voice broke off.

"It's okay," she said, even though we both knew it wasn't. "It's okay."

SEVEN

WHEN I WOKE up later that morning, my father was sitting by my bed. He looked exhausted. "How are you feeling?" he asked.

"Sore." My feet and legs still throbbed, and the rest of my body ached too. At first, I thought it was simply because of how tense I'd been the night before and how hard I'd worked to pull myself back to the ground. Then I realized I was still floating. I was several inches above the mattress, and when I looked down the length of the bed, I noticed that there were bungee cords holding me in place, their ends hooked to the bed frame on either side of me.

"Sorry about that," said my dad. "You fell asleep pretty hard, and we tried tucking in the sheet, but you didn't want to stay put. We almost brought you to the emergency room." His voice cracked a little, and he paused to regain his composure. "Dr. Liffey said if we could keep you down, it was okay to let you get some sleep and bring you to the hospital in the morning. So I found the bungee cords in the basement and we rigged this thing up."

It took both of my parents to hold me steady as I struggled into a pair of sweatpants and a hoodie, and then to wrangle me into the car. As we walked from the parking garage to Dr. Liffey's office, it was clearly a much greater effort for them to keep me near the ground than it had been after the time I got stuck on the ceiling. I tethered myself to a heavy wooden chair as soon as we got to the waiting room, but I was already floating like a balloon as Dr. Liffey walked in.

The three of them helped me into the exam room, and Dr. Liffey strapped me to the table. The straps dug in as my body pushed upward. The doctor, while always kind and compassionate, possessed a sense of calm remove that usually kept her from seeming too worried about my symptoms or prognosis. Not this morning, though. As I told her what had happened, she sat very still, her brow creased and her mouth turned down at the edges. "And you didn't have your tether on?" she asked.

I looked at the floor. "No."

"Why did you go outside without it?"

"I don't know. I didn't think. I just . . . went. I felt like I had to see the moon. It was so bright."

She nodded slowly, her face maintaining its concerned look. "I want to do a more sensitive light reaction test on you." She scribbled some notes on a lab slip and handed it to my father. She found a hospital map in the drawer and made a circle, indicating another of those mysterious labs deep in another basement hallway. My parents stood, and I was about to unlatch myself when she said, "Hold on. I better get you a grav chair."

She disappeared into the corridor, and I glanced at my parents to see if I had missed something. Grav chair? My mother let out a long breath, dark circles under her eyes. My father pinkened and barely seemed to be breathing.

Dr. Liffey came back about five minutes later, accompanied by an orderly rolling what looked like an ordinary wheelchair, only bulkier. "This is a gravitational wheelchair," said the doctor. "It'll help you get to the lab without floating off."

The orderly, a heavyset guy with a buzz cut and a thin mustache, pulled the chair around and angled it toward me so I could get in. As he brought it closer, I could see that unlike the regular hospital wheelchairs, with their folding vinyl seats and backs, this one was much more solid and made of thick metal. Underneath the seat was a large box that reached most of the way to the ground, and there was a series of switches and dials between the push handles in the back. Dr. Liffey and the orderly helped me off the exam table and onto the thinly padded seat, where they strapped me into a complex safety harness as though I were boarding a rocket. The orderly gave the chair a quick test push forward and back, then adjusted the dials. When he was done, he pushed me toward the door, and the chair's added gravity and my antigravity canceled each other out enough to make it feel like I was in a normal wheelchair, even though the harness straps were digging into me as my body pulled up against them.

We traveled along hallways and across bridges, went down elevators and through lobbies, my parents marching on either side of me like palace guards. When we arrived at the lab, they waited outside while the orderly pushed me into a boxy room filled with a soft light that seemed to be coming from every direction at once. It was the perfect sort of lighting for an art studio, I thought, everything nice and light without being too bright or casting any sharp shadows. It would be nice to have a studio in my house, to be able to paint with all those bright colors. Maybe I could talk to my parents about making one in the basement.

It was strange, letting my thoughts wander like that in such a weird and unfamiliar place. I felt oddly relaxed. My body still felt buoyant, but it stopped straining so hard against the grav chair's straps. The room was a perfect cube, and it occurred to me that the reason the lighting was so even was that the illumination was actually coming from every surface of the walls, floor, and ceiling. All of them were covered by translucent tiles, each maybe a foot square, the seams visible only up close. A single stool sat in the center of the room, a molded plastic seat with a low back and a seat belt, and a short pole running down to a wide base on the floor.

A woman in pink scrubs, who must have been the lab technician, came into the room. She looked young, like she was just out of college, and she smiled at me. "Hello!" she said in a cheery, high-pitched voice. "How are we today?"

Under normal circumstances, I would have found her chirpiness incredibly annoying, but now I was feeling too mellow to care. "I'm fine," I said dreamily.

"Excellent," she said. She knelt and opened a keypad on the back of the stool and pressed a few buttons. "Okay, so I'm going to have you take a seat here." The orderly helped me out of the grav chair and onto the stool. "Good," said the lab tech. "And clip that belt on nice and tight. Great." Even though the lap belt was the only thing securing me now, my arms and legs no longer pulled toward the sky, instead hovering around me as though I were suspended in water. The orderly wheeled the grav chair out into the hallway. "Now, before we get started, do you have any issues with darkness?" asked the lab tech. "Like, do you get scared or claustrophobic at all?"

My mellowness turned down a notch. "No," I said, "I don't think so."

"Excellent," she said again. "This room is a perfect darkroom, which can be a little weird. No light gets in at all unless we want it to. What I'm going to do is step out, and then the lights are going to shut off completely. They'll stay that way for a minute or so while your eyes adjust, and then different lights will come on around the room. What I want you to do is just relax, let your body do what it's going to do. You may feel yourself moving—that's okay. The chair will move with you, up and down, side to side as you follow the lights, and it'll record your movements for us. You don't have to do anything. Just go with it. Okay?"

I wasn't sure it was okay, but what choice did I have? "Okay," I said.

"Excellent."

She left, the door clicked shut behind her, and the lights dimmed to nothing. At first, it seemed to be a normal level of darkness, but then, as the tech had warned me, it did feel weird. Total darkness. It was disorienting. The blackness grew thick around me, like mud, and I struggled to breathe normally. Just as I was putting one hand in front of my face to try and see it, to make sure that it was still there, that *I* was still there, a low whirring started in the floor, and I felt the stool shift slightly. A faint light came aglow in one of the tiles on the wall to my left, and I stared at it, grateful to have something to look at, to step out of the fear that I might have vanished into oblivion while the lights were out. The square's brightness gradually grew in intensity, and I felt myself sliding toward it, my arms and legs shifting in its direction. I looked at the base of the stool again. I could see now that it was like a puck sliding across an air hockey table, and nothing was propelling it except me.

The light faded off, and a different square of light on the opposite wall shone to life. My body slowed, switched directions, and moved toward it now, drawn to its glow. A second light came on at the other end of that same wall, not as bright as the first, and my path swerved slightly but continued toward the first light. Then both of them switched off. Another came alive on the ceiling, and the pole attaching the stool to the base telescoped up, extending toward the light. I panicked, but then I remembered what the tech had said about letting my body do what it wanted to do. It wasn't like I could float away, confined in that cube of a room. I tried to relax as squares of light bloomed and withered all over the room, pulling me toward them.

Usually when I started floating, that sharp, prickly pain began in my feet and moved through my legs, up and up. But now, I felt a generalized low throbbing, an ache that pulsated throughout my entire body. It shifted as I slid toward the different squares, sloshing around inside me like liquid in a water balloon.

Finally, the last squares went dark and then, a second later, all the lights came back on to the same low ambient glow as when I first arrived. The floor whirred back down to silence, and my stool came to a halt near one corner of the room. I let out a deep breath. The throbbing ache stopped moving and dispersed evenly throughout my body. I felt wrung-out, limp. The tech came back in and asked, "How are we doing?"

I wasn't sure what to say, but it was okay; it didn't seem like she was expecting much of an answer. She beckoned the orderly back in, and it took both of them to help me off the stool and into the grav chair.

In the hallway, my father was fiddling with the sleeve of his jacket, which lay slung across his lap. "Don't go anywhere just yet," said the tech. "Let me call your doctor and see where she wants you next."

Under the hallway's fluorescent overhead lights, my body immediately began pulling toward the ceiling again, my achy muscles pressing against the straps and getting even sorer.

"Are you okay?" asked my mother. "You look a little pale."

I nodded, still not finding any words.

The tech came back a moment later. "Okeydoke," she said. "You can head back and see your doctor now to go over the results. Sound good?"

"Sounds great," said my mother. I could hear the sarcasm in her voice. Great, all of this sure was just fantastic.

My father came around and put his hand, warm and twitchy, on my shoulder.

"Well," said Dr. Liffey when we arrived at her office, "I think we're going to need to change your medications a bit. I want to increase your Coronide a little, at least until we get this flare-up under control." She scribbled a few notes in my chart. "I also want to try something new. This new drug, Luxitra, is a shot that we'll give you today, and then you'll get it once a month at clinic. We'll need to keep you here until we get you stabilized. The tether's use is limited after a certain point, and in addition to the health risks of letting things go unchecked, it's not safe for you to be out and about right now."

My skin felt clammy, and the harness straps dug into my chest and legs as my body surged upward again, like I was riding on an airplane in heavy turbulence. "What do you mean, it's limited?" I asked, my voice faint in my ears.

"Hmm?" said the doctor.

"The tether's use is limited?"

"Think about it like a piece of string," said Dr. Liffey. "You can use it to tie down a helium balloon, but you can't tie down a rocket."

It grew hard to breathe again. Until then, my only concern about the tether (aside from embarrassment about wearing it) was that I wouldn't have it on when I needed it. Now she was telling me it might not even hold? At what point would the ceiling itself become too weak to contain me? At what point would I simply crash through the roof and be gone forever?

Even my mother looked pale at this news. She managed to keep her voice as steady as ever, though, and she asked, "So what about the treatment?"

"Side effects aren't bad with this one," Dr. Liffey said. "You may feel a little drowsy. You might also have more intense dreams, which can be a little weird, but it's normal. It's also pretty common for colors to look more vivid and to see a bit of a halo around lights, but if you have any actual hallucinations, be sure to call me right away."

I went on nodding, overwhelmed.

She kept talking. "A couple other things: Your test showed you've become highly phototactic, which means you're drawn to light sources very easily. That's what the Luxitra is meant to reduce. But even with the medication, you'll need to be careful. During the day, it shouldn't be too much of a problem if you're in a well-lit room or outside, where it's pretty bright all around. But at nighttime, I would avoid going outside when you can, and if you do go, stay out of open areas. And you absolutely must wear that tether. Don't even step out the door without it. Got it?"

Some force made the word "Yes" come out of my mouth.

"You're also going to need some good, thick light-blocking curtains for your bedroom at home. You'll sleep better if you can block out the moonlight or streetlamps that shine through the window. Headlights going by. Anything like that. The nurse is going to put some curtains up for you for tonight. And whatever lamps you have in the house at night, it's good to make that light as even throughout the room as possible. It'll help you feel more relaxed."

I thought about that wonderful even lighting in the lab.

My mother was scribbling notes in her little book. My father kept glancing over her shoulder to make sure she got everything and nodding frantically at Dr. Liffey. "Got it," he said.

"For now, I'd like to give you a shot of something to relax you a little bit. It should calm you down and hopefully help your gravity while we get everything else going. Okay?"

"Okay."

Dr. Liffey got up and left the exam room. My parents and I sat quietly together. I waited for them to say something, but neither of them did. Dr. Liffey came back in and gave me the shot herself. It was an odd thing to see—normally she was just the one who gave the orders, yet here she was, rolling up my sleeve and swabbing my upper arm with an alcohol pad, pricking me quickly with the needle, like she did it every day. I imagined her younger, back in medical school, with less gray hair and a pair of scrubs instead of the white coat. She must have practiced giving shots, drawing blood, and taking blood pressure. What was she like then? Come to think of it, what was she like now, when she wasn't there in the office? I didn't even know if she was married, if she had children or friends or hobbies, if she spent her time doing anything other than seeing patients or doing research studies. She seemed able to be summoned at all hours of the day or night, no matter when we paged her, and I wondered what it was we were interrupting when we did that.

She pulled the needle out and pressed a gauze pad to my arm, deftly sliding the needle into the red sharps container on the wall at the same time. "I already called Admitting. We'll get you set up in a room, and I'll be in to check on you later."

I nodded, a little dizzy from the shot, as she applied a bandage to my arm.

The orderly came back in and pushed me to the inpatient ward. The medication must have been kicking in already, because he had to stop halfway there to adjust the chair's gravity to a lower setting. My mind drifted as the exhaustion hit me all at once. The constant lack of sleep, the tests, the motion—constant motion—from home to the hospital, through the maze of hallways, back and forth, up and down. Maybe it was the tidal wave of everything crashing over me, or maybe it was the shot, but I was feeling much heavier now.

I SLEPT UNTIL it was dark out and woke to find myself alone in a single-person room that didn't look like any others I had stayed in. There was something above me, and as I examined it, I noticed that it resembled a mattress. For a second, I panicked, worried that I was on the ceiling again, looking down, but then I realized I was lying on a mattress as well, and the world was right-side up. I was simply contained in an enclosure. It was like a bunk bed, but with clear plastic slats a couple inches wide, set about a foot apart all around the sides to keep me in. And the mattress-type thing above me on the underside of the top piece of the enclosure offered a soft place to crash if I flew up and hit it.

As I shook off the sleep, I discovered that my entire body from the neck down was tucked snugly under a sheet that seemed to be fastened to the bed. "Hello?" I said.

Nobody responded, and I started to panic.

"Hello?" I called out into the hallway, hoping someone would hear me.

A nurse and my mother came in. "You're awake!" said the nurse.

"What's happening?" I asked, still a bit groggy and edging toward claustrophobia.

The nurse walked over to my right and lifted a latch. The whole right side of the enclosure was connected in a wall of slats that she swung open, and she helped me free my right arm from under the blanket. It wanted to drift upward but wasn't shooting for the sky, like all of me had been before. She took my pulse and blood pressure, then tucked my arm back in and took my temperature. "Looks like you're doing a little better," she said. "Do you need anything right now? You slept through dinner, but I can get you something if you're hungry."

The whole day had passed. "Okay," I said.

She took the remote control from behind the bed and tucked it under the sheet next to where my right hand was pinned, leaving me just enough wiggle room to turn on the TV or press the call button. "Once that medicine kicks in a little more, we'll let you keep your arms out. For now, we'll keep them in except for eating and going to the bathroom." The nurse buttoned me back in, shut the cage door, and went to the end of the bed to adjust some dials I hadn't noticed before. The bed must have enhanced gravity just like the grav chair.

She tapped one of the cage doors. "It's not locked, but please call for a nurse if you need to get out so we can help you move around safely."

A tray of food came a little while later: small plastic-wrapped containers of steamed carrots, steamed chicken, steamed rice, all with the flavor of steam itself. The nurse came back and freed my arms, and I picked at my food and peered at the television, which I could see, mostly, through the slats. Nothing was on but the news: ominous stories of violence in faraway places and economic problems I didn't understand and couldn't control. I was tired but restless, antsy but trapped.

But better trapped than free-floating out in the world. I kept picturing those power lines emerging out of the darkness ahead of me as I drifted toward them, the view of my neighborhood from above. I kept thinking of all the ways I could have died: of electrocution, of exposure. Of lepidopsy.

And Dr. Liffey's words kept running through my head as well—*The tether's use is limited*—and I pictured all the other ways the disease could end me: Being sucked out of my seat in school so quickly and so suddenly that my head crashed against the ceiling. Smashing through the roof and falling up into thunderclouds. All the places I might float off to, even if I was able to get down: the ocean, the mountains, beyond the reach of anyone who could help me.

I finished my dinner and was tucked back in, swaddled like a baby. At least I was safe for now. My parents went to the cafeteria to get something to eat. After they left, I stared at the television for a few minutes while commercials flashed past like highway signs: Car dealer. Law firm. Fast food.

I fell into a choppy, dream-infested sleep and was only vaguely aware of my parents coming back into the room, my father stroking my hair through the slats, my mother patting my arm, and both of them disappearing again, into the maze of hospital hallways.

THAT NIGHT, WITH the light-blocking curtains up and the new medication circulating through my blood, I slept better than I had in months, even with the nurses coming in every few hours to take my vital signs. In the morning, despite still floating and being a bit achy, I felt more like myself than I had in ages.

With the immediate danger past, my thoughts drifted back to my thwarted conversation with Smilla. How hurt she had looked. She probably thought I was pathetic now, just as pathetic as she'd always secretly known. That I could be taken in by someone like Kristi. I was ashamed for going with her. I should have stayed and kept talking to Smilla, but it had all happened so fast, I hadn't had time to react.

My mother came to hang out with me soon after I woke up. We watched game shows on TV, but my mind kept wandering. I thought about my close call with death over and over again, interrupted only by waves of guilt, anger, and frustration about the situation with Smilla and Kristi.

Late that morning, my mom went to get a cup of coffee, and when she returned, she said she had run into Pam's mother. "Pam's here in the hospital too."

"Is she okay?"

My mother settled into her chair. "She's having some kind of treatment for her chrysalization."

I thought about how rough a time she'd had walking that day during clinic. What happened if chrysalization kept getting worse? I tried to remember what the book had said. Something about it being dangerous if it forms around major organs or restricts breathing. What if it kept getting worse and worse until it completely engulfed her?

Around midday, the phone rang in my room. My mother answered it, then helped me get my arm free from under the sheet. "It's Kristi," she whispered, handing me the receiver. She seemed to be taking pains to keep her expression neutral.

I held the phone away from my face. "How did she know I was here?"

"Maybe she heard from someone in Mr. Halsing's office. I mentioned it when I called to tell them you'd be absent." She moved for the door. "I'm going to go find some lunch."

Once she was gone, I lifted the receiver to my ear. I didn't say anything for a moment, unsure how much I actually wanted to talk to Kristi. But the other choice was to hang up on her, and I didn't feel like I should do that either. "Hello?"

"Anna! Are you okay?"

"I'm all right."

"But you're in the hospital? You want me to come visit you?"

I didn't feel ready to see anyone. To relive the story of that terrible night of floating by telling it again, especially to someone I didn't totally trust. "That's okay. I'm just resting. I'm probably not very good company right now."

"Aw, come on. I don't mind! I can bring you some drawing supplies. You can capture everything while you're right in the middle of the action."

The action? I frowned. "Sorry, I'm just not really feeling up for it. How's school?"

"School is pointless—you know that. Besides, you're the one we should be focusing on."

Out in the hallway, the meal cart clattered out of the elevator and began making its deliveries. "Listen," I said, maybe a little too quickly, "I have to go. But thanks for checking on me. I'll call you when I'm home to get the geometry homework." I'd have to get my other assignments directly from the teachers. I hadn't been in the hospital since back when Smilla and the girls and I were still on good terms, and I didn't think they would be quite as willing to help me out this time around.

I hung up just as the orderly came in with my lunch tray, but I felt uneasy. Talking to Kristi had unsettled me somehow. Between that, my concern for Pam, my guilt over Smilla, and the horror of my latest flare-up, I just wanted to hide in my cage and never go back out into the real world.

LATER THAT AFTERNOON, Pam passed by my doorway. Seeing someone so familiar in this strange place was like discovering bipedal life on an alien planet: commonplace yet unexpected. She was hooked to an IV, limping along with the assistance of a physical therapist and a gray walker instead of her bejeweled cane. Her movement had become stiffer since our walk together only a few weeks earlier. "Hey," she said, pausing briefly. I wondered if she had ever been stuck in a cage like I was. She didn't seem surprised when she saw me in it.

When she passed by my doorway again on her way back, she paused once more. "I'm almost done with PT. You want company?"

I thought about it for a second. I wanted to be better about figuring out what I actually wanted and saying no when I meant no. I realized that although I'd told Kristi I wasn't up for visitors, I didn't mind the idea of hanging out with Pam. I wouldn't have to explain myself like I would with anyone else. "Sure."

She disappeared for a few minutes and then reappeared in a regular wheelchair, pushed by her mother.

My mother stood. "Why don't you girls talk for a bit?" I sensed a hint of relief from her at having a few minutes to herself.

Pam's mother rolled her next to the bed and put on the brakes, then slipped out into the hallway with my mom.

"How are you feeling?" asked Pam.

"Okay, I guess. What about you?"

She tried to shrug, which came out as her whole upper body bobbing stiffly to the side. I noticed for the first time that she had what looked like a gauzy white scarf around her neck, and when she caught me glancing at it, she said, "More chrysalization. It's a little hard to move and breathe. They're having me do ultrasonic therapy to try and control it." She frowned a little. "It's the first time I've ever had it on the outside."

That worry I had felt for her bubbled up inside me again. I didn't know what to say. Her situation sounded terrifying. But then I remembered that mine was, too, and I almost laughed at myself. "I'm sorry. That's awful."

"Yeah, well. You had another flare?"

I paused, wondering how much to tell her. But then I realized she was the one person in my life who would actually understand. "I was outside without my tether."

"Ooh," she said knowingly. "Was it the moon?"

I nodded.

She adjusted herself in her chair, getting as comfortable as she could manage. "So, what happened?"

I told her. Everything. The floating, the drifting, the

power lines, the skunk and the tree and the owl, the lost slippers, the phone booth. She listened and nodded, reacting with horror and sympathy at every turn. I was so grateful for her understanding, to finally have someone to talk to about everything, that I almost cried.

We compared notes about our medications. Pam had taken Coronide, but she'd had better luck with another drug I hadn't heard of before, and she had never taken Luxitra. "Floating's never been my main problem," she told me. "I mean, there was a little at the beginning—almost everyone has that at first—but since then, it's been mostly the chrysalization. I started getting it in my elbow, too, and my neck, as you can see." She bent her left arm stiffly, demonstrating her restricted range of movement, and then gazed at the muted television, which was showing a talk show in which a tall man in a suit was interviewing a crying woman. "You know, I used to be a tennis player. Now I've got a wonky knee and a messed-up elbow."

"I was a runner for a while," I said, remembering my brief window of solid performance. "Hard to run when you can barely breathe and you can't keep your feet on the ground."

We gave each other sympathetic smiles.

"Helloooo?" called a familiar voice from the doorway, and my stomach dropped. I looked over to see Kristi standing in the doorway, draped in black as usual, a shadowy ghost lingering where she didn't belong.

"What are you doing here?" I asked. I had told her not to come. *Why did she come?*

"I came to visit you, obviously. I had to make sure you were okay." She looked over at Pam. "Even though I *thought* you said you weren't up for company." A hint of annoyance tinged her voice.

"This is Pam. She's staying in the hospital too. Pam, Kristi."

"Hey," said Pam.

Kristi didn't say anything, but she kept her eyes fixed on Pam for an uncomfortably long time.

At that moment, Pam's mother appeared in the doorway. Pam gave me a strained smile as her mom walked over to wheel her out. "I guess I better get back. Can't stay off the ultrasonic machine for too long."

"Thanks for visiting," I said. And I meant it.

When she was gone, Kristi turned to me, her mouth hanging open in a wide grin. "Wow."

I was feeling more and more irritated by the minute. "Wow what?"

"Did you see her neck? What was that? And, oh my god, why are you in a cage? You're like a wild animal or something."

It seemed like she wanted to comment on everything more than she wanted answers to any of her questions, so I lay there silently, still wondering why she had come and how she had gotten here.

"Anyway," she said, "here. I brought you a present." She handed a small plastic bag through the slats and placed it next to me.

"Thanks," I said flatly.

"Aren't you going to open it?"

I sighed. My arms were still pinned under the sheet. I was supposed to keep them there, but I was able to slide them out if I really tried. After a minute, I worked them free and looked in the bag. There was a new-looking set of drawing pencils and a small sketch pad, which I hoped weren't stolen. There were also a package of gummy candies and a chocolate bar. "Thanks," I said again, setting the items on the tray table.

"Don't you want to have some candy?" she asked.

As much as I'd indulged lately, I now wondered if all those treats, over time, had made things worse. And even if they hadn't, eating candy where my mother, the nurses, and my doctors could potentially catch me wasn't something I wanted to do. "Not right now."

"Aww, come on. You're in a damn cage in the hospital. Treat yourself!"

Why wasn't she getting it? I went with a different tactic and tried to play off my response as a joke. "What, are you *trying* to make me float?"

She tilted her head to one side and shrugged. "I mean, I've never seen you do it. And you're in that thing, so you'd be safe, right?"

I was so shocked by this that I couldn't think of anything to say at all.

And she wouldn't stop. "Being able to float? And going through something this intense? You literally see the world from a different point of view. Do you know what a gift it is for an artist to have that kind of material?"

"Are you kidding me?" I said, the words bursting out of my mouth without my thinking about them. "A gift?"

"What?" she said, like she honestly didn't know what she'd done wrong.

I shook my head. "I thought you actually cared about me, but it sounds like you're just in it to see a freak show."

Now she looked as mad as I felt. "What the hell, Anna? I'm trying to help you be the artist I know you are. And you said it yourself: Nobody else gets it like I do. Who else is going to listen to you? *Smilla?*" She spit out the name like a curse.

"But you're *not* listening to me," I said, realizing the truth of the words as they left my mouth. "You're doing exactly what Smilla did. You're putting your own story on me. It's a different story than hers, but it's still not mine."

"I am *not* the same as her," hissed Kristi.

I ignored her and continued, talking as much to myself as to her. "Smilla thought I was this hero who was going to magically overcome an incurable disease. And you think I'm this tragic figure who should just focus on all the bad stuff and, god, even try and make it worse so I can make art about it. But you're both wrong."

"You are *so* ungrateful," said Kristi, grabbing back the bag of presents sitting on the table. "If you don't appreciate me, then just forget the whole thing."

"Kristi," I said, but she was already storming out.

On the silent TV, another woman had joined the first onstage, and now they were both crying, tearfully addressing each other and then collapsing into a hug. Cut to the applauding audience.

OVER THE NEXT few days, the medication continued to kick in, and I left the cage only for the challenge of going to the bathroom. But once the floating stabilized enough that I hovered just a few inches up, Dr. Liffey had me start physical therapy. "It's not good to float, but it's not good for your circulation to stay pinned down for too long either," she told me.

For my physical therapy sessions, an orderly came with a grav chair and brought me to a gymnasium-type room, where I was strapped into a device that latched around my waist, arms, and legs and let me move like I was walking. It was sort of like a cross between a treadmill and a bicycle, with my feet in stirrups that moved with me in a walking motion about a foot above the ground. The whole apparatus was bolted to the floor so that I couldn't float away.

"Good for you to get some exercise," the therapist said. "Helps the medicine work better."

And it was working. Each day, I felt a little more solid, and by the third day of physical therapy, my feet stayed on the ground without my having to hold on to anything. I still felt lighter than normal, but I was able to walk the halls with the therapist instead of using the machine, and I was steady enough that Dr. Liffey let me sit in the chair in my room for a little while instead of in the cage, as long as I kept my tether on.

But the better I felt, the more I worried about going back to my life. Everything was so controlled in the hospital: I didn't have to go to school; there wasn't anyone I didn't want to see; I ate what they gave me; I was inside and safe. Out in the world, there were classes I couldn't seem to catch up in, lost friends, and candy and soda whenever I felt like sneaking some. And a sky I could float off into anytime.

In addition to worrying about myself, I was concerned about Pam. While I was getting better, it seemed like she was getting worse. At first, Pam had shuffled past my door a few times a day with her walker, but it had been a long time since I'd seen her. The next time the nurse came by to check my vitals, I asked if Pam was still here.

"She is," said the nurse as she wrapped a blood pressure cuff around my arm.

I waited for her to take the reading and then asked, "Would it be okay if I went to visit her for a little while?"

The nurse looked me over and nodded. "I think it should be fine for you to walk over there as long as I keep an eye on you. Let me check and see if she's up for company."

I waited a little while for the nurse to get back to me. It was late afternoon, but it was one of those rainy gray days when it was hard to tell exactly what time it was. My mother had left to run errands, and I was tired of watching TV, so I sat quietly, watching the raindrops pelt off the window and looking out over the drab, wet slice of cityscape.

The nurse came back and escorted me to Pam's room. "Hey," she said as I sat down in the chair next to her bed and tethered myself to it. She lay very still. She inclined the head of the bed so she could see me better, but she didn't really move her neck.

"How are you feeling?" I asked.

"I've been better." Her eyes flicked toward a boxy gray device humming on a pole near the bed, with knobs and handles all over it and wires coming from it and disappearing under the blanket. "That's the ultrasonic machine. I don't even know why they're still having me use it, for all the good it's doing. If the chrysalization keeps getting worse, I might need surgery." She sounded tired, resigned. It seemed hard for her to move her jaw, and the shape of her words was slightly distorted. We were both quiet for a minute. "And what about you?" she asked. "It seems like you're doing better."

"Yeah, I guess so." I didn't know what else to say. I felt a little guilty about improving when she was getting worse. My eyes kept traveling back to the lacy white chrysalis forming around the beige skin of her neck. The webbing was slightly shiny and had a hint of the palest green to it. I thought about the day she and I had walked around the hospital, how much worse she had gotten in a matter of weeks. Even in the past handful of days.

"So what's up with your friend?" she asked.

"Hmm?"

"The one who came by the other day?"

"Oh," I said. "Kristi. I'm sorry about her. I don't know if we're friends anymore. Actually, I'm not sure we ever really were."

Pam shifted slightly in bed. She looked like she couldn't get comfortable. "Is she the one who thought you were going to miraculously recover through sheer willpower?"

I sighed. "No. Kristi and I only started hanging out after

I got sick. I thought she was interested in *me*, but I think she was just into my weird disease." *Our* weird disease, I realized after I said those words to Pam.

"Eww."

"Yeah. Anyway, I kind of fought with her about it. She probably hates me now."

"I hate that I'm about to sound exactly like my mother," said Pam, "but if she doesn't like you for who you are, then she's not a real friend."

I smiled. "You sound like my mother too."

The ultrasonic machine, which had been humming along quietly, changed pitch to a slightly higher note. "So who is the real you?" Pam asked.

I thought about that and realized I wasn't sure what to say. I was Smilla's friend and then Kristi's. I was a runner and then I wasn't. I liked music and clothes, but those interests didn't add up to who I was, exactly. I *was* a sick kid, I realized, but I was more than that too. "I guess I'm trying to figure it out."

"Yeah," said Pam. "Me too."

"I feel like I've been going along with what other people want and who they think I am for so long, but I don't think I can anymore."

"That's good," said Pam. "And it's hard. People do the same thing to me. Like, ever since I got sick, they want to talk about how brave I am. I'm not brave. I'm scared to death." She let out a sad chuckle. "Bad choice of words."

I sat in silence for a minute. "Do you know . . . I mean, do you think there's anything you did . . . anything that triggered your chrysalization?" Tears welled up in my eyes, and I sniffed and tried to push them back down.

"What do you mean?"

I pictured myself soaring over my dark neighborhood. "I haven't always done what Dr. Liffey said," I admitted softly. "I've been eating sugar, not wearing my tether, doing whatever I want. And now . . . I think maybe I broke myself."

"Anna," she said, "come on. You didn't break anything."

"How do you know that?" The tears were getting harder to hold back.

She gave me a weary smile. "Yes, there are things that help. I feel better when I don't eat sweets and I get a little exercise. So I try to do that. But some of it's just out of our control. I mean, god, I *wish* I could fix this just by not eating candy, you know?"

I sat there and tried to take in her words. Was it unsettling to know that I couldn't control everything, or was it in some strange way a relief? To know that I could let go a little, not worry as much about my every move, not feel guilty about screwing up, as I frequently did?

She went on, quieter now. "And anyway, there's already so much stuff we don't get to do. You don't have to be this model patient. You deserve to have a life. We both do."

"I guess."

The gray of the sky was getting heavier. We sat together in the dim light and the quiet. "Hey," said Pam after a few minutes, full of fake cheer, "it could be worse."

"Ha, right."

She looked more intently at me, still smiling but her

tone more serious now. "I mean, it could be. Have you ever read any books about lepidopsy? I found one in the library that was twenty years old, and trust me, it was way worse back then. All these medications we take with the terrible side effects, they didn't even have them. If Coronide didn't work, you either hung in the air until your body gave out or you floated away. Or you got completely consumed by chrysalization. Or thoraxing. Or whatever. The point is, you can't worry about that stuff all the time. You could waste your whole life worrying."

What neither of us needed to say was that no one knew how long that life would be. We could live a normal life span, like many people with lepidopsy apparently did. Or not.

We were quiet again. I looked over at the nightstand, where there was another of her thick books with a spaceship on the cover. "How's the book?"

"Pretty good. It's been hard to hold it up in front of my face, so it took me a while to read, but I finally finished it. Feel free to borrow it if you want."

I wondered what it would be like to be in space, if I would be pulled in any particular direction or if the natural weightlessness of zero gravity would counteract my floating. "Sure," I said.

The nurse popped her head through the doorway. "The meal cart just came up. Ready to head back?"

"Okay," I said, unhooking my tether and carefully standing. I took the book from the nightstand. "Thanks."

Pam gave me a careful smile. "You're welcome."

"I'll be back to help you with dinner," the nurse said,

and it occurred to me how little Pam had moved the entire time I'd been there. I wondered at how the same disease could make her fight so hard against gravity and make me fight so hard for it. I imagined linking arms with Pam, letting my floating even out her heavy stiffness, letting the two of us move at floor level down the hall, out of the hospital, into the world. Leaving all the medications and machines and lab tests behind.

AFTER ANOTHER COUPLE days, Dr. Liffey said I was stable enough to be released. I arrived home on a Thursday afternoon, and that night, I lay in bed, flipping and sighing. After being so light for all those days, it now felt odd and itchy to be pressed against my mattress by normal gravity.

My parents let me take the next day of school off to rest and to start catching up on the assignments my mom had picked up for me. But I still didn't know quite what to do with myself. I paged listlessly through textbooks for most of the morning, but I was too distracted to take much in. In the late afternoon, I thought about calling Smilla, but I still wasn't sure what to say to her. I thought about calling Kristi, too, but I didn't actually want to talk to her.

What *did* I want? I had to really stop and think about it. I liked the woods Smilla and I used to run in, but I couldn't run anymore. I liked the art projects I'd worked on with Kristi, but I wanted color in my life, not just black and white. I liked having people to hang out with, but I needed people who I could be myself with.

And, I realized, I liked Pam. Despite how hard I'd pushed her away at first, despite how much I didn't want to admit we had in common, I liked her, and I was worried about her. In that moment, what I truly wanted was to talk to her and see if she was okay.

When I called her room at the hospital, a woman who wasn't Pam answered. She had a faster and more fluid voice, lower, sharper, yet still ragged like Pam's was when I'd visited her room a few days earlier. "Hello?"

"Hi, is Pam there?"

"Who's calling, please?"

"It's Anna," I said, unsure whether the person I was talking to knew who I was.

But she did. "Oh, hi, Anna. This is her mom. Pam's resting right now."

I had talked to Pam's mom a little bit in the waiting room at clinic, but she sounded different somehow. "Is she okay?"

The voice grew heavier. "She's having surgery early tomorrow morning."

I took that as a no. My breath rattled. "I guess . . . maybe if she has time tonight, she could call me? If she feels up to it?"

"Maybe," said Pam's mother, though I could tell from her tone that this, too, was a no.

That night, I lay in my bed in the deep darkness, worrying about Pam and fighting off the urge to peek around the edges of the new light-blocking curtains my father had installed in my room. Because of the Luxitra, my body wasn't pulled toward the light as much, but I still felt the desire to look at it. Even though the moon was almost new,

I could sense other lights out there: porch lights, the head-lights of cars passing by, the icy glow of the stars. *Don't look,* I told myself. *Just close your eyes and sleep.*

But as hard as I tried to convince myself to stay under the covers, I couldn't seem to get still, and I found myself up and walking around, as if I had no say in the matter. I wandered my room, seeking out even the faintest slivers of light, trying to pull myself back from the danger that lurked there. *Stay away from the windows,* I kept thinking. Each time I did, a vision filled my mind of pulling back the curtains and my body smashing through the glass. "Stay away," I growled to myself out loud.

The following day, I waited until what seemed like a rea-sonable amount of time had passed, and then I called Pam's room again to see how her surgery had gone. But no one answered. I dug up the home phone number she'd given me the first time we met, but the answering machine picked up. I called several times in a row, in case someone had tried to answer but hadn't made it to the phone in time, but I got the machine every time. It was already midafternoon, but maybe it was still too early.

I tried again that night after dinner, but again, nobody answered. I watched TV with my parents for a while, but all I could do was stare blankly at it as I thought about Pam. Later, after my parents had gone to bed, I went back into the living room and found the lepidopsy book. It wasn't stashed away on the high shelf where I'd left it months before, so I suspected one or both of my parents had been reading it, maybe while I was in the hospital. I looked up chrysalization in the index and found a couple of page references. The first led back to the section I had read before: *Chrysalization is difficult to treat, though it is typically not dangerous unless the chrysalis forms over the face, restricting breathing*...

The next reference led to a more detailed section about treatment, and there I found more information about the procedure I believed Pam was having.

> For cases that don't respond to medication or ultrasonic therapy, surgery may be an option. Surgery to remove chrysalization is difficult and risky, as growth strands are often widespread and must be removed individually to avoid damaging the surrounding tissue. This procedure has a success rate of around 40 percent, although it is often combined with immersion therapy to increase the overall success rate to around 65 percent. Because of the high risks of tissue damage, disfigurement, and death, surgery should be considered only for the most severe cases.

I read the paragraph twice, and then I found myself shaking, and I couldn't stop. I felt cold all over. I put the book away, went upstairs, and got into the shower, blasting myself with hot water to try and warm up, but I couldn't stop shivering. What if she died? What if she died, and then what if I died? I shook and I cried until the hot water ran out, and then I buried myself under a pile of blankets in my bed, but I still couldn't seem to get warm.

THE FOLLOWING DAY was Sunday, and the impending school week was weighing on me. What would Kristi say when she saw me? Or would she go back to ignoring me, as she had before I got sick? And what about Smilla? How was I going to look at her after abandoning her to go with Kristi? What about these growing mountains of homework and missed assignments?

But, honestly, it was hard to think of much besides Pam. I tried again to call her room and her house to see how things had gone, but I couldn't get ahold of anyone. With each unanswered call, my panic grew. What if she was already gone? What if the surgery had failed? I had just realized how much I might actually get along with Pam, that she might be the only person in the world who even came close to understanding me anymore. And now what if she had been yanked away, along with some part of my future? Some part of myself?

I couldn't eat dinner. My parents offered to make me something else, but for once, I wasn't hungry. My father suggested TV shows we might watch, music I might listen to, board games, books, but nothing was appealing. I took the cordless phone to my room and tried calling Pam again, and I still couldn't get through. I pressed the button to hang up, and I couldn't breathe. The world spun, and I dashed to the bathroom, just barely making it in time before I threw up.

My parents must have heard me banging around, because they both ran to where I lay, crying, on the bathroom floor. "Honey?" said my father, putting his hand on my head. I was clammy, maybe feverish, but still his hand felt warm by comparison. I lunged for the toilet and threw up again. Maybe I was having another flare. Maybe this was the beginning of the end for me too.

My father brought me a glass of water and a damp washcloth, and when I was ready, he helped me to my room while my mother went to page Dr. Liffey and let her know what was going on.

I sat there staring at the carpet while he took my temperature and told me it would be okay, that I was all right, that he was there. "It's normal," he said, looking at the thermometer.

My mother reappeared with a cup of chamomile tea and set it on my nightstand. "Dr. Liffey doesn't think this is a symptom or a side effect of anything," she said. "Probably just a bug."

I was apparently regular sick, not capital-S Sick. But I couldn't trust any of that anymore. Who could tell what would or wouldn't turn out to be serious, what horrors my cells might be cooking up in the shadows? My body felt wrung-out; my brain, numb. I didn't move, but tears began rolling down my face.

"Honey," said my mom, "what's going on? Please, talk to us."

But it was hard to know where to start. I had been keeping so much to myself. "I don't know what to do," I said, my voice catching in my throat.

"About what?" asked my father.

"About anything."

I caught them looking at each other in my peripheral vision. "I know it's scary," said my mother. "Especially this latest flare. But you're okay now. You're going to be okay." Was she trying to reassure me, or herself?

"You don't know that!" My body again shook with sobs.

"Sweetie," said my father. "We're going to get through this. You have the best medical care—"

"So does Pam! She has the same doctor and everything, and look at her. Did you know she had to have surgery yesterday? And I can't even get anyone to tell me if she made it through!"

There was a long moment of silence. Then my mother said, "Listen. You're here, right now. And we're here for you. And you're going to keep moving forward one step at a time, and you're going to keep taking care of yourself, and you are going to be okay. I know it's hard right now. And it's been hard for a while. But I don't want you to get stuck in sadness and worry. I want you to have fun, happy things too. Things to look forward to. Parties and the prom. Finishing high school. Going to college and building a future for yourself."

I laughed. I actually laughed out loud at her. A hard, bitter laugh. "A future. Okay."

Her eyes grew wide. It took a lot to surprise my mother, but I had just done it. It was the first time I had acknowledged any doubts about the future, specifically whether I would be alive to see it. "Anna," she said, softly but firmly, "you're going to have a future."

I wasn't so sure, but what use was arguing about it? Instead, I went back to something else she'd said. "And who's inviting me to parties or the prom? I don't even have any friends."

"That's not true," said my father.

"Smilla hates me now, and so does everyone else from the team. Even Kristi hates me."

"I seriously doubt they *hate* you," said my mother. "I know you've had your differences, but maybe you can still work things out. And," she said, hesitating for a second, "you and Pam seem to be getting along well lately. I know you're worried, but don't give up on her yet, okay?"

"But what if she doesn't make it?"

My mother put her hands on my shoulders and turned me gently to face her. "We have to hold on to hope that she will." She stayed like that for a moment, and then she stood. "I'll be right back."

I looked at my dad. He gave me a tired smile and put his arm around me, pulling me into a hug.

My mother returned a minute later holding a plastic garment bag. "I got you something." She lifted the plastic to reveal a gorgeous ruby-red crushed-velvet dress. "I was doing some shopping, and I saw this. It seemed like your style."

I ran my fingers over the plush fabric. The dress was beautiful. It was stylish, too, and not in a conventional way, but in a cool way. It would look good with high heels or army boots. It even had long sleeves in case I wanted to cover up my scales. I smiled a little. "What's this for?"

"For the things I said," she replied. "I wanted you to have something nice for parties or dances or whatever. You've been spending so much time by yourself lately, and I don't know how much of it is self-consciousness, but I want you to have things that make you feel good about yourself. You deserve that. I know you've got a lot going on, but I don't want you to look back on this time and feel like you missed out on all the regular teenager stuff."

I held tightly to the dress. "Thanks." I still didn't know what to make of her unshakable expectation that I had a future, one that would be different enough from my present to look back on this time and have opinions about it. And I didn't know whether I'd ever been a "regular teenager," whatever that meant, or if I ever would be. But it mattered that she cared. And she really had picked out a great dress.

My father sighed, and I turned toward him. "You know, your mom and I thought the support group would be enough to help you through all this, but maybe we were wrong. If you need to talk to someone else, we can find someone."

"Like a therapist?"

"It might not be a bad idea," said my mother. "This is a lot for anyone to go through."

"Course you can always talk to your old dad, too," said my father, and it was so cheesy, I couldn't help but crack a smile.

They left to let me get some rest. My queasiness having subsided a bit, I tried on the dress and checked myself out in the full-length mirror. I'd put on some weight, but the dress fit perfectly. Maybe I actually could wear it to parties, if I ever got invited to another one. Or other events. I didn't know what those might be, but maybe I could hope for them anyway.

And maybe if I could have hope for myself, I could have it for Pam too. The whole weekend had passed since her surgery, and I still didn't know how it had gone. I wanted her to be okay, needed her to, but it seemed like if she were, I would know by now.

I brought the phone into my room and held it tightly against my chest. I didn't believe I had the power to change anything at that point, and I barely even believed in hope anymore. Still, I took a deep breath and whispered, "Please," before dialing her home number.

The phone rang once, twice, three times, and then there was a click. My breath caught. But again, it was only the answering machine. "Hi, this is Anna," I said after the beep. "From clinic." I didn't want to address my message directly to Pam, in case she wasn't around to receive it, but I didn't want to not direct it to her either. "I'm just calling to see how Pam . . . how things went with the surgery. Could you please call me back?" I left my number and hung up. It was scary to hope for anything good, but I had to try.

EIGHT

I WENT BACK to school the next day. I'd been out for two weeks, but it seemed like ages longer. In French class, I kept my eyes on my notebook and avoided looking at Jennie or anyone else. I tried to pay attention to the teacher, knowing how much catching up I had to do, but I still couldn't get my mind off Pam.

I thought and wondered and worried about her almost constantly, and any peace that came when I got distracted vanished in a hurry. Halfway through class, I was twirling my pen, my mind gone blank for a moment, the sounds around me like a mist obscuring the worries in my head. And then the pen slipped from my grasp and clattered onto the floor, and in a flash, the mist cleared, and there everything was again. My heart rate jumped. The teacher looked at me, some other kids snickered, and my cheeks burned as I picked up the pen as quickly as possible. But even the embarrassment rapidly dissipated, making way for my worry. All the questions I didn't dare speak aloud: *What if this happens to me too? What if the surgery didn't work? What if I never see her again?* She was only fifteen. What if she only lived to fifteen? I knew from the stories she told in group that she was the oldest of six children, and Ashley, the youngest, was only three. Ashley adored her big sister. But what if Pam died and Ashley didn't even remember her?

What if Pam died?

I shuffled through the corridor and into study hall and was the last one into the room. I couldn't focus at all. All the colors I saw, psychedelically vivid thanks to the Luxitra, reminded me of Pam's beautiful clothes and bejeweled cane: the girl in front of me in her purple sweater, the neon-pink and yellow flyers on the bulletin board advertising clubs and events.

As I walked through the crowd toward English class, I felt a low dread simmering at the thought of seeing Smilla. I didn't even look to see if she was there as I entered the room, instead heading straight for my regular back corner. But as class began, I glanced up, and there she was, looking back at me. I ducked my head and focused on my notebook, but I continued to feel her eyes on me.

I doodled abstract shapes in the margins, alternating between worrying about Pam and wondering what Smilla thought of me now. And suddenly, in that moment, I understood something that hadn't occurred to me before: How Smilla must have worried about me as much as I was currently worrying about Pam, if not more. What must it have been like to come upon her best friend unconscious, *floating*, in the woods? To watch me go through something she had no way of understanding?

A deep ache bloomed in my chest. She just wanted me to be okay and things to be normal. And didn't I want that, too, at least at first? Before I understood that there was no going back? She wasn't wrong that I had kept her at arm's length—in fact, I'd done so for the same reason: to pretend that things were fine.

As class ended, Smilla gathered her stuff and headed out the door unusually quickly, and this time, I didn't dawdle. She disappeared into the crowd on her way to study hall, but I saw her ponytail bobbing ahead of me. She rounded the corner, and I followed, going the opposite direction from the library, where I usually spent fourth period. She was getting too far ahead, and my feet were growing sore as I struggled to catch up. If I ran, I would float.

"Smilla!" I called.

A few people turned and looked at me, some stepping out of my way. But she didn't stop.

"Smilla, wait!"

I saw her slow down and watched her shoulders droop before she turned toward me. "Yeah?" She sounded tired.

I approached her and tried to catch my rattling breath. "I just wanted to talk to you."

"Okay, so talk," she said softly, not moving out of the middle of the hallway.

I had so much to say, but I didn't know where to start.

"I'm sorry about the last time we talked. Kristi pulled me away, and I just . . . I didn't react fast enough. I should have gone back to finish our conversation."

Smilla bit her lip and looked at the floor, nodding.

I stood there waiting for her to say something, and when she didn't, I thought she was going to walk away. But she didn't do that either.

"Do you think we could just talk sometime?" I asked. "Like, for real?"

She twisted her face, as if considering something, and then looked at me and said, "Okay, let's go." She began walking back in the direction from which we'd come.

I swiveled around and walked by her side. "Don't you have to get to class?" I asked. Smilla never skipped.

"It's just study hall," she said. Maybe I had underestimated her ability to change.

We walked down the corridor as it cleared out, people filtering into classrooms. We came to the outside door at the end of the hallway. I decided I felt stable enough to be out there, and I pushed through into a pleasant, almost-warm almost-spring day.

She was quiet for a while, and then she said, "You were gone for weeks. I thought maybe something was really wrong."

"It was," I said softly. We kept walking.

Our feet carried us naturally toward the wooded cross-country trail, which was still slightly muddy but passable. The earth smelled damp as it woke up, and red buds festooned the maple branches. It was strange to be in these woods again. For a brief moment, I had the impulse to set down my backpack and jog along the trail, but I didn't really want to. It was just something about being in that place, with Smilla.

We strolled down the trail for a while. "I'm sorry I kept everything from you, and about how it all came out," I said at last. "I guess I just felt like you wouldn't want to hang out with me if I complained all the time. You were so set on me staying positive, but I didn't *feel* positive. And if I didn't make a miraculous recovery, I was afraid you'd think I was a failure. But that's not how it works. This illness is just something I have now."

She shook her head. "Talking about what's going on with you is not the same as complaining all the time. And I *never* wanted to stop being your friend." She sounded a little indignant but not angry.

"It's just that you always wanted to hang out with your running friends," I said, "and you have so much in common with them. I never really felt like part of that."

"Of course you were part of it! That was our group. You were on the team."

We walked. I still wasn't sure I felt like part of their group, but I believed she thought I was.

"I'm sorry too," she said. "I didn't mean to be unsupportive. I was just trying to help."

"I know."

Her voice got softer. "I read a bunch about lepidopsy."

I looked over at her. "You did?"

She nodded. "After you said all that stuff about how I didn't understand how you were feeling. I wanted to."

I kicked at a pebble as guilt and sadness and longing for my friend competed within me.

"I'm sorry I made you feel left out," she said. "I wasn't trying to pull away. I guess if I was pulling, I was trying to pull you back to being happy. You just seemed so . . . sad. And lost."

I listened to our footsteps for a little bit. "I think I needed you to be where I was instead of bringing me somewhere else. I should have been more honest about that. I guess I didn't really know what I needed either." After another minute, I said, "There's this girl I go to clinic with, Pam. She's the only other person I know who has lepidopsy." I caught myself using the present tense, and hoped it was still the right one. "She's not doing well, and I'm worried about her. I guess it made me realize how hard it must have been for you to watch me struggle."

"Oh, Anna, I'm sorry about your friend. I'm sure—" She caught herself. "I hope she'll be okay." She paused and then asked, "So are *you* okay? I was worried about you being out so long . . . If you want to talk about it."

I took a moment to think about what I truly wanted, and found that, yes, I did want to talk to her about it. So I told her what had happened when I went outside to look at the moon. As I got to the part about my mother picking me up at the elementary school, Smilla stopped walking. She was crying. She turned and hugged me. It seemed she understood how close she'd come to losing me, really losing me, how dangerous this thing could be.

After we let go, Smilla took a long, deep breath.

"Anyway, how have you been?" I asked lightly, and she laughed.

She told me about the indoor track season, how she liked it but not as much as being outside, and how she was looking forward to getting back out when spring track started in a few weeks. "Running isn't as much fun without you there, though," she said. She talked about some books she'd read and the music she'd been listening to, and it felt a little like talking to a stranger, like the time away from each other had confirmed that we were growing apart in our tastes and interests. But I felt a greater sense of acceptance about that. Maybe it was still possible for us to be a different kind of friends.

"How are things with Kristi?" she asked finally. I could tell she was trying to be upbeat and nonjudgmental, but I could still hear the sigh in her voice.

I considered what to tell her. I didn't want to trash-talk Kristi. She seemed like not the happiest person, and I understood from recent experience how easy it was to lash out when you were unhappy. "I'm not sure that's going to work out," I said. "But I started working on some art projects with her, and I may want to do more of that."

"Oh, that's great! You've always had such a great sense of color and style."

"Really?"

"Anna, of course! Why do you think I'm always borrowing your clothes?"

We smiled at each other. As we headed back toward school, a bright blue jay landed on a branch up ahead. The first green shoots pushed up through the earth. Maybe there was a chance things would be all right.

I FELT A little calmer in my afternoon classes, though when I got to geometry, I waited nervously to see what Kristi would do when she arrived. Just before the bell rang, I caught a flash of black across the doorway. She must have seen me and not wanted to deal with me. I knew sooner or later I'd have to talk to her, but it was a relief to have one less heavy emotional thing to do today.

That night, my father decided we could all use a little break, so we went out to dinner at an Italian restaurant. After I finished my eggplant Parmesan, I looked longingly at the dessert menu but decided on a cup of peppermint tea instead. My parents and I talked and laughed together in a way we hadn't in a while, not about anything serious but just silly stuff: a weird guy at my dad's work, a funny thing my mom had read, the latest episode of a TV show we liked. It was nice.

A few minutes after we got home, the phone rang, and someone else picked it up while I was in my bedroom. A moment later, my mother appeared in the doorway, clutching the phone to her chest. "It's Pam," she said, and everything else fell away.

"Wait," I said. "Her mother? Or . . . or her?"

"It's her." She was smiling and holding the phone out to me, her eyes teary.

"Hello?" I said tentatively.

"Hey." Her voice was weak and a little creaky, but it was Pam, all right.

"Oh my god, how are you?"

"I'm okay," she said, and I could hear the smile in her voice.

I was trying not to cry now. "I was so worried about you. You're really okay?"

"I'm okay," she said. She told me about how she'd woken up submerged in a tank of pink goo, as she put it, and had to stay there for almost forty-eight hours. "It was so weird. I'll tell you about it later when I have more of a voice." She still had to stay in the hospital for another few days of observation, but then she'd get to go home.

"So, did it work?"

"Yeah, I think so. I can move my neck again, and I'm breathing well. I can move my other joints more easily too. I have to do physical therapy for those, but I think they're getting better."

"I'm so glad you're okay."

"Thanks. I mean, I guess you never know what the future will bring. But I'm all right for now."

I didn't want to let her go after waiting such a long time to reach her, but she needed to rest.

I took a few minutes to myself after hanging up just to breathe and let the relief wash over me, and then I told my mother what I'd learned. She hugged me tightly for a long time.

I couldn't stop smiling with relief for the rest of the evening. As I thought about Pam, I remembered the book she'd loaned me, which I had stuffed in a bag in the hospital and hadn't touched since then. Now I felt inspired to do something in Pam's honor, so I found the book and read it for a while before bed, and it felt good to lose myself in the story. As the cover suggested, the book was about an astronaut who finds herself stranded alone in space after an accident aboard her shuttle. When she's picked up by an alien ship, she knows how strange the situation is, yet the ship feels familiar somehow. It turns out that the astronaut is actually one of the aliens and was sent to Earth as a baby to be raised there, but her destiny is among the stars. Weightless.

I imagined Pam could relate to it as much as I did. Maybe it was our destiny to be weightless too. At least we weren't alone.

THE NEXT DAY, Kristi was back in geometry, though she sat on the opposite side of the room, and when Mr. Takahashi called for us to pair up with our assignment partners, she made no move to come any closer.

So I went to sit near her. The room was rumbling with conversation as the other pairs worked on the assignment. "Hey," I said, but she was silent. "What do you think about this first question?"

She scribbled in her tiny handwriting on her paper, her

hair a curtain hanging over her work so I couldn't see it. She still didn't respond.

"Kristi," I said. I knew she heard me even if she was pretending not to listen. "The last time we saw each other . . ." I kept my voice as calm and kind as I could make it. "I need friends who are going to respect me and support me in being as healthy as I can. You know?"

Nothing.

"I know you're going through your own stuff too. If you ever want to talk about it with me, you can."

Did I imagine it, or did the scribbling slow down a little?

"And you don't need to make up tragic material to be a good artist. You're already good."

I left it at that and worked on the worksheet by myself.

THAT WEDNESDAY ON the way to clinic, we had just pulled onto the highway when my mother remembered something. "Oh!" she said. "I picked up something for you to look at. Grab my purse."

I took her purse from the center console, opened it, and found a couple of brochures. They were from a local art museum.

"They have classes," said my mom. "I thought you might want to do some this summer."

I flipped through the pamphlets to find offerings in drawing, all sorts of painting techniques, sculpture, photography . . . the list went on. "Oh wow. These are great!"

My mother smiled. "Let's talk about it some more soon and see what you might want to sign up for."

When we got to the hospital, I was surprised when a tall young woman in a white lab coat strode into the exam room instead of Dr. Shiel. "Hello, I'm Dr. Chandra," she said, extending her hand to shake mine. A good, firm grip. "I'm the new resident in manifestology."

"Hi," I said. I didn't want to be rude, but I couldn't help but ask what happened to Dr. Shiel.

She smiled warmly. "His residency ended. But I'm very happy to be here working with Dr. Liffey. She's wonderful, isn't she?"

I let my guard down a little and nodded. I wasn't sad to see Dr. Shiel go, exactly, just acutely aware of the passing of time. Dr. Chandra checked my flutter, my skin, all the usual things, and I found that I felt comfortable around her. I couldn't tell if it was because she was a comforting presence or if I had grown more at ease with my situation. Maybe both.

When Dr. Liffey joined us, I told her I'd been having a little trouble sleeping. As usual, she said she'd look at my lab results and maybe adjust my medications, or maybe we'd just wait and see how things went. But the uncertainty didn't bother me as much as it used to. Maybe it was because I knew that since I had gotten this far, I could keep going. Maybe it was because I didn't feel so alone anymore. Or, again, maybe it was both.

I walked into the conference room when it was time

for group, and there were Carrie and Elaine, just like they were the first time I went. Marina was there, too, now not-so-newly diagnosed, looking ashen and lost, a slight hum coming from her direction. I felt for her. Lisa turned to Carrie to check in first, but before she could speak, the door opened again, and Pam walked in. Everyone cheered.

"Hey!" I said. "You're here!"

She smiled and came over to sit next to me. She was moving slowly but more fluidly than she had been, and she wasn't using her cane. "I had some follow-up tests downstairs. So, what are we talking about?"

Carrie gave an update. Someone she liked had just asked her out, and she was beaming. "Of course, my parents are *so* overprotective. They'd rather I just stayed in my room till I was thirty. But they're letting us go out to the movies this weekend." We grinned and demanded she come back with details next time.

Elaine talked about the summer music program she was doing this year. "I'm so excited! There was a camp I was going to go to last year, but I got sick and had to cancel it. This one's local, so I can still do all my appointments and stuff. They do a whole concert at the end of the season with a professional conductor and everything."

Marina's turn came, but she didn't feel much like talking. I caught her eye for a second and gave her an encouraging smile. She gave me a quick smile back and then looked at the table. I understood.

Pam went next. The others had heard about her surgery but didn't know all the details, so she gave us a quick update on her condition. "Everything looks good so far. And I feel a lot better too. It's amazing how fast it works. Well, at least that's how it felt to me." She shook her head a little in wonder. "It was so strange," she said. "You know, when they put you out to have surgery, it's like no time passes. I remember from when I was a kid and I had my tonsils out. They tell you you're going to feel sleepy, and the next thing you know, you're trying to get your eyes open and it's over. I was in surgery for eight hours, they said, and then I was in that tank of goo, and I kept going in and out of consciousness. It was a weird couple days."

"It was a *long* couple days," I said. I didn't say how convinced I'd been that she hadn't made it through. The words *normal life span* flickered across my mind again, and for the first time, I wondered, truly, what if they were right? What if Pam and I lived to be old women? It was scary to think about having lepidopsy for years, for decades, but maybe I could try to focus on the living part.

Pam smiled at me. "Yeah, my mom thought so too." There was a faint pale outline on her skin where the strands of the chrysalization had been, but she didn't seem self-conscious about it. She ran her hand down the side of her face and neck. "It's so weird that it's gone," she said softly. "I mean, it doesn't look totally gone, but it feels gone."

"Are you going to keep it covered up?" asked Elaine. "Because I think it looks kind of cool."

"I don't know," said Pam. She thought about it for a minute. "Maybe I'll let it all hang out, and everybody can just deal with it." She gave us a wicked grin.

"Thanks, Pam," Lisa said. "We're glad to have you back. Okay, last but not least, Anna. How are you doing?"

I looked around the table and saw everyone looking back at me, waiting patiently to hear whatever I had to say. Even Marina was peeking at me a little bit. I hadn't shared much beyond the surface with these girls, but I now had the feeling that I could be honest with them. That maybe it would even feel good to do it.

I took a deep breath. And then I told them my story.

AUTHOR'S NOTE

ALTHOUGH THIS BOOK doesn't follow my own exact story, Anna and I do have a lot in common. I was fourteen when my wrists began to ache a little during field hockey practice. In the weeks that followed, my joints grew more painful and swollen, and I became more and more fatigued. By late November, a month and a half after those first mild aches started, my hands and feet were so sore and swollen that it was hard to use a pencil or walk, and I was sleeping thirteen hours a night but still exhausted all day in school.

I was terrified about what was happening to me. Fortunately, I had a smart and attentive pediatrician who referred me to the right specialist, and she was able to quickly and definitively diagnose me with lupus. It was a relief to have a name for what was happening to me, and even more of a relief to start medication that made me feel better within a day. But like Anna, I was only at the beginning of the roller coaster.

For years, I looked for other stories—in books, on TV, in movies—of people with lupus or people who had been through similar experiences with other chronic illnesses. These stories were few and far between. When I did find them, they often treated chronic illnesses as terminal illnesses, with a dramatic death scene at the end. Once in a while, the character got to heroically triumph over their illness, which felt just as unrealistic. Either way, these characters usually served as objects who existed only to teach Valuable Life Lessons to the people around them.

I wanted stories where chronically ill people got to live their own lives rather than existing as plot devices—stories about what it was like to live with an illness that went on for a long time, the ups and downs of it, the effects it had on a person's relationships and sense of identity. As time went by and I still had trouble finding stories like mine, I realized I needed to write such a story myself. It's now been over thirty years since I was first diagnosed, and I'm happy that I am now bringing this book into the world.

I used a made-up illness in this story for a couple of reasons. First, getting seriously ill out of the blue is a profoundly weird and life-changing experience. Writing about a reality-defying illness seemed like a good way to capture that surreal feeling. Second, I wanted to break away from the typical story arcs I was used to seeing. My hope was that a made-up illness would limit the preconceived notions readers would have about what would happen to Anna so that they would feel just as uncertain about her future as

Anna did. I believed that would allow room for them to see her as a real person with her own complicated thoughts and feelings—not as a two-dimensional brave hero or tragic figure. Just a regular person going through something tough, as we all do at some point.

A single book can't possibly represent every story of chronic illness or disability. In many ways, Anna is lucky. She receives a clear, fast diagnosis, which many people don't. She has access to good medical care, a supportive family, and (despite their missteps) friends who care about her. For many people, the challenges of developing a chronic illness are compounded by a lack of those things, as well as systemic racism, sexism, homophobia, transphobia, economic struggles, and other issues.

I recognize that a diagnosis story is only one kind of chronic illness story. I would love to see not only more stories like this, but many other kinds of tales featuring chronically ill characters as well. Bring on the books where people with chronic illnesses and disabilities fall in love, solve mysteries, do magic, make scientific breakthroughs, go on adventures, and do everything else our imaginations can come up with.

Most of all, I hope this book will help teens with chronic illnesses feel less alone and will inspire them to share their own stories, whether through writing, art, music, activism, or simply telling their truths to a friend. The world benefits from hearing our stories in our own words. Even more importantly, we deserve to tell them.

ACKNOWLEDGMENTS

Thank you, thank you, thank you to:

The wise and steady Alexa Stark, who believed in this story and helped it find its home, and to Ana Ban for helping it find its way into the wider world.

Arianne Lewin, who brought true passion to the process and pushed this book to be the absolute best it could be. Thank you to Hsiao Ron Cheng, Kristin Boyle, and Suki Boynton for turning my daydream into a beautiful object, and to Ariela Rudy Zaltzman, Cindy Howle, Jacqueline Hornberger, and Elizabeth Johnson for polishing the text to a shine. Many thanks as well to Elise LeMassena, Jen Klonsky, Ashley Spruill, Anna Elling, Felicity Vallence, Shannon Spann, and James Akinaka for their support and behind-the-scenes magic.

The friends who shared their insights to help shape this story: Liz Thurmond, Susan Stinson, Natalie Dougall, Jaime

Leon Lin-Yu, Rich Buckley, Linda Rowland-Buckley, and Kasey Corbit. Thanks as well to Helena Maria Viramontes and my fellow Bread Loaf workshoppers for their advice early on, which helped point the book in the right direction, and to Nova Ren Suma and my fellow NESCBWI workshoppers, who helped later on to fine-tune the beginning. Shout-out to Lillie Lainoff and Katryn Bury for swooping in with last-minute advice and fake band names.

Sera Rivers, tireless champion, confidante, and partner in crime. Cheers, friend!

All the wonderful writer-friends who have provided community and support along the way, in particular Bethany Webster, Caitlin Sabourin, Karen Frasca, Loretta Kapinos, Lillian Baulding, all the Millsians, and the '22 Debuts.

Dan Blask and everyone at the Massachusetts Cultural Council. Your support not only allowed me to take advantage of opportunities to grow as a writer but provided a booster shot of confidence at a moment when it was especially appreciated.

The many health care providers who helped keep me alive long enough to tell this story, and the many literature, creative writing, music, and art teachers who did the same.

The high school friends who were there for me with laughs, books, video games, music, companionship, silliness, kind words, and Jurassic Park trading cards.

Mom, for being my first fan, for knowing I was a writer even before I did, and for jotting down everything the doctors ever said on that little notepad. And, of course, for raising me on a steady diet of the *Twilight Zone* to make sure I grew up nice and weird.

Andrea, for all the conversations through the radiator, on the stairs, after bedtime when there was to be not another peep, and every other place and time. You're the best sister a girl could ask for, and the coolest to boot.

Dimitri, for seeing me for who I am and loving me because of it. Your unwavering belief in me has meant everything. Thank you for celebrating with me, comforting me, and making me laugh every single day.